## THE CRESCENT AND THE NORTHERN STAR

Edited by
**Muhammad Aurangzeb Ahmad**
**& Joshua Gillingham**

ALTHINGI: THE CRESCENT AND THE NORTHERN STAR

*Speaking with Giants* © 2021 Linnea Hartsuyker
*The Blasphemy of the Gods* © 2021 Sami Shah
*The Short Tale of Thurid the Exasperated* © 2021 Genevieve Gornichec
*Torunn Unhoused* © 2021 Emily Osborne
*What a Miserable Drink, and What a Terrible Place* © 2021 Alex Kreis
*The Saga of Aud the Seeress* © 2021 Siobhán Clark
*Dragoslava Dreadkeel* © 2021 Giti Chandra
*The Gold of Iskander* © 2021 Nicholas Kotar
*Wave Runners* © 2021 Kaitlin Felix
*Exiles* © 2021 Shannon Sinn
*A Clash in Kaupang* © 2021 Eric Schumacher
*Sif the Fair* © 2021 Jordan Stratford
*Sky of Bronze* © 2021 R.F. Dunham
*So do I write and color the runes* © 2021 Bjarne Benjaminsen

Published by Outland Entertainment LLC
3119 Gillham Road
Kansas City, MO 64109

Founder/Creative Director: Jeremy D. Mohler
Editor-in-Chief: Alana Joli Abbott

ISBN: 978-1-954255-07-4 (Print)
ISBN: 978-1-954255-08-1 (eBook)
Worldwide Rights

Editors: JM Gillingham & Muhammad Aurangzeb Ahmad
Cover Illustration: Lada Shustova & Pedro Figue
Cover Design: Jeremy D. Mohler
Interior Layout: Mikael Brodu

Printed and bound in China.

Visit **outlandentertainment.com** to see more, or follow us on our Facebook Page **facebook.com/outlandentertainment/**

# — TABLE OF CONTENTS —

"I saw the Rusiyyah when they had arrived on their trading expedition and had disembarked at the River Atil. I have never seen more perfect physiques than theirs—they are like palm trees, are fair and reddish, and do not wear the qurçtaq or the caftan. The man wears a cloak with which he covers one half of his body, leaving one of his arms uncovered. Every one of them carries an axe, a sword and a dagger and is never without all of that which we have mentioned..."

—From the journal of Ahmad ibn Fadlan,
emissary of the Caliph al-Muqtadir in Baghdad, 921 A.D.
(Adapted from the english translation by J.E. Montgomery)

# — SPEAKING WITH GIANTS —
## Linnea Hartsuyker

*Vidar the Strong*

Rashid's fever rises during the day, when the heat of the Baghdad sun bakes the walls of his building. Vidar drapes wet towels over Rashid's forehead, which dry quickly, even as he sweats his sheets sodden. The boy Vidar hired to fan him often grows tired and must rest.

The last time Vidar remembers hating the very air around him was after a week becalmed in the Black Sea, the sky shimmering and misty, the sea's marine scent turned lifeless. Rashid had been full of energy, though, writing in his book when he wasn't watching the water intently, hoping to see a Leviathan.

Now he spends his time groaning softly in pain, or sleeping, and then Vidar dozes too, curled up on the rug next to the bed. Fever has pared the flesh from Rashid's face; planes of cheek and jaw that

Vidar once found beautiful have sunk away. Only his eyes are the same, brown and too large in his narrower face.

During the day Rashid can only speak a word or two at a time, requests for relief that leave him breathless. Sometimes Fatima takes Vidar's place by her father's bed, but even then, Vidar can't make himself retreat very far. He lingers outside the door, listening, waiting, hoping. Hoping this is the day that Rashid's fever breaks and doesn't return.

At night Vidar opens the windows and lets in the cool desert air. Earlier in Rashid's illness, Vidar would carry him to the roof at night. There, they watched sunset glimmer orange on the Tigris River, and then ships' lanterns blinking awake, moving like slow dancers across the water. On those nights, Rashid sipped cool mint tea, propped up on pillows, and told Vidar stories of his youth on Baghdad's docks, begging tales from sailors about the savages to the north.

"That was when I learned about the Land of Darkness," said Rashid. "It made me more determined to travel. I loved the world so much I hated to imagine it ending."

Loved. Vidar's Arabic is good enough to understand the past-tense, to know that Rashid is withdrawing.

"What are you going to do when I am gone?" Rashid asked him.

Vidar stared down at his huge hands, useless for fighting Rashid's illness. He never let himself think of anything beyond shifts in Rashid's breathing, and signs of pain in the tightening of his jaw.

"You are meant for more than to be my servant," said Rashid. "Still, I would ask something else of you."

"Anything," said Vidar.

"We have spoken before of the new land, this Iceland. It may be where the giants live, the ones who will end the world. I will not ask for your promise, but if you wish for another task, go there. Claim a farm, find a wife, sons as tall as yourself."

Vidar shakes his head. "What about Fatima? You asked me to guard her."

"Drink Odin's mead, and ask the giants of Iceland how to prevent the world's ending. Guard Fatima that way."

This long speech made Rashid's breath come in gasps. He closed his eyes and did not wake when Vidar picked him up and carried him back down to his room.

These days Rashid can hardly speak at all and cannot bear to be moved. Vidar sponges his limbs with mint water, hoping to draw down the fever without hurting him too much.

Today Rashid's cousin Umar has come again to check on Rashid, or so he said. He seems more interested in peering into his rooms, and running a finger along the dusty wall-hangings, than sitting by Rashid's bed. When Vidar shows him to Rashid's room, he demands tea and pastry, a footstool, for the boy fanning Rashid to turn and cool him instead.

"Are you his slave?" Umar asks Vidar in sharp Arabic. "Tell me, how many slaves does he have?"

Vidar pretends not to understand. He doesn't know how to answer. Rashid was his master. Once Vidar had been a slave. Perhaps he still was, enslaved by bonds of love and loyalty. But he will not be Umar's slave.

When Umar first visited, Rashid had laughed when he left, and said to Vidar in Norse, "Umar has a coin-hoard for a heart."

Vidar thinks of dragons, dwarves, the glowing of gold under the earth.

Umar reaches out to cuff the child fanning him. "Come here little boy," he says when the child flinches away from his blow.

The anger Vidar feels is an echo of an older rage. Those same words, spoken in a different language on the bank of the Dnieper River, below Kyiv's cliffs, brought Vidar to Rashid, ten years ago.

Sun beat down on Vidar's shoulders as he helped unload the foreigner's ship. His fellow slaves complained, but Vidar enjoyed the power of his arms and back as he lifted the foreign merchant's heavy trunks and carried them down the gangplank. A pulley system at the base of the cliffs would raise them up to the city proper.

"There is still ice in the river," Vidar overheard one of the foreigner's servants say, haltingly, to Agmund, warrior for the Grand Prince of Kyiv, who was supervising the unloading. The servant had dark eyes that widened when an ice-chunk the size of a small boat passed near. Its depths shone blue like a summer sky at midnight. The servant's skin was nut-brown. One of Vidar's fellow slaves had said that it was from the bright sun in their land, burning them dark as logs in a fire.

"Yes," Agmund was saying to the servant. "Spring comes late here."

Vidar's boots crunched in the spidery tracings of ice at the edge of the vast river. Mist clung to its surface even as the sun sparkled above.

He hefted another box and his eyes caught Agmund's. A few years ago, Agmund had said he would free Vidar when he grew to his full size, find him a place among the Prince's warriors. But time had passed, and Vidar tried not to let himself hope. Agmund let him train, sometimes, with his men. He had a special nod for Vidar, and greeted Vidar in the dialect of their shared stretch of Norse coastline. Vidar replied in words that tasted strange now, after so many years away. In Kyiv they spoke a mix of Slavic and an oddly accented Norse that Vidar had barely understood when he first arrived.

"Come here little boy," Vidar heard Mani say from somewhere beyond a stack of boxes. Vidar tightened his grip on the trunk's handle, splintering wood. Mani was another of the Grand Prince's warriors. "I have a sweetmeat for you," Mani added with a laugh.

The last time Vidar had tried to save a slave boy from Mani, Agmund had threatened a beating. Vidar still wished he had tried harder, learned whether Agmund would carry out his threat. Most of Agmund's men feared Vidar's size.

The slave boy had looked haunted for two weeks, especially in the mornings when he came from Mani's bed, though after Mani tired of him, he became a palace servant, so perhaps he judged the price worth it.

Vidar deposited the trunk in the pile of those waiting to ascend the cliff and trotted back to the ship. Mani had cornered the boy against a pile of stacked crates. The boy's shoulders shook, his dark eyes scared and defiant.

This child didn't belong to anyone in Kyiv—not dressed in those scarlet trousers, a color no Kyiv master would waste on a slave. If Mani wanted a night with him, he should at least compensate the boy's owner. The thought sickened Vidar. He could not have seen more than seven summers.

The child glanced up when he saw Vidar approaching, and darted toward him, hoping, it seemed, to duck between Mani and the wall of crates. Mani saw his movement and backhanded him, sending him sprawling onto the frosty ground.

Something in the way the child had fallen made Vidar think this was a little girl, not a boy. Mani might not care, but it made Vidar even more determined to save her.

Mani lunged for Vidar, who ducked so Mani's fist swung over his head. Few expected someone of Vidar's size to move quickly, and Mani looked affronted that his blow had missed. The girl scrambled to her feet, and as Mani glanced at her, Vidar shoved a box toward Mani's feet, hoping it contained nothing breakable. The girl ran around behind Vidar.

"I'll see you gutted for this," said Mani. "They'll flay the flesh off your back and leave you for crows to pick."

"Maybe," said Vidar. He waited to see if Mani would try to attack him, even now that the girl had gotten away. He half wished he would. He wanted to feel how hard Mani's blows might be, if he could resist by tensing his muscles enough to ward off the worst of the pain. Could he break Mani's wrist the way he had the handle of that last crate?

"What's going on?" Vidar heard Agmund say from somewhere behind him.

"Mani wanted to take one of the visitor's...boys," said Vidar. If the child wanted to be thought a boy, he would let her. "I didn't think it would be good for business."

"Perhaps," said Agmund. "Perhaps not."

The child said something in her language, her voice high and harsh. Vidar turned to look where she did, and Mani's blow caught him on the cheek.

He staggered a few steps before regaining his balance and the most beautiful face Vidar had ever seen swam into view. A man's face, floating above crimson and saffron, symmetrical and finely cut. His beard could not disguise the line of his chin, or his lips, shaped like a nomad's bow.

"The child tells me that you helped," the man said in deeply accented Slavic that Vidar could hardly understand at first.

"I did, my lord," Vidar mumbled.

He said something else in his language, which his translator repeated as, "Who is this man?"

"An ugly liar," said Mani. "The boy was lost. I was finding his way."

Vidar clenched his fists, but otherwise kept his eyes cast down.

"This is no boy, but my daughter," the traveler said. "Fatima bin Rashid, Fatima daughter of Rashid."

Vidar's anger ebbed somewhat. He had been right to see a girl child in boys' clothes. He dared a glance up at the foreigner— Rashid—and saw the man's clear, kind eyes resting upon him, as though they saw through to his heart. Vidar's throat burned and he had to look away.

Rashid continued, through his translator, "She likes to explore. Her nurse should keep better track of her, but I had not thought her in danger as a guest in your land."

Servants and warriors murmured to one another. To abuse a guest was a crime even Mani should understand. The Prince would lose standing with the great merchants of Constantinople and Baghdad if news of this reached them.

"A girl," Mani scoffed. "You cannot believe a girl."

"I believe my daughter over a blustering coward who would harm a child," said Rashid.

Another wash of murmuring. Mani must answer Rashid's words with a sword or be thought no man at all.

"Do guests insult their hosts where you come from?" Mani asked. "You will defend your lies and I will defend my honor."

Rashid looked unperturbed by Mani's anger. He exchanged a few low words with his translator, who then said, "Lord Rashid did not name a particular coward," he said. "There is no insult."

The crowd that had gathered laughed at that. Agmund, standing near Mani, said, "He has you there."

"But who is this man who has aided my daughter?" Rashid asked. "I would reward him."

Agmund raised a hand as if to push away Rashid's offer. "He's only a slave, my lord. He does the Prince's bidding. It is the Prince you should thank."

Vidar looked at Rashid again, and felt an understanding pass between them, though it faded as soon as someone else caught him in conversation.

At the feast that night, Vidar sat in his usual place, on the low benches with the other slaves, eating scraps leftover from those of higher rank. He hunched in his shoulders out of habit. Every time he reached for the ladle to pour some broth to soak his stale, coarse bread, his elbow hit one of his fellows.

A Slavic man with a tan too deep to have been burnished in Kyiv approached Vidar at his seat. "My lord would like you to join him tomorrow at his ship in the morning," he said. "He also warned you not to find yourself alone with that man." He sniffed fastidiously. "And you should bathe first."

Vidar inhaled a whiff of dog shit hidden among the rushes, mixed with the scent of rotten food, and his own sweaty reek. He nodded.

Vidar used the bathhouse in the depths of the night, when no one else wanted it, and kept himself awake until dawn, wary of an attack from Mani. By the time he joined Rashid on the deck of his ship, sleeplessness made his head spin.

He stared at one of the sailors lowering the yard that held the triangle sail, so different from square-sailed Norse ships. A breeze blew down the Dnieper River, carrying scents of forest and fish, making ripples and eddies on its broad back.

Rashid and his translator appeared at Vidar's elbow. His head came nearly to the top of Vidar's nose. A tall man, by most measures, and as perfectly formed as Vidar remembered.

"Do you have anything binding you here, in Kyiv?" Rashid asked, speaking for himself, in his deeply accented Norse. Vidar had to watch Rashid's lips form the words to understand him and forgot to be embarrassed by Rashid's beauty. A man like Rashid should not be easy to reach.

"No," said Vidar. Nor anywhere else. His kin were dead or scattered in the raid that had brought him here.

"Then why do you stay?" Rashid asked. Vidar hardly noticed when Rashid switched to Arabic and his translator continued, "You are strong. You could run off into the woods. Any village nearby would be glad to have a man like you to lend your strong back to the work. No one would follow you or make you return. I have spoken with Agmund and I am sure of that."

Shame burned Vidar's face. Why had he stayed? Too little imagination to leave? Or had he been grateful for a place to belong, even as a slave?

"Not every man is born to lead," he said, quoting the Norse proverb.

"Perhaps not," said Rashid through his translator, "but I think you could learn to lead yourself, at least. How old are you?"

Vidar thought about it. "I had seen twelve summers when I was captured. Now, I have seen six more, I think." Or was it five? It was easier to count winters, when so little happened that one event defined the season. The first winter: cold and always hungry. The second: still hungry, with hands and feet grown huge, making him trip whenever he moved. His bones ached that winter. The third: he learned to sleep among the cows for warmth, and his fellow slaves mocked him for the dung on his clothes. The fourth winter: his shoulders broadened and a local girl with an aged husband took him to her bed a few times. The fifth: when Agmund had noticed him and began to train him for a place among the Prince's warriors. And this last winter, when he had fought with Mani for the first time.

Rashid was laughing a little, his eyes shining. "Oh, you are very young. I did not realize. I am bad at judging the ages of you Northmen, and still worse with a giant like you."

Vidar looked down at his hands, massive, shovel-like, and wanted to fold into himself.

"I could use a man like you on my travels, though you must be expensive to feed." Vidar winced to be compared to livestock. "But it would be worth it for your kindness. You are wasted here, and that man will find a way to punish you if you stay. If you will not come with me, take my advice and find a place away from Kyiv. I will give you some silver to ease your way."

"You want me to come with you?" Vidar asked, not believing.

"Yes," Rashid replied in his own voice. "I think you are a man I can trust, and I need more of those. You have shown you will fight for my daughter. You will be her guard."

Vidar joined Rashid's ship, carrying nothing more than his eating dagger and a winter cloak. Rashid offered him an eastern sword, but when Vidar said he didn't know how to wield it, let him choose for himself. He decided upon an ax that he could use for slaughtering a cow or defending Fatima. He wore it on his back and practiced unsheathing it quickly.

Fatima didn't require that kind of guarding though. Instead she slipped away in every port, wending through narrow passages, and down crowded alleys. Vidar learned the narrow streets of Baghdad, of Constantinople, and the forests of every trading town in Rus and Pencheneg territory, following her through them, though he missed many marvels looking for her little sandaled heel as it disappeared around a corner.

He learned that, even among their people, Rashid and his daughter were thought strange. Rashid let her dress as a boy and go unveiled. He said he would not marry her off unless she asked him to, and he did not think that likely.

The first time they returned to Baghdad, Rashid's home, Vidar lost Fatima when she pursued a crying kitten. He had been learning Arabic slowly, and Persian too, enough to ask the street-sellers of Baghdad if they had seen his charge. When he found her, she pointed to a fallen wall until he moved the stones and retrieved the creature, small enough to nestle in the fold of his palm.

In Sarkel, Fatima asked her father to purchase a little slave boy who did nothing but get underfoot on the ship and perform little tasks that the sailors set for him. Vidar longed to ask if he had been acquired the same way.

"Why?" he asked Fatima, instead, in his few words of Arabic. She would have to answer simply for him to understand. "Why do you always flee?"

"Practice," she said stonily. "Someday I will have to flee for good, and I want to know how."

"Flee your father?" Vidar asked.

She laid a hand on his forearm, her fingers light like a bird's bones. "I would never flee him. But I will flee anyone but him who tries to cage me."

Vidar frowned, and tried to keep a closer eye on her.

At Rashid's request, Vidar taught them Norse, speaking the language of his childhood with pleasure after days when he felt as though his mind and tongue had to traverse a maze more challenging than the streets of Baghdad.

Rashid treated all his men according to their abilities, none as slaves, none as masters. Every season, a young Arab man accompanied him, each the son of a friend who wanted to learn the merchant life. These he taught with patience, and sent them back to their families, wiser, stronger, and quieter men.

He kept a notebook of his travels, bound in calfskin, in which he wrote with a feather. In Norway, only sorcerers knew runes, and used them in rituals rarely glimpsed by common men. Rashid wrote as a matter of course, and often made Vidar fearful. Was the peace and generosity that surrounded him unnatural? Vidar had never known a man who did not cuff his servants, did not laugh to see a fight break out between his men.

Vidar had been traveling with Rashid for three years before he summoned the courage to ask what he wrote each night. They were sailing before a spring gale across the empty vastness of the Caspian Sea. A Norse captain would stay in view of the coastline to keep his bearing, but Rashid and his pilot read the stars and the weather to cross open sea and thus brought their goods more quickly to market.

"My lord, what sorcery do you make with that feather every night?" Vidar asked in Norse, when they practiced one night.

"Sorcery?" Rashid asked.

"Runes?" Vidar replied. "Norse has no word for 'writing.'" And here he used the Arabic word, which he thought must mean sorcery.

"It is not sorcery," Rashid answered in Norse. "It is…I record my thoughts and the things that I have seen so the Caliph can read them. But also, so Fatima can read them when I am gone. Perhaps a man in Baghdad with no legs will read them and be able to see in his mind what I have seen. Perhaps the Ulema—the religious scholars—will read them and add to their vast store of knowledge about…"

He trailed off and regarded Vidar thoughtfully before continuing. "The Ulema say that the end of the world will come when the descendants of the great giants, Gog and Magog, come down out of the North, bringing snow and cold with them." He spoke in Arabic now, slowly, so Vidar could translate each word in his mind.

"Their snow will smother the fertile lands of the Tigris and Euphrates, and blanket even Kaaba in Mecca. Then God will call all of His people home to heaven. It is not something to be wished. Allah has given us this world as a blessing to care for. The Ulema has asked me to find out what I can about these giants, and whether they will one day destroy us."

He gave Vidar a fond look. "I have met you, though. You are a giant, but you do not seem to desire destruction. Indeed, you seem more peaceful than most of your fellow Norse, though you are the largest of them. So, what am I to make of this? Is it the truth, or is it a tale that may only be true in the empty desert, like the djinns and ifrits, the Cyclops on their wandering islands? I have traveled many places and I have not seen those things, though other men may swear to them. What do you say?"

Vidar roused himself from the spell of Rashid's words and replied in Norse, "We too, believe that giants from the north, from the Land of Darkness, will one day destroy us. We call it Ragnarok, the end of Fate. The giants will fight the gods, and their fighting will destroy the earth."

"Is that so?" Rashid asked, fascinated. "I have not known Norse well enough to ask, and the Slavs are mostly Christian with a different idea of the end of the world. Do you know what must be done to avert it?"

"No," Vidar tried to remember the tales. "They say that many wolf-years will come before the end, when men fight men in hungry packs and tear one another apart."

"We are also taught that," Rashid replied. "The Masih al-Dajjal, the false one, will rule the earth during a time of terrible violence. But at the end the dead will be resurrected in body, and then will never die. Will your dead live again?"

"Yes. The brave warriors will fight on the side of the gods, and the cowards and oath-breakers will fight on the side of the giants."

"And then all will live forever?" Rashid asked.

"No, all will perish, and the world be full of darkness." At Rashid's frown he added, "Some say a new world will rise, with new gods."

"Ah, that is different from our tale. I would know more of this. We do not know when it will come, but I fear it will be soon."

"Why?" Vidar asked.

"I have met too many wolf-like men," he said. He shook his head. "Is there anything else you know of it?"

"I heard in Kyiv that the frost giants live in Iceland, a new land that some Norse have settled."

Rashid sat upright. "Is that so? I would like to go there."

"It is a rumor," said Vidar. "It would be easier to ask Odin himself, I think." He yawned.

"Can that be done?" Rashid asked.

"They say the berserks who drink Odin's mead can speak with him," said Vidar. "I do not know how, though."

Vidar gazed up at the dark sky overhead, his huge, heavy body sinking into last year's leaves, and the loam underneath. The full moon raced across the sky, the stars wheeling around it. He closed his eyes and opened them again. The moon had returned to where it started, staring down at him.

They had encountered some of Odin's brethren, berserker warriors, in Staraya Ladoga, near the Baltic Sea. Because Rashid wanted him to, because Vidar would do anything Rashid asked, he had fought on the side of these berserkers when they raided a nearby town.

Never before had he quaffed Odin's mead, strong and sweet, but bitter too, and musty like he lay his tongue on a stone. In that cave, his mouth tasted death, and then he emerged and slaked death's hunger with his ax and then his hands. He followed a Valkyrie into battle. He had a memory of pulling on a man's limb with all his might, hearing bone snap, tendon and flesh tear. No weapon could touch him. They wouldn't dare.

He returned from battle with his face and hands covered with blood until Rashid washed it from him with a rag, gently, and then used a broken stick to pry blood from under his fingernails. Vidar had gone shirtless into this battle on the edge of winter but did not feel cold until Rashid's touch.

"What did Odin say?" Rashid's voice was gentle and insistent. "Tell me."

Vidar flopped his head over, heard a snap as his movement broke a twig. The prickle of splinters pained him distantly. His arm wouldn't move to brush the pieces away. Rashid leaned up on one elbow, looking at him, his eyes black in the dimness.

"You are beautiful," said Vidar.

Rashid smiled ruefully, pleased and sorrowful at the same time.

"You're drunk," he said.

"More than that," Vidar replied, and looked away. Rashid's face was too much for him right now, his eyes growing wide to swallow up his cheeks, his teeth, his close-cropped hair. Odin's brethren had made Vidar drink too much of their drugged mead. He'd been lucky to stagger out of the cave and into battle without falling on his face.

"Are you angry that I asked this of you?" The worry in Rashid's voice made tears spring to Vidar's eyes.

"I am not a berserk," said Vidar. "I have never done this before. I suppose Odin is my god now."

"Did he speak to you?" Rashid asked. "Did he tell you about the end of the world?"

Overhead, the moon was covered with blood. Vidar's eyes had been open when he looked into the mystery, but he had seen nothing that Rashid wanted to know.

"When you're drinking Odin's wine you cannot die, and if you do, Odin and his Valkyrie maidens come for you," Vidar said.

"What was it like?" Rashid asked. His voice was beautiful too, full of patience, but cruelty also, because he sent Vidar to take the mead of the brethren, to learn what it was to fall upward into the bloody sky.

"What *is* it like," Vidar countered. "I have not left."

"The others are sleeping now," said Rashid. "I hear their snores, but you are still awake."

"You won't let me sleep," Vidar grumbled. He'd never spoken to Rashid like this before.

"I'll let you sleep if you tell me," said Rashid. "Did you see him? Did you learn anything about the giants? Where to find the Land of the North?"

Did he see Odin on his eight-legged steed? He saw the limbs of men and horses, moving through the air, wielding hooves like weapons, swords like hooves, limbs severed on the ground, white bone and red blood. He saw the sky clawed by dead fingers. He was speaking now, letting the words spill out of him. "I could not die. I could not live. I could only kill. I am still drunk on the blood."

Vidar wanted to help him understand. But maybe it was like his mother used to talk about the pangs of childbirth. Unless you've gone through them, you can't know, and even on the other side, the memory slips away. Pain and effort like that can't stay in the body. It's too much: body and spirit turning themselves inside out, trying to approach a god.

"Odin makes the killing feel inevitable," said Vidar. "Not easy, but impossible to do otherwise."

"Perhaps this Odin does not fear the end of the world," said Rashid.

"He wants warriors for it," said Vidar. "So, he can win. Does your god want warriors?"

"Warriors of the faith," said Rashid.

"Then we will fight together," said Vidar.

Rashid sighed. "I suppose that's all I can hope."

Vidar holds Rashid's limp hand in his own. His breaths come so slowly now. Vidar thinks each one will be the last, until another rattles his chest. Fatima sits on his other side.

Three years of winter should have come first, the great Fimbulwinter, the wolf-years, the horn of Heimdall announcing the doom of the gods.

This day is cool, a fall breeze stealing around the curtains. Vidar sends the fan-boy away.

Rashid's other servants have left. Vidar does not know how to pay them and there's little enough for them to do.

Then Rashid breathes no more.

Vidar hears city sounds. Fatima sits, shocked and still, then utters a cry and flings her father's hand down. She flees to another room, and still Vidar sits. He has no plans for this. He never needed to plan, not when he followed Rashid.

If Rashid were Norse, he would be burned on his ship, with a crowd of warriors to drink his farewell. He should have a dog killed and burned with him, to guide him to Valhalla, and a wife too, or concubine, to go with him so he would not be lonely. He should have Vidar and Fatima.

But that is not what he asked of Vidar.

Rashid's cousin Umar arrives that afternoon, leading an army of servants he sets to removing everything from Rashid's chambers, including the shutters nailed to the outside of the building. He speaks in simple phrases that Vidar can understand, particularly the one he keeps repeating: "All of this belongs to me."

And later, "Where is the girl? I am allowed one more wife."

"The girl is with a friend," says Vidar loudly, to warn her.

"If you were his slave, you belong to me too," Umar tells him.

"I am not a slave," Vidar says, walking slowly toward Umar. His servants look cowed when Vidar rolls his neck. Umar himself has a bit more heft than Rashid did, broader in the shoulders and waist, but Vidar doesn't think he would be a problem, not if Vidar wraps his hands around Umar's neck and does not let go until he is dead.

"This house is mine, and you'll have to clear off," says Umar, in a more conciliatory tone. As if he saw the thoughts of violence passing through Vidar's mind.

"Tomorrow," says Vidar. "Come back then."

"Tomorrow," he agrees. "Bring the girl back and there's a reward in it for you. I'll hire you, if you like."

"Tomorrow," Vidar repeats.

He stares after Umar and his entourage as they leave, meeting the eyes of any who turn back. As soon as they're gone, he finds Fatima on the roof. She has her knees drawn up to her chest, her arms wrapped around them, her face pale.

"He's come," she says. "I thought he might. Father told me of him. Too much..." Her face crumples.

"What do you want of me?" Vidar asks. Fatima looks so much like Rashid, her beauty angular and androgynous like his. He would serve her, follow her, for Rashid, and for herself.

She rushes toward the roof's edge and he follows her. She holds a finger to her lips and points down. Below, two men stand, swords curving from their waists.

"There will be more tomorrow," Fatima tells him in a whisper.

"What do we do?" Vidar asks.

"I don't know!" Fatima's voice rises and Vidar puts a hand over her mouth.

"I promised your father I would guard you," says Vidar slowly, letting her go.

"He's dead." Now she sounds like a stone given speech.

"What do you want to do next? Do you have relatives I can bring you to?"

"Yes, Umar," says Fatima with a broken laugh. "But I do not want to marry him. I do not want to marry anyone."

"You don't have," Vidar replies. "You don't have to do anything."

This is more than they have ever spoken to one another, even when Vidar guarded her. He saved his words for Rashid, and so did she. He looks out the window again. Two more men have arrived, talking purposefully to the others.

"They're not waiting until tomorrow," he says. "If we're to leave, we have to go tonight."

"To where?" Fatima asks. "Neither of us have anywhere to go."

"Your father wanted me to go to Iceland," says Vidar. "I thought guarding you was more important."

Fatima raises her head. "I can go to Iceland. I would like to see it."

"The giants, and the end of the world?" Vidar asks.

"I don't know if my father ever wanted to find answers," she says. "He just liked searching."

He also advised Vidar to find a place where his strength was needed. A new minted land, with giants in the mountains. He might be needed there.

"I have some jewelry hidden in my mattress to pay our way," says Fatima. "But how can we get out? That's the only exit."

The building backs up against one much higher—they cannot escape on the roof. And two more men have joined the others. Surely, soon they will have enough to confront Vidar and a slender girl.

"I have a packet of Odin's herbs," Vidar tells her. "If I take them, I will be able to fight my way out. But I will not be in my right mind. You will have to guide me to the docks so we can hire a ship."

She looks fearful, but only asks, "What about my father? He should be buried tonight. It is our way."

"My way would be to burn him," says Vidar. "He will still reach the gods. And it will be a good distraction."

Fatima doesn't like it, but she lets herself be convinced. They do not have time to wash him and dress him properly, a task, Fatima says, that his male relatives should undertake. Vidar carries him up to the roof, along with his bed and mattress, and stacks some broken pieces of furniture around him.

Fatima has a bottle of spirits used for some of Rashid's medicines. She pours some on the pyre to help it catch, and Vidar drinks the rest, swallowing down dry bits of Odin's herbs. He prays in Norse, and Fatima prays in Arabic, and when Rashid's skin starts to crackle in the heat, the drugs take hold.

Fatima towers over him. *Follow me,* she says, somehow in Vidar's mind, not his ears, one of Odin's Valkyries, her black eyes gleaming death. He follows her down a narrow set of stairs to a door she opens quickly, before springing back.

A man's head appears in the doorway, and Vidar slices down with an ax he does not remember picking up. Now the man lies on the ground, his head and shoulder half severed from his body.

Two come through together. One trips over his fellow and Vidar kicks him in the chin so his head snaps back. He catches the other in the gut with his ax.

*They'll trap us in here,* the Valkyrie says, so Vidar pulls the bodies in one-handed, still holding his ax in the other.

Another attacker slices along Vidar's arm with a blade, but Vidar cuts off his hand and then his head. He picks it up and tosses it out the door. He hears it hit the wall on the other side of the street and then hears feet slapping stone, growing quieter.

*They've run away. Let's go.*

But Odin does not yet have his fill of blood and death, and Vidar longs to give it to him. Bring him more. Let these men be the wood for the pyre on which Rashid burns.

The Valkyrie takes his hand, though, sticky with blood, and leads him out into the night, where black stars shine down from a white sky. Vidar looks back at the bodies in the street, until the Valkyrie tugs on him again. He nods. She is Odin's creature. She will know where he can find more blood.

They hire on a ship that night bound for Cordoba.

The sun rises before Odin's herbs depart from Vidar's senses, and he remembers what he did, and why he is here. His hands are cool where Fatima has scrubbed a wet rag over them. Vidar remembers Rashid doing the same, and he weeps. Fatima weeps with him, for a time, but then she wipes her eyes with the edge of her veil and says, "In Cordoba we can find a ship going north to Iceland. There, it will be safest if you act as my eunuch guard. Further north, perhaps I should act as your slave instead."

"Perhaps," says Vidar. "But I serve you. Always remember that."

"Perhaps," she echoes back. "Perhaps we both serve him."

# — THE BLASPHEMY OF THE GODS —
## Sami Shah

*Bjorn the Berserker*

**B**y the Grace of Allah, the merciful, the all-seeing, and by the grace of the final Prophet sent to us, may peace be upon him, what I am about to convey is the truth. For those that would read my words and blame upon me falsehoods that they might perceive in my tale, all that I may say is that were I you, I too would consider that which is being told here to be too fanciful to be true. Yet, the truth it is; for all that occurred, I was not only a witness, but also a participant, and my experiences are undeniable, try as I have to find ways of denying them. If you would call me a liar then consider only this before you do: what do I gain from lying? In telling this the way I am about to, do I not risk bringing ruination upon my own name? I have considered omitting some details for just that reason and have agonized over the price I will pay for my honesty. But my honesty is what I have valued above all other traits I might be blessed with. Indeed, it is what has been considered by others as my most respectable attribute. Even the Caliph, may Allah bless him always and keep him in virtue and prosperity, marked my adherence to the truth as the cause for sending me on the mission he set for me.

I was summoned to the court of the most gracious, Caliph Abu l-Fadl Ja'far ibn Ahmad al-Mutadid, in the month of Rabi' al-thani, on the 318th year of the Hijra. It was not my first time being commanded to serve my leader, for in my capacity as ambassador of the Abbasids, I had previously been sent far beyond our kingdom. In truth, only three full moons prior had I returned from far off Constantinople, where I had been sent to take full seizure of captured soldiers of our Ummah from the Empress Karvounopsina. I stood in the presence of the regent known for her eyes as black as coal—and that they were—and asked that she honor her commitment to our Caliph for the ransom he had paid. It was my shame to see the followers of Isa being ruled by a woman and for our own warriors to be her slaves, and so it was with relief that I had brought them back to the land of their fathers. The Caliph had entrusted me with the sum of one hundred and twenty thousand gold pieces to be delivered in the exchange, knowing full well that my forthrightness in the eyes of Allah would mean that not a single coin would be amiss. This reputation was my birthright, for my father had served in the court of the previous Caliph, Abu Mansur Muhammad ibn Ahmad al-Mutadid, and had earned the title of "The Trusted". It was a day of great pride when I too had that bestowed upon me, referred to in the most recent summons as "Bilal ibn Hammad, al Maqthuq".

My wife, who should be forgiven for her dismay at my being asked to leave her and our two sons so soon again—for it is the provenance of women to wish their husbands spent more time with them—asked when I would return. I answered as I always have to that question: 'When Allah wills it.'

I departed our home in Tikrit, and rode with the Caliph's guard to the capital. There, presenting myself to the ruler of our lands and the defender of Islam, I received my orders.

'In the West, beyond where I've sent Ibn Fadlan, are the Rusiyah,' he said. His voice was that of a young man steeped in luxury, but not yet secure in the knowledge that the comforts were his by right. 'Do you know of them?'

Prostrated still, my forehead cooled by the marble floor, I said I did. I knew of Ibn Fadlan, the great explorer, who had left just a few months prior on a journey to discover all he could of the Volgar Bulgars, those men with eyes the color of a clear sky and skin so pale you could see the blood beneath the skin.

'A man of the Rus is here now, with me. Look upon him, O' son of Hammad.'

I lifted my head and saw first the Caliph, seated upon a small hill of cushions, cooled by peacock feathers, and festooned in robes of golden silk. Next to him, standing and looking down upon me, was a man I had never laid eyes on before. His eyes were not the blue of the few Bulgars I had seen on my travels, but a dulled grey, much like the steel of the axe hanging from his belt. The scar that stretched across his right eye and down his cheek was old, and his beard was not as soft and oiled as my own, but a slab of jagged ice. He wore a patchwork of leather and coarse cloth, clothing that might have been brighter in appearance once, but had not been so for a long time. Much like many of his kind, I could not tell his age, for he could be a man in his thirties or fifties, his features afforded no such specificity. Next to the explosion of color that was the Caliph, he looked as drab as an etching in charcoal.

'This man is named Bjorn,' announced my eminence. 'He has been training my warriors in ways of war.'

'I did not know you had retained the services of men from so far away in your army, lord,' I said, instantly regretting the impertinence of the question.

'Oh...and is it my duty to consult with you before I decide who can and cannot work for me Bilal,' snapped the defender of Allah's will.

'Forgive me, O' Gracious one,' I requested, and with a laugh he did.

'Bjorn comes from a land far away. Farther than any of our people have gone. In that land, there is to be a gathering of his people. A...what did you call it Bjorn?'

'The Althingi, Grace,' said Bjorn. His voice was the sound of heavy snow cascading down the side of a mountain.

'Yes. Bjorn is to return to his land to attend this...Althingi. He is to inherit a parcel of land left to him by his brother who has died and he must present himself at the Althingi to claim it. I require that you go with him.'

What I asked next was not to succumb to further impertinence, but so I could have some measure as to why I was once again being deprived of the warmth of my family.

'To what end my lord? What would you have me do at this Althingi?'

'To observe it, Bilal Ibn Hammad. It is a gathering unlike any that we have in our kingdom, and I would learn from it. Perhaps it is something we can all learn from. Perhaps it is a folly that is exclusive to the people of the lands of ice. But, I would know more of it. From what Bjorn has told me, we could find great allies in his home, warriors to aid us in our battles against the Christians. Knowing of their ways could benefit us all. After all, did not our Prophet Muhammad, peace be upon him, not say, "One who treads a path in search of knowledge has his path to Paradise made easy by God"? I would like my path to Jannah made easier. Will you do this for me Bilal?'

And so was my task set. I departed before the next prayer, with the pale man as my guide.

'I'm sorry for the loss of your brother,' I offered, as we rode our horses with the rising sun at our backs.

'He was a great warrior,' Bjorn said, with some sorrow tinging his words.

'Did he die in battle?'

'No,' said Bjorn. 'He was gored by a walrus, the damn fool.'

'What is a walrus', I asked.

'It is like a bear with fins instead of paws, and two giant teeth as large as your arm.

'That sounds fearsome,' I said.

'It isn't. They're slow and easily dodged. My brother had the wits of one of your mules.'

I looked over and saw Bjorn's face was split by a grin. It looked like a glacier had broken in two.

The journey was not without events worth retelling, and if I am fortunate enough to live a longer life, then I shall endeavor to describe it in greater detail. I will write of being beset by bandits in Armenia, and how it was only the ferocity of Bjorn that saved us. Of the man in Abkhazia who ate the raw intestines of a goat as he offered to divine our future for gold; we did not take him up on this offer. In the land of the Khazars we met a people in such familiarity with their horses that you could be forgiven for thinking they were formed from the beast's parts. When, on the rare occasion, they did climb down, they walked with legs widely set. It was they who led us through the oceans of grass that would have drowned us had we not their guidance, shooting birds from the sky with arrows truer than their sight. The Livonians with their strange music and the Estone with their hatred for that music. And finally, the Norsemen who greeted Bjorn with a language they both spoke and set us on a ship for his land.

On the journey, Bjorn told me of his gods. They are a heathen people, still deprived of the truth of Allah and His Messenger and so worshipping the many instead of the One. He told me of Odin, their one-eyed king of gods, with two ravens upon his shoulder, and of this son who controls the lightning and rides a chariot pulled by rams. I tried to make sense of his belief in a tree older than the world, and of the day of judgement that he called "Rag Nah Rok". Bjorn told me these tales and I did not tell him he will burn in the fires of Jahanum[1] for believing in them, for it is rude to say so to your guide.

We moored at the mouth of a village, where there were many who had heard of him and a few who knew him, and from them did we buy fresh horses and furs. It is here that I would pause in my tale of my travels to dwell on something that needs understanding: this land that I have been brought to is cold. I have seen ice and snow before, on a journey through the mountainous North of the Abbasid empire; I have felt the bite of winds that carry ice. But not like this. Here there is no refuge from the cold. It mocks the heat of a fire and infiltrates even the thickest of coats and furs. I shiver from dawn to dusk, meagre as those daylight hours are, and then in my sleep I shiver still. I feared my teeth would shatter and my eyes would freeze in their sockets. Snow covers everything so thickly, one would have to dig for a lifetime to find the earth beneath. And in this cold, Bjorn seems most at ease. As I sit curled around fires, he walks bare-chested, rubbing ice on his skin and laughing at my frailty.

'It is because you do not drink mead,' proclaims Bjorn with a laugh, taking a long drink from a horn full of the fermentation of honey and berries he keeps on his hip.

---

[1] Arabic term for hell

'My belief prohibits me from any drink that would rob me of my senses,' I offer as a justification, but he waves his away with more laughter.

'What god is worth trusting if he would not let his follower enjoy that which is best in life,' he says, and warms himself with another drink. If there was a dulling of his senses caused by the mead, I could not tell. For he provided evidence of his sharp senses by throwing his axe a mighty distance and killing a fox, the meat of which was all the warmth I could enjoy in that land of endless cold.

The people of this place are simple in their presentation, from their clothes to their homes, there is little ornamentation to be seen. This was made clearer to me when we reached our destination. It was not the first gathering of leaders I had seen in my lifetime; tribal chieftains, warring commanders, and even emperors and caliphs—I had seen many of their meetings in person, and had read in detail the descriptions of others. There is pomp and ceremony and displays of extravagance, for even the poorest of tribes would not allow their poverty or simplicity to be known by others. I had heard of one gathering, where the king of a small state that was presenting its arms to our Caliph, put his people into a debt that would take a hundred years to repay, just so no one could say he was not capable of the same comforts as any others. These Rusiyah care little for such indulgence. When we arrived at the hall near the vast field where the Althingi was to commence the next day, I might have been forgiven for thinking it the stable for our horses; a single long hallway with a triangular roof, heated by a fire in the center, the only adornments being the tables and chairs on which attendants would be seated. There were no paintings, no carvings into the walls, no way at all of telling this place to be any more prestigious than any of the homes we passed along the way.

We were amongst the last of the attendants to arrive, myself and a follower of Isa from a land called Bremen which I had not heard of before. His name was Thangbrand, and his mission as he proclaimed it was different from mine. Whereas, I had been sent to observe and learn, he had been sent to convert all he would encounter in the ways of their Prophet of the Cross. Despite our two peoples being at war for as long as either of us could remember, we found a great affinity in each other's company, combining my meagre Latin with his surprisingly fluent Arabic to converse.

'This gathering of theirs is not held under the light of Christ,' he said. 'However, in my visitations with the king of the land East of here, he said their practices of putting faith in pagan gods and ways is coming to an end. Soon, even these men of this frozen land will come to my lord Jesus Christ.'

'Better they follow a holy book,' I agreed. 'Even if it is to be your Bible and not my Quran.'

'What are you two foreigners conspiring on,' said Bjorn, collapsing on the ground next to me. We were in a visitor's lodge close to the main hall, and he had consumed enough of mead over the course of the dinner to slur even his words.

'We are wondering what you think of tomorrow's proceedings,' asked Thangbrand of Bjorn, speaking in a language native to this land that I knew not, but was grateful to Bjorn for his translations, somewhat inconsistent though they were at this particular point.

'This is a great thing,' Bjorn said, motioning to the many gathered at the lodge. 'Nowhere before has it been done, and no one else dare do such a thing. But I care little for its success. I am here for the land of my brother, and these collectors of law will see to it that I get what is mine. I have relatives that would see it taken from me, but I have paid a fair sum of gold to ensure that does not happen.'

He was speaking, of course, of the Althingi. Tomorrow, a gathering of men numbering nearly five score would begin dispensing legal judgements based on a compilation of laws, collected after being forced out of their ancestral lands, with no benefit of writing. They compiled the laws as the Meccans related fables before Allah showed them the wisdom of the written word, with just memory. They would agree on the payment of debts, the settling of scores, and the minutiae of life lived on this isle. Those five-score men would be the deciders of these rules, and their decision-making was the cause of great spectacle, for hundreds had gathered in tents across the hills of the area. After it was done, I would return to the Caliph and describe its successes and failures. He would be unlikely to institute such a system in our lands, where we had long been accustomed to a single lord who decided all in the wisdom of Allah, but he should know of it nonetheless.

Bjorn's breath had grown rank, and the follower of Isa had taken him up on the challenge to see which of them would succumb to stupor first, so I headed out into the cold wind to regain some clarity of thought. The sky here is peculiar, rejecting the darkness of night even at a late hour. Instead, it looks much like the hour of Maghrib does, with fingers of sunlight still casting light. I had heard tell of such things from the writings of other explorers and travelers, but to now stand under a deepening day while the body yearned for the sleep of the midnight hour was a peculiar sensation. I walked through them, listening to men and women conversing in a language I knew not, singing songs I struggled to find the melody in. This is a land so different from whence I came, a people so far removed from mine. We have grown accustomed to comforts, to foods flavored with spices from far away, and music constructed with instruments so delicate one has to dedicate a lifetime to their mastery. We wear silken garments with ornate patterns sewn into them, and our conversations are of philosophy and the discoveries of optics and medicine. Here, there is none of that indulgence. They talk of survival, of making it through the next winter and the next battle. They sing of the same, and no doubt their food is eaten with the same limited ambition. Yet, in this bare existence, there is hope for a future that will extend past their children's children. They have the considerations of legacy, for why else would you gather to create a new governance, to codify in it laws that would guide and bind one and all.

The cold exhausted me, and my legs began to ache from the exertion required to walk through the snow, so I returned to the heat of our lodge and lay in my bed. The room was small, and I was sharing it with Thangbrand, who was well into a drunken snoring sleep. Asking Allah to wake me for the Fajr prayer, I too lay down. It was how I always managed to keep my prayers; just before sleeping, I make this request of the Almighty, and he obliges by waking me in the minutes before the sun makes its creeping ascent over the horizon. I do not wake with a start, there is no sudden jolting of my person, no sound sent from Allah, just a gradual release of sleep's hold, until I can rise to attend my duties. Which is how I awoke when I saw the death of Thangbrand.

When I travel I dream of home, of my wife's smile and my children's laughter. Waking from that missed life is always a torture, but I do not begrudge it too much, for what better way to start the day's work than by bowing your head to Allah's grace and wonder. This time, however, the dream was struggling to hold on to me, my wife pleading with me to stay with her, just a little longer. 'Until it's safe,' she said. And behind her, somewhere in the depths of our home—which is always far more expansive in the dream than in reality—I could hear the grunt and snore of a massive beast searching for me. I pulled free of her, angry at her for making me risk missing the Fajr prayer, and forced myself awake. I lay in my cot, covered by thick furs, and realizing that the hungry sounds of the beast had followed me out of the dream. There was a growl to my side, then the wet rending of something being chewed. I looked over and made a loud invocation of help to the Almighty.

Standing over Thangbrand was what seemed a wolf. It was too large to be a wolf, too strangely thin, with its ribs heaving visibly under scant fur, but it had the head of a wolf, and the teeth of a wolf, and the tail of a wolf. Where there should have been paws were hands, hands like mine and yours, but large as my torso, and with those hands it gripped the missionary's limbs. His stomach had been opened to the world, and the wolf was pulling his intestines with its teeth, feasting on them with slow savor. It heard me, large ears twitching as I prayed, and lifted its snout to face me, teeth glistening like black pitch in the dark.

'O' Allah have mercy on me,' I whispered.

The wolf spoke with the voice of a man. This I do swear, for I heard it as clearly as I heard my own voice.

'Your Allah is not here. Just I,' growled the wolf, and then I began to scream. I screamed though the scream was involuntary, coming from me even though I had not willed it. I had on my person a sword, gifted to me by the Caliph several years before. It was a thing of exquisite beauty, and had drawn so much attention over the years that I had grown to resent it. The hilt was golden and sparkled with jewels, and the curved blade sharpened to an edge so fine I could slice through parchment with it. More than once had it given me cause to defend myself against bandits who attacked for only the greed the sword inspired in them. I pulled it now from the scabbard and rushed at the wolf, but the distance between us was too great. It laughed a human laugh, then turned and leapt. There was a window and it was closed, and even had it been open it would be too small for the wolf to fit through, for even a child would have struggled to get through it. But the wolf went through the window, silently and easily, and was gone.

My scream had woken those in the rooms adjoining ours and they came rushing in, Bjorn in the lead with his axe held ready for battle. I could not know what it was they saw when they entered, but Bjorn would later describe it to me. There I had stood, over the body of Thangbrand, my sword in my hand, his entrails around my bare feet. Before I could react further, Bjorn had snatched the sword from my grasp, and put himself between the others and my person.

'He has killed the preacher', they cried out, and my protestations were for naught. Nor do I blame them, for who would believe my tale of a wolf with hands like mine, who spoke to me in Arabic and vanished through a small window.

'What have you done Bilal,' Bjorn asked, holding me by my arms as you would a child who is in the throes of a tantrum. I tried to explain to him, but he was as unbelieving as any of the others, and allowed them to clap chains on my hands and feet, and lead me away from the scene of steaming death.

I do not know what occurred in the first Althingi, I was not allowed to witness it, but Bjorn did tell me later that they talked of my supposed crime and decided I had forfeited my protection as a representative of the Caliph by committing murder.

'They will behead you tomorrow Bilal, though I did beg them not to. I spoke of your good character, but their trust in my word does not outweigh the evidence in that room. You say a wolf did this, but there were no marks of teeth or claw on Thangbrand. What was done to him could only have been done with a blade and with hands.'

'But there was no blood on my sword. Or on my hands. Even you saw that,' I pleaded.

'I did,' he said after a long silence. He offered to pray for me. 'I will ask Thor for mercy, for he is also the dispenser of justice. Though I should tell you he is unlikely to hear my call, for I dedicate myself to Odin who aids me in making war, and have not made any sacrifices to Thor in my life.' I thanked him for his care, then asked for parchment and ink that I may write this accounting of what occurred, and that he take it back to the Caliph when he returns to Baghdad.

He left a few hours ago, and though I cannot see the sun in this small room where I am to spend my final night, I know it has descended from the sky. As I finish my prayer and prepare to write my tale, I hear laughter. The room can barely fit a person other than myself, and the door has stayed closed since Bjorn's departure, so I wonder if the laughter has come from me.

'It is not you laughing,' says the thing in the corner. It is a man, but it is also a wolf. It is also a snake, and it is a flame. It is all these things at once, and yet when I look at it directly, I see that it is mostly a man.

'What are you,' I ask of it.

'I am the son of Fárbauti and Laufey, and the brother of Helblindi and Býleistr' it says, and the smile shows teeth. 'I am the father of Hel, of Fenrir and of Jörmungandr, of Sleipnir and of Narfi. I am Loki. And I am a god.'

'There is no god but Allah, and Muhammad is his messenger,' I say, though it is difficult for me to speak.

'I am a god nonetheless,' it says, and begins to laugh again.

'Why did you kill Thangbrand? Why have you done this to me,' I ask.

'I killed that fool because he would dare bring his new beliefs to my lands. For already so few are left who still believe in me and believe in the All-Father. Soon there will be no more who pray to us. Who curry our favor. Who fear our wrath. Killing him will delay their abandonment of us.'

'But why me? I do not seek to convert your followers to the way of Allah. I came only to witness.'

The thing rises up and stands taller than a djinni, its head brushing the ceiling. Each eye is larger than my hand, and in them I can see my frightened form reflected.

'You were there. And you annoy me. And your death for this will amuse me,' it says. And then I am alone again.

In the morning they will come and take my head for a crime I did not do, one committed by a bitter and angry god. I will die knowing that there are other gods than mine in this world, and that I can do nothing with that blasphemy in my heart.

I pray that the Caliph, in his compassion, can trust in what I have conveyed here, though I know that it is too much to believe. I pray that my wife and children can forgive me for not writing to them. Most of all, I pray that Allah will have mercy upon me, and take me from this land of ice and vengeful gods.

# THE SHORT TALE OF
# — THURID THE EXASPERATED —
## Genevieve Gornichec

*Eystein the Unlucky*

**M**other! Mother!"

Thurid looked up from her spinning as her eldest son Bjarni hurtled through the door. Around her, the serving women looked up from their own work from where they sat on their benches lining the hall, seeming irritated at the disruption on what had promised to be a calm, quiet night.

It was late in the evening. Most of the men from the settlement had gone to the *godi*'s daughter's wedding feast, leaving behind the women, the children, and the older farmhands who weren't up for the trip. The latter two groups were already laid out and snoozing on their own benches, but a few of them stirred or lifted their heads at Bjarni's premature homecoming, earning him irritated looks from the mothers or wives.

Thurid set her wool and spindle aside and rose to her feet. "What's happened, Bjarni? You weren't supposed to be back until the morning. Where is your father?"

Bjarni was doubled over, panting from exertion. When he straightened, he said, with all the gravity a ten-year-old could muster, "Father's challenged someone to a duel!"

The hall was silent.

Thurid's eye twitched. *Not again.*

"Of course he has," she said, as calmly as she could. "Where is he?"

"Chasing ghost-walruses off the beach with Weird Uncle Skeggi," said another voice as Thurid's middle son Bolli appeared behind his brother.

Thurid sighed. "Bolli, there are no ghost-walruses on the beach."

"But Weird Uncle Skeggi says there are!"

"Don't call him 'Weird Uncle Skeggi.'"

"But he's weird, and he's our uncle," said Thurid's youngest son Bork, aged seven, as he sat up on his bench, where he'd been sleeping until approximately thirty seconds ago. "And his name is Skeggi," he added helpfully.

In her head, Thurid counted to ten. Then she turned to Bjarni and Bolli and said, "Will *one* of you go get your father, please?"

True to form, not one but *both* of them spun around and launched themselves back into the darkness, hollering, *"Father!"* As the last people still sleeping in the hall began to stir at their shouts, Bork sprang off his bench to join his brothers. Thurid caught him by the back of his tunic and said, "Oh no you don't."

"But *Mother!*" he wailed, struggling.

"No buts," said Thurid. "You don't want to be eaten by a ghost-walrus, do you?"

"But you said there were no ghost-walruses!" Bork plopped back down on his bench and folded his arms, pouting. "Things can't only be true when you want them to be. They're either true, or they're not."

Before Thurid could comment on the validity of his statement, there were shouts from outside as the door opened and Eystein appeared, flanked by his two sons and followed closely by his brother Skeggi. It seemed that the two men were deep in an argument, and not about ghosts, walruses, or any combination thereof.

"I'm only saying," said Skeggi, "if you make an offering to the gods for a good duel—"

"And *I'm* saying that we need to eat this winter, and we can't go sacrificing our livestock all willy-nilly whenever we have a hangnail," Eystein said in his deep, rumbling voice. He kicked the doorframe with the side of his foot to shake the sand from his worn leather shoes, then stepped inside.

"A duel to the death is hardly a hangnail," Skeggi said, offended, but he and the boys followed suit and trailed after Eystein as he went inside and discarded his hood, cloak, and haversack on a bench at the front of the hall.

Thurid straightened and said, as evenly as she could, "What's this about a duel to the death?"

Eystein startled as if just realizing she was there, and then took in the sight of the entire household—some twenty people—all awake and staring at them, from the shepherd boys and the old field hands to a serving woman's fussing baby.

"Oh. Hello, all. Did we wake you up?" he asked, blinking.

Thurid resisted the urge to roll her eyes. Instead she put on her most placating face and said, in honeyed tones, "Husband—a moment of your time?"

———◖ ✳ ◗———

What grated on Thurid the most about her husband's daily misadventures was the simple fact that both of them were far too old for this: Eystein had seen nearly fifty winters, and Thurid herself was nearing the end of her childbearing years, although she had not become pregnant again since Bork was born, for which she was secretly grateful. Perhaps her body had decided to prematurely decline the notion of bringing any more of her husband's progeny into the world.

Not that Thurid disliked Eystein. She loved him, truly. She'd chosen him, after all, and she could've picked anyone; she'd definitely had enough offers. She'd been wealthy and twice widowed already when she accepted his marriage proposal some fifteen years ago. A reformed Viking adventurer-turned-farmer was a far cry more exciting than her first two husbands, who had gone raiding maybe once or twice in their lives and never returned with much plunder to speak of, and died of disease before they could get any children on her.

Eystein, at least, had tales to tell. Although this got him into trouble more often than not.

Some called her husband "Eystein the Unlucky." The fact that Thurid's first two husbands had perished may have made her worry that *she* perhaps had something to do with his bad luck. But since Eystein's nickname predated their marriage by at least two decades, many had questioned Thurid's decision to legally bind her fate to his.

But if you asked Thurid, her husband was not unlucky. He was just very, very unwise, to the point of stupidity.

Besides consistently offering his support to the losing side of nearly every legal dispute he'd been involved in—which made Thurid wonder why anyone asked him for his support in the first place, as they weren't a particularly powerful household—there was also the time he accidentally burned down half the house when making an offering to Thor.

There was also that other time he got shipwrecked on an iceberg when he went out fishing and wasn't rescued for a week, and Thurid thought herself widowed again until Old Gunnar from the next fjord over picked him up and brought him back, blue-lipped and starving.

Then there was the time he told their foster-son Atli that he wasn't "shepherding correctly" and tried to "show him how it's done," only to fall asleep in the hayfield and spend the next three days chasing down all the sheep who'd wandered off rather farther than usual.

And before he even came to Iceland, he was shipwrecked three other times on various raids in England, Frankia, and al-Andalus. That's why they called him "the unlucky," when really, Thurid thought, he'd been rather fortunate to have survived, and to have kept surviving against all odds.

*Maybe,* Thurid sometimes thought, *that really does make me the unlucky one.*

"You challenged someone to a duel to the death," Thurid said tonelessly to Eystein once they were outside and out of earshot of the others. She knew from careful experience when it was appropriate to shame her husband in front of others to incite him to act, and when to have a serious, private shaming session with him to provoke a true response and hear what was really on his mind. She stared him down, one hand clutching the rope of the wood-and-rawhide lantern, the other hand clutching the shawl about her shoulders to protect her against the frigid wind blowing in from the sea.

"Not just anyone," said Eystein. "Illugi, that young Norwegian upstart, the *godi's* nephew-in-law or what have you."

Thurid stared at him.

"Illugi," she echoed in disbelief.

"That's the one."

"Illugi the young Norwegian."

"That's him."

"The one they call Illugi *the Dueler*?"

"Well, yes—"

"Why," said Thurid, fighting to keep her voice even, "would you challenge a man called Illugi *the Dueler*—"

"Well, the thing of it is—"

"*—to a duel*?!"

"For honor!" boomed Eystein, shaking his fist. "I was telling the story of my adventure in al-Andalus—"

"Your *shipwreck* in al-Andalus," Thurid corrected him.

"Of my *adventure* in al-Andalus," Eystein repeated, like he hadn't heard her, "and Illugi had the nerve to call me a liar."

"The first of *three* separate shipwrecks, in three separate lands—"

"He said I'd probably never even left Norway before I came to Iceland, let alone met any Arabic scholars like my friend Ibrahim. I tried to tell him all about it and he wouldn't listen, and called me a liar again."

"—all of which contributed to you earning your nickname. Three separate shipwrecks, Eystein. Do you think the gods were maybe trying to tell you something? Something akin to, 'Maybe I shouldn't test my luck by challenging a man called *the Dueler* to a duel?"

A beat passed.

"He called me a liar," Eystein said again, but this time it fell a little flat. Then his voice gained strength. "How can I call myself an honorable man if I let an insult like that stand?"

Thurid sighed. "So a duel was the first thing you thought of? Is there no other way to prove your story was true?" She paused. "What about the chest?"

Eystein stiffened and said, shifty-eyed, "What chest?"

"The chest of Arab silver that may or may not be buried somewhere on our property?" she prompted.

"I don't know what you're talking about," Eystein said defensively.

"You told me about it before we married?" Thurid said. "You said you got it after your shipwreck, after you met your friend Ibrahim and fought off two dozen raiders—?"

"*Shh!* Woman!" Eystein hissed. "No one is supposed to know about the silver!"

"Well I damn well should know about the silver, considering it was my bride-price," Thurid said loudly, and he shushed her again.

"Okay, *okay,*" Eystein said. "Just keep it down! If the rest of the household finds out—"

"Just dig up the silver and show it to Illugi as proof, and you won't have to duel," Thurid said. "Simple, yes?"

"Right." He nodded once. "Dig up the silver."

"Don't you think that would be enough to convince him?"

"I think it certainly would," Eystein admitted.

"It was enough to convince me, after all," Thurid pointed out. The story of Ibrahim was one of the very first Eystein had told her, before they'd even married, and she herself had been skeptical until Eystein had shown her the chest of gleaming silver, stamped with images and characters that signified their origin in far-off lands.

Eystein shifted. "Yes, well, you're—" Thurid knew he was about to say *a woman* and cut him a look, which made him stop and clear his throat. "You're more confident in me. Although sometimes that isn't saying much," he added in a mutter.

"And when is your duel?" she asked, ignoring that last bit.

"Tomorrow at midday."

"I see. Well, that's plenty of time to dig up the chest, then, isn't it?"

"I'd say so, yes," said Eystein, making no move to do so.

Another beat passed.

Thurid said, "You forgot where you buried it, didn't you?"

"It was fifteen years ago!" Eystein protested before she'd even gotten the last word out.

Thurid took a deep breath and let it out slowly.

"Then I suppose you'd best get digging," she said, nodding at the storehouse where the spades were kept. "That is, unless you want to die tomorrow."

Eystein stuck out his lower lip. "I've survived other duels."

"Yes, but those weren't duels to the *death*, now were they?"

"You truly have so little faith in me?"

"Perhaps," Thurid said as she brushed past him and opened the door. The warmth of the hall hit her in a comforting wave, but it did nothing to quell her anger, which was so violent that her hands shook where they held her cloak and the lantern. She slipped inside, glaring over her shoulder at him. "But perhaps if Illugi doesn't kill you tomorrow, I'll do it myself."

Then she closed the door in his face.

Thurid awoke alone in the bedcloset she shared with Eystein, which was unsurprising considering the reprimand she'd given him last night.

What was also unsurprising was when she emerged into the daylight to find the immediate area outside the hall filled with holes. The sheep meandered around them as they grazed, *baa*-ing irritably.

She squinted against the sunrise and saw shapes moving about on the next hillock, and it didn't take her long to figure out that it was Eystein, Skeggi, and Bjarni frantically digging. Bolli and Bork, ever unhelpful, yelled and chased each other in twisting patterns around the holes.

Thurid supposed she should bring them some breakfast.

One of the serving women had awoken before Thurid and had prepared a breakfast of cold porridge for the farmhands. Thurid transferred what was left of the pot into a large clay serving bowl, grabbed several wooden spoons, and headed out into the crisp morning after donning her thickest homespun shawl and pinning it in place at her throat with a brooch.

The sea breeze was bitter cold, but that was nothing new. Unlike her husband, she had been born and raised on this island, and had gotten used to it over the years. Eystein had grown up in southern Norway, and had ended up here after finding himself feuding with one of the lesser jarls and getting expelled by King Harald Fairhair, who seemed to have exiled so many people that Thurid was surprised there was anyone left in Norway at all.

Nevertheless, part of Thurid wondered if Eystein would ever love Iceland the way she did.

"Ibrahim always said he'd come see me one day," Eystein told her once, back when they were first married and she'd still delighted in hearing tales of his adventures. "But that was when I was in Norway. I doubt he'll ever come here. What's here, anyway? Lava fields and glaciers. I miss forests, I'll tell you what. Good thing I'm not a woodworker or shipbuilder by trade, or I'd be out of a job on this treeless island, eh?"

Thurid had laughed good-naturedly at that, but it had become less funny every time she heard him say it over the years. Iceland's native scrub birch was disappearing, and in this particular fjord, it had been just about used up by the earliest settlers for firewood. Now that most of the arable land on the island was settled, they burned turf to keep warm in the winters and to thatch their roofs, and most of their lumber had to be brought in from abroad.

For his part, Skeggi had gone the same way as his brother and had been exiled by King Harald, but for altogether different reasons: for claiming that the king was displeasing the gods by doing something or other. Skeggi had allegedly been touched by the gods after surviving a near-death experience in battle and now professed to know their will. In Thurid's opinion, he was just as unwise as his brother.

And if the gods spoke through Skeggi, well...Thurid could draw her own conclusions about the gods, then, though she wouldn't say them aloud. Especially when she never knew who was listening. Just because she didn't think much of the Aesir and Vanir didn't mean she wanted them as enemies.

"It's not too late to ask the gods for aid in this duel against Illugi," Skeggi was saying to Eystein as Thurid approached. He was waist-deep in the hole he was digging, and a few feet away, the top of Eystein's head was just visible from his own hole. "We could make an offering, call upon—"

"Eystein doesn't need the gods' help with the duel," Thurid said, stopping in front of the much shallower hole that Bjarni was working on digging. "What he needs to do is to find that chest of silver, which I see you men are doing a great job of looking for."

Bjarni puffed his chest proudly at being grouped in with the *men*, but Eystein didn't look up and Skeggi merely snorted.

"Fifteen years of marriage and I still can't tell if you're being sarcastic or not," said Eystein as he hefted his spade and flung a clod of dirt straight into Skeggi's face, sending Bolli and Bork into a fit of giggles. Even Bjarni let out a snicker.

"If I didn't know better, Thurid," said Skeggi with gravity as he shook the dirt from his long beard, "I'd say you *wanted* our Eystein to lose the duel today."

"You know that's not true," said Thurid mildly. "Come, take a break and eat some porridge."

Bjarni threw down his spade without a second's hesitation as he and his brothers crowded Thurid, snatching spoons from her outstretched hand and digging into the porridge pot like they hadn't eaten in weeks.

"Hey! Save some for us." Eystein hauled himself out of the hole and wiped his brow with his sleeve. Thurid handed him a spoon and passed the pot from her sons to her husband, who dug in with equal fervor.

Skeggi had paused in his digging, but made no move to rise and get some food. He was eyeing Thurid and the boys with a look on his face that was somewhere between pity and outright contempt.

"Aren't you hungry?" Thurid asked him. "You need to keep up your strength if you're going to be digging all day."

"This is a waste of time." Skeggi stuck the tip of his spade in the dirt with such force that it held fast, standing straight up. "No silver chest is going to get Eystein his honor back. We should be practicing for the duel and picking out your best sheep to slaughter as an offering to the gods. Without their favor—"

"*No sacrifices,*" said Eystein through a mouthful of food. Thurid reached forward involuntarily and wiped away a blob of porridge that had caught on his beard, and he gave her a wan smile in return.

"Oh? And why not?" Skeggi demanded. "Because you need your sheep for *food* and *clothing*?" He said this as if he scorned such mundane, *mortal* necessities, as if he did not also eat food and wear clothing just like the rest of humanity.

"Yes," Thurid said without hesitation. "Exactly."

Skeggi leapt out of his hole and rounded on his brother, wagging a finger in his face. "You won't *need* food and clothing if the gods decide you're better off dead for not honoring them. You're so terrible at fighting that Odin wouldn't even want you in Valhalla. You're absolutely going to die in this duel."

"Ah, but if I die in this duel, won't that be where I go? Valhalla?" Eystein took another spoonful of porridge and raised his eyebrows.

There passed a long moment wherein Skeggi kept his finger raised and opened and closed his mouth like a fish. Then he said, "A duel isn't a battle. You have to die in *battle* to go to Valhalla."

"Semantics," said Eystein tiredly. "If it's as you say, that Odin doesn't want me, then why would I fear dying with a sword in my hand? Illugi is the better fighter; the gods would rather see him in Valhalla than me, no? So why should I make an offering for their favor if I already *have* their favor by being so bad at fighting that Valhalla wouldn't even let me in?"

"You're *proud* of being bad at fighting?" Skeggi sputtered, clearly for lack of anything better to say.

"It's kept me alive this long," said Eystein with a shrug. "I wouldn't want Odin's favor anyway. I'd rather live, thanks."

Skeggi had nothing to say to that. After a moment he leapt back into his hole and resumed digging with a renewed fervor, muttering darkly under his breath.

As Eystein scooped out the last of the porridge and he and the boys deposited their spoons in the empty clay pot, Thurid hid a smile as she turned away and headed back to the croft.

Perhaps her husband wasn't so unwise after all. She only hoped that Odin's lack of blessings upon Eystein would be enough to save his skin today.

The sun rose higher in the sky, although it was never directly overhead at this time of year, not even at midday. Thurid went about her daily chores with the other women as the men mowed hay in the fields and her husband, sons, and brother-in-law continued to dig up the property in search of the misplaced chest.

Eventually they came back, dirty and haggard and empty-handed, and wordlessly donned clean clothes or took off their tunics to shake the dirt from them outside. When Eystein was done dressing, he said, "Where is my sword, wife?"

"Here," said Thurid, taking it out from behind a box where she'd set it. She'd spent part of the morning sharpening it, and told him so.

He pulled it partway out of the sheath to examine it. Satisfied, he re-sheathed it and said, "You had so little faith that we'd find the chest, did you?"

"I just think it's always best to be prepared," Thurid said lightly. Now was not the time for shaming, after all. Eystein needed all the confidence he could get if he was going to survive the afternoon.

At midday, Illugi the Dueler and his kinsfolk crested the hill and approached the farmstead on their fine horses. With him was his uncle the *godi* and several other upstanding men of the district, all come to watch the spectacle.

Thurid had never much liked the look of Illugi. He was a grown man with a boyish face set in a permanent sneer, his limbs muscled but gangly. If the tales were true, he'd been outlawed from Norway for too much dueling, and he never lost. Many a man had been slain by his blade, never to return home to his wife and children, never to enjoy another bowl of ale by the hearth.

Or so she'd heard.

They marked out the place where the duel was to happen: a flat stretch near the beach. The witnesses assembled, Thurid and Skeggi on one side, the *godi* and his men on the other. As they watched Eystein attempt to don his tight, rusty chainmail from adventures past, Bork meandered down from the hall and stood at his mother's side, mouth agape.

"Papa has armor?" he said in wonder, for few enough men in the district owned chainmail, let alone a helmet and sword, even those as ill-maintained as Eystein's. Such items were expensive, and pointed to either a wealthy family or many successful raids, or both. "He really was a Viking, wasn't he?"

"Go wait inside, Bork," said Thurid, shooing him away. "You needn't watch. Where are your brothers?"

"I don't know," the child said sullenly. "And I'm staying right here. If Papa dies—"

"Let the boy stay, Thurid," said Eystein as he wiggled into his ill-fitting mail. "The others should be here, too. If I die, they'll have to avenge me, after all."

"It's not too late for an offering," Skeggi said to Eystein out of the corner of his mouth. Then he looked over his brother's shoulder at the beach and said, "At least one to get rid of your haunting. Your property is absolutely infested with walruses."

Thurid saw nothing but an empty strand, and turned to her husband and handed him his helmet once he'd buckled his sword belt over his mail. "Eystein, my love?"

"Yes, wife?"

"If you die," she said, "I'll be very unhappy."

Eystein swallowed heavily as he put his helmet on and buckled it in place under his chin. "That makes two of us."

Across the dueling ground, Illugi waved his sword around. His helmet was polished, his chainmail oiled and shining. Thurid could tell even from a distance that his sword was just as fine, as was the seax that hung horizontally at his belt. He had both his family's wealth *and* a history of successful raids behind him—and the latter had happened far more recently than Eystein's, whose own mail had fit him better when he was twenty years younger.

"You ready, old man?" Illugi called.

Eystein turned away from Thurid and set his jaw. "Are *you* ready, you little whelp?"

Illugi only laughed, and the two began to circle each other. Illugi's steps were light and quick, Eystein's heavy and measured.

Thurid wrung her hands, suddenly nervous. It struck her then that, between Illugi the Dueler and Eystein the Unlucky, the victor would be obvious by name alone.

It had not occurred to her until this moment that her husband *would* actually die today.

"Mama," said Bork, tugging on her apron, "what's that on the beach?"

"Not more walruses," said Thurid. She did not look away from Eystein, and out of the corner of her eye, she saw the *godi* signal for the duel to begin.

Illugi lunged, faster than Thurid could blink, and she gasped. Miraculously, Eystein dodged and parried a blow as Illugi swung for his shoulder, then blocked another blow aimed at his thigh. Illugi swung and swung and Eystein continued to parry, but he was on the defense with no room to strike a blow of his own—until finally Illugi delivered a swing with such force, and Eystein blocked it with equal force, and their swords were pressed together as each tried to overcome the other. Then Eystein twisted his sword such that Illugi's own weapon was wrenched from his hands and fell onto the ground.

Thurid pressed her clenched hands to her mouth. She could scarcely even breathe.

Beside her, Bork tugged at her apron more insistently. *"Mama!* There's someone on the beach! They're walking this way but you can't see them behind the rocks—"

"The ghost-walruses are made up, Bork," said Skeggi before Thurid could even respond. His own eyes were glued to his brother and he didn't give his young nephew a passing glance, even when he made a surprised, angry noise. "Now *shush!"*

"You lied!" Bork cried, pointing a finger at Skeggi. "Mama *said* you were lying, but I'm *not* lying. *There's someone on the beach.* They just came around the corner from Old Gunnar's fjord and dragged their boat up to—"

Just as Illugi reached behind him and ripped his seax from its sheath at his waist and bared his teeth at Eystein, shouts went up from the hillock behind the *godi*'s men.

"We found it! We found it!"

Bjarni and Bolli appeared over the crest of the hill, dirt-encrusted and grinning, each holding the handle of a weathered wooden chest. The *godi* and his group parted to let them pass, and Illugi and Eystein both lowered their weapons and stared at them. "Stop," said the *godi* loudly to the two duelers. Then, to the boys: "What's this about?"

"Father, we found the chest!" Bjarni said to Eystein, as he and Bolli entered the dueling space and set it down. He pulled back the lid to reveal a hoard of stamped silver coins. Eystein and Illugi, both panting from exertion, peered into the chest and then looked at each other.

"Well done, boys," said Thurid in surprise. Relieved, she turned to Illugi and then to his uncle the *godi*. "That settles it, then, doesn't it? Eystein's stories are true. He's not a liar, and he has nothing to prove. The dispute is settled."

The *godi* nodded without so much as pausing to consider it. Thurid knew he'd be reasonable, as he had little personal stake in Eystein dying. And a thrice-widowed Thurid would be nothing but trouble for the district.

"This seems reasonable to me," said the *godi*. "Illugi, do you revoke your insult? And Eystein, do you revoke your challenging Illugi to a duel to the death?"

"Yes," said Eystein, sagging with relief. He loosened his grip on his sword and held it limply at his side, turning to give Thurid a small smile.

"*No*," said Illugi fiercely.

And before anyone could stop him, he swung at Eystein with his seax.

Eystein blocked the blow at the last possible second by raising his sword: a clumsy deflection that was just enough to stop Illugi's blade from sinking into the space between his shoulder and neck. But his loose grip on his sword meant that the force of the blow sent it flying from his hand, and he fell back onto the grass as Illugi rounded on them.

"I'm sick of you, Eystein the Unlucky," Illugi snarled. "I'm tired of weak men like you telling tall tales. Everyone knows you're only full of hot air, you old blowhard. The chest means nothing. You could've stolen it for all I know. I name you a coward, and I name you a liar. Illugi *never* backs down from a duel."

Thurid could only stand there in horrible silence as Illugi raised his sword above his head with both hands and brought it down.

She gasped and looked away at the last possible second, expecting to hear Eystein utter a strangled cry as Illugi dealt him a killing blow. But that never came: instead, she saw a flash of red out of the corner of her eye, and what met her ears was not the sound of her husband's dying cries but the clash of steel upon steel.

"*Mama*," Bork whispered in awe, "look!"

A man had come out from behind the rocks, and his sword had stopped Illugi's from killing Eystein. He twisted his blade in the same way Eystein had earlier, disarming Illugi and making him step back in shock as the tip of the newcomer's sword was leveled at his throat.

Thurid's jaw dropped.

Her husband's savior was one of the tallest men she had ever seen, and was clad in a strange mixture of Arabic and Norse clothing: fine red silk, loose pants, and a stamped silk tunic, but also a heavy woolen traveling cloak about his shoulders, his black-streaked gray curls tucked under a cap. Though he bore deep smile lines from a life full of good humor, and his shoulders stooped a bit as if he were used to spending his life hunched over, his dark face was stern as he gazed down at Illugi.

"That," said the strange man in perfect Norse, "wasn't very honorable. Eystein, my friend, you told me that the Northmen had more integrity than this. I hate to think that I've come all this way only to be met with the godless heathens everyone says you are."

"I-Ibrahim?" Eystein said, wobbling to his feet. His eyes were huge. "How—how did you get here? How did you find me?"

"I brought him here," said a quavering old voice from the rocks, and Old Gunnar from the next fjord over appeared. "He landed on my beach and asked for directions. I thought it might be easier just to take him here myself."

"And before that, your cousin in Norway pointed me in the right direction," said Ibrahim. His expression remained stony as he continued glaring at Illugi. "Do you yield?"

Illugi nodded, too shocked to do anything else.

Ibrahim sheathed his sword and turned to offer his hand to Eystein, who took it and allowed himself to be pulled to his feet. Eystein pulled off his tarnished helmet and said breathlessly, "It's really you, isn't it?"

Ibrahim spread his arms and chuckled, seeming a bit winded himself. "In the flesh. What, do you think you imagined our adventure together after I rescued you from your shipwreck? We saved a whole town in Córdoba from raiders, and were justly rewarded, eh? I see you still have the chest, after all."

"Ha!" Eystein embraced him and clapped him on the back, and Ibrahim finally smiled and let out a booming laugh.

On the other side of the dueling ground, the *godi* and his men talked amongst themselves, some of them berating Illugi, others just looking annoyed. Without another word to Eystein's group, they headed to their horses.

"Well, I'll be damned," Skeggi muttered to Thurid. "You know, *I* didn't even believe the story about al-Andalus..."

Thurid elbowed him in the ribs and said, "You believe whatever the gods whisper in your ear but don't believe your own brother? Have a little faith, Skeggi."

"You're one to talk," Skeggi snapped, but he was smiling. He, like Thurid, was relieved that Eystein wasn't dead. They finally had something in common. Then he straightened and said pompously, as if simply to ruin the moment, "If I didn't know better, I'd say the gods led Ibrahim right to—"

"Oh, come off it," Thurid sighed.

"How long has it been?" Eystein was saying to Ibrahim, grinning like Thurid hadn't seen him grin in years, and he and Ibrahim set off toward their humble hall with their arms over each other's shoulders, like old friends. Like brothers.

Skeggi rolled his eyes and set off after his brother and their unexpected guest, leaving Thurid standing there with her three sons and Old Gunnar. Thurid turned to the old man and said, "Would you like to join us for supper? You must be tired from rowing, and I think a feast is in order tonight. You very well have saved my husband's life. It would be an honor to have you at my table, Gunnar."

A feast would be tough to put together on such short notice, of course, but Thurid was up to the challenge.

Old Gunnar gratefully accepted her offer and thanked her for her generosity, and Bjarni and Bolli picked up the chest together and led him off to the hall, gleeful at the thought of filling their bellies with more food than usual that evening.

Bork lingered with Thurid, his eyes on the beach.

Thurid knelt down so she was at eye level with him and said, "What troubles you, Bork? Your father's alive and your brothers found the silver. And we'll eat so well tonight you won't even be able to move afterward. Why are you sad?"

"Weird Uncle Skeggi lied to me," Bork whispered, putting his chin to his chest. "And you didn't listen to me when I tried to tell you about the man coming from the beach."

"I'm sorry I didn't listen to you, Bork," Thurid said gently. "And Weird Uncle Skeggi doesn't know up from down most of the time, so I wouldn't take his word for anything. Things can't only be true when you want them to be, after all."

Bork's face lit up. "You really think so?"

"Yes. They're either true, or they're not," Thurid went on. "Illugi thought your father was lying, but what he was saying was true, and not just because he said so. And no amount of Illugi saying he was a liar made your father's story untrue. So just because Weird Uncle Skeggi says ghost-walruses aren't real doesn't mean he's right."

"I knew it!" Bork ran off to the beach, waving his arms and laughing as he dashed along the black sand in search of his spectral animal friends.

And Thurid smiled as she watched him, letting him frolic until he tired himself out, and then led him back to their home.

She had a feast to prepare, after all, and she looked forward to getting to know Ibrahim; she wondered how long he would stay, wondered of his life and his travels and all the wonders he must've seen, all the things he and Eystein had seen together. Her heart lifted at the thought.

*Unlucky Eystein may be,* she thought with a smile, *but his misfortunes certainly make for wonderful stories, don't they?*

And even though she'd heard them all a million times before, for the first time in years she looked forward to hearing all the tales her husband had to tell.

# — TORUNN UNHOUSED —
## Emily Osborne

*Torunn the Wild*

It was the first of the four evenings of the *Fardagar*, the time in late May when many Icelanders travelled to new homesteads and were temporarily unhoused. Torunn Svanadóttir dropped her heavy sack upon a mossy patch and arranged her sleeping mat on the least lumpy spot. The moss was fragrant and damp. She had walked until the sky was seeped with deep-water blue. From previous travels during *Fardagar*, she knew that she would sleep only in the mere four hours of semi-dark. As soon as the horizon was tinged with fish-gut pink, she would wake, restless to make progress.

During her short sleep, Torunn roused enough to sense that someone had lain down beside her and was breathing spine-to-spine, rump-to-rump. She tried to turn over and inch away but felt immobilized, as though by a person's full weight. Dimly she perceived dread intermingled with a welcome warmth. Then these sensations faded into that space where the day's labors meet the dream's release; the intrusions became her heavy sack throttling her back as it had all day, her clay bowl and cup grating rhythmically against vertebrae. Always there were things to carry. They never left her.

"Share my breakfast. I shared your mat last night."

Torunn sat up swiftly and saw a broad-shouldered woman with long honeyed braids spit on hard rye cakes and pry them apart. The woman held out to Torunn the larger of the freed chunks.

"Young women shouldn't sleep alone during the *Fardagar*," the woman gestured at Torunn with her cake, and spoke while chewing, "Too many men roam the land, thinking they are outside the law before they reach their next residence. And maybe they are right." She added wryly, almost proverbially, "It's hard to witness what happens behind geysers and under rocks."

"Or where moss sinks deep and people walk softly as spirits," Torunn quipped, accepting the criticism and the cake. "You took me unawares, as we both see this morning."

The woman smiled, showing white, chipped front teeth. "I've been told my big bones tread heavily, but I'm skilled at covering and uncovering tracks. Where are you going and why are you disheveled, with hair unbraided and skirts torn? I gather from the cleanness of your bag and mat that you are not generally sloppy."

This woman did not hesitate to enter Torunn's personal life with her questions or her body. Oddly, her ease made Torunn, who was both guarded with her own person and matter-of-fact in her dealings with others, feel companionable and willing to share her story. "I'm going to Narfi Uggison's farm near Reykholt."

"Why do you go there and where did you reside before?"

"Narfi is my dead husband's brother and his farm will be the sixth that I've lived at since I was born. My parents were poor and my father said to be a scoundrel, so I was fostered at three different farms until I reached my independence. Then I married two years ago and lived on my husband's small farm near Bergþórshvoll. That's now razed and absorbed into Jarl Hámundar's holdings." Torunn paused, searched her pack for something to offer her unexpected companion, found dried dulse and trout. "As to my hair and dress, I'm in mourning for my husband. Outwardly, at least. My husband has been called a villain and coward, and I never disagreed. Really, I mourn my razed farm, but the attire keeps most people from asking too many questions."

The woman held her palms up, acknowledging she had trespassed without backing off. "I agree it can be useful to have a weapon that turns away unwanted questions. I am sorry for your lost farm, and I do not envy you, going to Narfi's farm. I have heard dark stories of that place. Have you no other option?"

Torunn knew these sayings to be true. Narfi was like his brother. His hands were hot and searching and unwanted, his breath sour. When discouraged he flung words like dirty daggers, always in the largest companies for the greatest chance at spreading slander. Torunn clenched her fists, crumbling her food.

"Not at present. My farm was razed in twisted circumstances, and there are many who saw me throw harsh words and more Jarl Hámundar. Men leveled these accusations against me when I petitioned to keep my land at the last Thing. Some people said they'd heard this verse composed about the incident:

Torunn's farm was pestered by piss,
the jarl's stream staining the fence.
Men can't keep their shortswords sheathed.
Some say the jarl drinks to dump
his bladder, so his farmers bless

their wasted weapons for unfair
fights, lose lands. I say no one cared
he made Torunn's earth a toilet.

The woman snorted approval. "So you're a composer of libel verse and a mock mourner. It seems, Torunn Feral-Hair, we both wear cloaks that cover our true selves. I am Gerda. You might call me Gerda the Sleep-Trespasser based on your knowledge so far, but I might call myself Gerda the Strong-Shouldered. As for my story, there's libel in it too, but perhaps you'll hear that later. I have not yet secured myself lodgings for this year. Last year I stayed at the farm of Ölvir Brandison in the southern quarter after many years abroad. At Ölvir's farm I kept to myself, and few people care to track my whereabouts. This suits me well." She stood and arched her shoulders, grimacing at kinks before repacking and slinging her bag on her back.

Gerda held her hand out to Torunn. "I do have a destination in mind right now, and it will take me along your path to Reykholt. Let's walk together today and then tomorrow until we arrive at the turnoff to Reykholt, and then we may part company."

Over gentle hillocks, across swollen streams, and through sucking mud they trudged, keeping track of the sun's position, the distant glint of glaciers on their right, and the frayed pathways ahead of them. Sometimes they maintained companionable silence. Sometimes they talked smoothly. Torunn felt grateful for Gerda's company. The women looked like unequal cartwheels that were nevertheless impelled to move at the same pace. Torunn was cord and whip: sinewy, her light brown hair hanging in unkempt ropes, her step light and quick. Gerda was broad and solid as a cart. She strode heavily and purposefully, with her shoulders bent forward from the weight she carried. Sometimes she twitched her shoulders back violently, as if shrugging off an unwanted hand.

They passed many of Iceland's unhoused, trailing sacks and carts: children and the aged, couples, a lone pregnant woman. Torunn wondered aloud what it would feel like to carry that huge mound of stomach in addition to a large sack on one's back.

"I have heard from travellers tales of animals from the East called khámels," she said, "They are like horses or donkeys tamed by desert dwellers. When the khámels are pregnant, the baby grows on their backs. If they are having twins they have two mounds. I have never been with child but think perhaps it would be easier to be pregnant in this way, seeing we are used to carrying heavy loads on our backs."

Gerda chuckled and said she had heard on her travels marvelous tales of the East, though not this story of the khámels. Then she shook her head firmly. "If you have ever carried a person on your back for any length of time, you would know it is an unimaginable weight. This is so whether they are born or dead."

It was a partial answer to a question Torunn sensed she could not ask.

That night when they lay down to sleep, Gerda arranged her mat overlapping with Torunn's and told her they would sleep back-to-back like last night.

"It will give me comfort to feel you breathing at my back."

Torunn was not happy about this arrangement, but decided not to object as they were only travelling together one more day. The warmth, at least, was a comfort.

The first drizzly hours of their second day passed uneventfully, apart from a minor skirmish with a ratty dog that followed Gerda for several miles, snuffling and whining at her rear.

"Go! Go home!" Gerda yelled, pointing ineffectually in different directions. "Hmph, that mutt must smell that my red tide is flowing out."

When they arrived at Skorradalsvatn, the thin lake that sign-posted where to turn for Reykholt, Gerda held Torunn's arm gently and said, "This is where we part company, or perhaps not. I am going to a small farm northwest of here that is empty and waiting for an occupant. I knew the owners, but they reside now in Norway and will not be returning. They have no descendants to claim this stead and no one else I think knows of its whereabouts, for it is in a remote valley. I will give you a choice: we can part ways here, you to Narfi's nasty farm and me to claim this waiting house. Or, you can travel with me and help me establish this new stead. It will not be easy. We will need to buy some animals and grain on our way. I have coin, and we can make these purchases at a nearby farm..."

While Gerda outlined her plans for acquiring essentials, Torunn's mind rapidly forged images. Herself stretching an animal skin to a fine transparency across a window, while sheep grazed on moss in the yard. Gerda singing and hanging fish to dry. The two women enjoying a quiet meal during winter downpour. A memory she carried from childhood, of hiding a pink shell beneath her mattress while her father dragged her mother outside. There was a treasure, she sensed, in what Gerda was offering, one that she could carry and conceal in the thin bones of her hand. And yet she felt a vague discomfort and displacement, as though she were entering a dream in which a familiar path leads to an unknown place. Narfi's farm was rumored to be mean and harsh, but it was a guaranteed roof for the next year. Gerda's stead was also a rumor and might be unlivable, or Gerda might prove impossible to live with, or to sleep beside. But for someone who had been unhoused as many times as Torunn and who had been roughhoused by as many fists and words, rumors were a weighty currency.

Torunn realized Gerda was silent and waiting for a response. "Why would you offer this to me?" Torunn asked.

"Because a farm needs at least two occupants. One to watch the stead in case the other must travel. One to work inside while the other works outside. Four hands to carry the heaviest loads and wrangle the unruly animals. And at this point you are my only free acquaintance in Iceland, and I do enjoy your company. But I give you full warning, Torunn, if you choose to live with me you will do very hard work. Man's work. You will not be in the house stirring pots all day."

Hard outdoor work appealed to Torunn, who had never had much patience for cooking and weaving. She would rather swing an axe and feel it bite.

"There." Gerda pointed to the opposite ridge of the narrow valley below them, where a small moss-roofed farmhouse nested under the cliff overhang. Implements of work lay around it, looking from this distance like twigs and eggs. Its owners had obviously left with confidence that no one would disturb their stead. Gerda and Torunn smiled at each other, and Gerda said, "Thanks be to Freya for providing for us." At her words, Torunn felt a force at her back like a strong wind, impelling her forwards. Perhaps the gods, she mused, were finally walking with her.

The journey down into the valley was slippery and chaotic, as they led the sheep and goat and Torunn carried two angry chickens in a sack. "They are my Huginn and Muninn[2]," she joked. "They remind me this will not be a journey to make twice."

In the yard the women found respectable tools and fishing poles and lines. Inside, a small stable waited opposite the door. There was a good fire pit for cooking and, Torunn noted with satisfaction, two firm mattresses. A few more personal items remained: a string of painted beads, dress, bodice, two clean daggers and a handsome spear. Torunn hefted this, feeling its energy and

---

[2] A pair of ravens in Norse Mythology that fly all over the world and bring information to Odin.

flexibility. Looking around, she pointed out runes carved on the lintel. She could not read them and was surprised when Gerda said: "Words do not burn."

"Perhaps not," Torunn considered, "for it seems they spread and reproduce forever. But certainly they can brand a person."

The women did not need to consult on how to make the farm habitable; setting to work was a kind of homecoming. Those first weeks, as darkness disappeared from the night sky and sleep eluded them more, they laid out moss for the sheep, milked the goat and fed the chickens, scrubbed the surfaces of the stead with cold water from the stream, and beat the dust from the window-skins and mattresses in musty clouds. Torunn watched these clouds sail up and away down the valley, like spirits departing. Evenings were companionable, as Gerda shared stories of her travels along the coasts of Europe, and Torunn spoke of her scattered childhood and her violent but short marriage. It astonished Torunn how quickly they made this stead their own, how soon they became domesticated to it and it to them.

Alongside her new freedom and attachment to this stead, Torunn also felt wild. Her muscles ached from new chores: wrangling the animals back into the stead at night, sitting on hard shore rocks while fishing. She enjoyed how firm her limbs had become, the feeling of Gerda's strong fingers working out the knots in her back in the evening, and the feeling of Gerda's fleshy shoulders as she returned the favor.

They existed, and yet who knew of their whereabouts? Not residing at a recognized farm, they were outside the law. What had the law been to her anyway? Words bandied about, and set against other words that lawspeakers declaimed, that some jarls memorized and others wielded. There were word-laws that dissolved people of rights for words they were said to have spoken. Maybe she had or had not composed libel, but those mere rumors of her words had robbed her of any right to claim back her land. It was better, she decided, to step outside the law, to protect whatever came into her hands with sinew and wit. And she felt certain that so long as she and Gerda lived together, they would protect each other. Partly because, she admitted to herself, Gerda seemed to need her in ways she had not spoken.

Gerda was increasingly ill at ease with stepping beyond the stead. Torunn wondered why Gerda never desired a change in her daily chores, by going fishing or gathering moss for the fire on the drier cliff side. Gerda was always engaged in a task within the stead before Torunn had a chance to suggest one outside it. Even by high summer when the sun ceased to set, when the day's work was done and sleep evaded them, Gerda would not join Torunn to sit outside in the fresh air, to listen to the subdued sounds of the not-quite-night.

It was on such a pink-bright night as she lingered outside on the cool moss, that Torunn first heard footsteps on the roof. Cautiously, she moved for a better view, but could see no one. She called to Gerda in a loud whisper, hoping her friend would answer from above. No answer came apart from a shuffling noise, a low laugh and a rock that thudded the earth beside her. She ran inside to find Gerda sleeping soundly.

"Wake up! There is someone on the roof. Wake up!" Torunn shook Gerda and pulled off her blanket. Gerda was half-naked and unperturbed at being uncovered.

"I am not happy at being woken from the most comfortable sleep I've had in months, friend, but I will get up with you and look around." She slung the blanket round her shoulders and marched outside barefoot.

They searched the yard, the stable, along the cliff, even scrambled up onto the roof to make sure no one was lying flat on its mossy thatch. It was clear no one had been up there in a long time.

"The footsteps and laughter were clear," Torunn insisted, "And I am sure that a rock was hurled down at me."

"Perhaps the cliff bent the wind so it stirred the roof. And perhaps a bird came down at you. It would not surprise me if you dozed off while sitting out here on your rock, Torunn. You have not been getting enough sleep these weeks past."

She gave Torunn a look of genuine concern, and led her gently back into the stead.

Torunn was not satisfied by this explanation, but did not push the issue. Her sleep did not improve. Often now at night she roused at scrabbling noises on the roof. Sometimes the rafters buckled, like a horse under a heavy rider. She questioned Gerda repeatedly to see if her friend had heard the noises, but Gerda only shrugged and said the windy cliffs blew as strong as a forge's bellows. Torunn began to feel that Gerda was guarding a secret.

It was not long before she found out what Gerda guarded.

On an unusually hot mid-summer day, Torunn was putting the sheep out to pasture when she heard Gerda's voice say clearly,

"I will not go to Norway before next spring. I will not leave Torunn alone now, without any guarantee that I will be back before winter. Stop asking me to do this. I have done the first part of what you asked and returned here. Look what we have done to care for this farm!"

Torunn thought she heard a rasping voice reply, indecipherably male or female. Immediately she went inside. No one was there but Gerda.

"Who were you speaking to? I heard your every word clear as a horn and thought I heard a strange voice respond."

Gerda's face adopted its habitual open expression, and she began to speak in her usual hypotheticals, "It might be, friend, that I am growing lonely already, for I do sometimes find myself voicing my thoughts aloud, and even responding to my own thoughts with another voice. I am not in the habit of dividing myself into two persons just to have company, especially when I have you nearby, but I do sometimes talk to myself while working, or sometimes I sing, which I have been told sounds like many cows in competition for fodder."

Torunn's patience had worn thin as a fishing line. She advanced on Gerda and spat words in her face, "Tell me the truth. Where is this invisible person, or have you invited the gods to stay in our lodgings?"

Gerda slid nimbly around the other side of the table. "The gods indeed, Torunn! I have never heard their voices, and I think that if you are hearing them speak you need to lie down and rest. I will get you some bone broth."

Torunn brought her fists down hard on the table. A mug rolled to the floor and shattered. "You won't skirt around this with jokes or by making me sound like I've misplaced my wits. Speak truth: how do you make the air respond, and why were you speaking of returning to Norway and leaving me alone for the winter?"

"Please, Torunn, sit down by the fire. Let us both think." Gerda walked round the table, put her hands firmly on Torunn's shoulders and pushed her back into a chair. When Gerda used her full strength, Torunn could not resist. "I will get you the bone broth."

"I do not need bone broth! Curse you Gerda! You need to talk and I need to listen."

Gerda's face crumpled. "Do not curse me, friend. Not you, please." She sat down wearily in the other chair. "Yes, I will talk. I have always meant to tell you the full story of this stead, though the time has come earlier than I had hoped."

Gerda sighed and raked her fingers through her loose tresses, which were shining, for the women had washed each others' hair that morning. "Last year I set sail from Norway with my then-husband Eiðr. He was a trader, with wealth in swords and coin and with friends and enemies in Norway because of his success. We were set to buy land in Iceland. The captain of our ship, Ölvir, was a good man, but there were two scoundrels on board, Bjarki and his wife Boga. Bjarki was a poet who had been at King Haraldr's court for a season. Bjarki had a high, squeaky voice and entertained the court by mocking the king's thegns. While everyone had many chances to laugh, no one liked it much when it was his turn to be mocked. When it came Eiðr's turn, Bjarki's verse was most brutal, saying he lured squirrels to him with nuts and then took them from behind for pleasure. Now the thing Eiðr hated most was to be called small. I joked sometimes to him that his size was the reason we had no children, that his penis never got far enough inside me, but then he would joke that it was my bottom that was the problem, saying it was so wide he could never find the right spot. This was just our way with each other and in fact we enjoyed our differences. But when Bjarki called Eiðr small in front of the court, my husband vowed to strip him of his pride.

So when we found each other on board Ölvir's ship, Eiðr said to me one night as we lay together, 'I've composed a verse to shame Bjarki. We will see if he lets the matter rest after I've recited it for the ship's company, or whether he wants to escalate this feud.'

The next morning, Bjarki was rowing, for that was how he paid his passage. Eiðr knew this was one of Bjarki's sore points, that he might not be a good enough poet to pay his and his wife's passage to Iceland. Eiðr stood at the stern and looked down at the rowers and declaimed this verse:

'One boy I see who rows rougher
than most men. He must, for his verse
is shoddy as eagle shit, his voice
squeaky in the gold-hurler's hall.
But this runt's skilled at sculling for
he has no beard beneath his belt
or his cheesy armpits to chafe
when he pumps his puny ring-lands.'

Bjarki immediately jumped up from his rowing station, his skinny limbs taut and quivering. He lunged at Eiðr and drew his shortsword, and Eiðr did the same. It was not a fair or long fight, for Eiðr made up in brawn what he lacked in bed. When Boga saw Bjarki had been slain, she wept sorely, and I did feel sorry for her then. Ölvir, who had been at court and knew how it stood between Eiðr and Bjarki, said Bjarki was the instigator, and there were many on the ship who could attest to this at the next Thing. But Boga would not have the matter settled. She had been robbed of much and I know not what marriage she would have made next, considering she was ugly and unpleasant. That night while most of the ship slept, Boga came at Eiðr with Bjarki's shortsword, wanting to even the score."

And at this point, Gerda paused, choking back tears. "That witch, she was quick in her death-dealing. But Eiðr's cry roused me and the night watchman. The watchman grasped at her and in the scuffle, Boga fell overboard.

So you see, Torunn, we are both mourners, though I do mourn my husband greatly. Ölvir allowed me to mourn while living at his farm, and I paid him ample coin to allow me to stay without working much, and to keep suitors at bay. His wife was kind to me, and over the months I became eager to work, but not to be courted. And then a few weeks ago, a strange thing occurred, and this is the twist of the tale where you, Torunn, and this stead are intertwined.

Bjarki and Boga, their spirits, came to me. I was kneading bread and they were there suddenly, nightmares, attached to my back. They rode my shoulders and cackled. They told me their bones had washed ashore in Norway and they wanted a proper burial. They have hounded me now for weeks. They tell me to go to the beach in Norway where their bones have washed up, to retrieve the bones and bring them here for burial. This was their farmstead, Torunn. They pestered me to come here, told me I could use it, told me to find someone who would keep their stead safe and working while I voyaged to Norway. I resisted at first. I tried to ignore them, which was impossible, for they only became more insistent. At Ölvir's farm, people saw how it was for me, that I was being pursued by fiendish spirits. Some taught me spells, which did nothing. Bjarki and Boga only laughed, clinging at my shoulders throughout the burnings and incantations.

Only since I have been here, Torunn, have they relaxed and dismounted from my back. If I go beyond the stead, immediately they are on my back. When I'm here, they seem to sit on the roof most of the time or watch us at our work. These past weeks they have begun to hassle me more fiercely, urging me to go to Norway. I am divided, my friend: I do not want to leave you and this stead but I cannot live much longer with their demands and taunts. What do we do? We could live with our ghosts until spring and then hire help for you while I go to Norway. But what do you say, Torunn? I got you into this mess and I think it's fair for you to decide how I get you out of it."

Gerda bit her lips anxiously and reached for Torunn's hand, which Torunn drew back. Torunn clasped her hands firmly in her lap. In them, she realized, she held both a property and a friend, and could determine the future of each. But what kinds of friend and property were hers to hold? She loved Gerda's bravery and jocularity. She pitied Gerda, in mourning and pestered by nightmares. She resented Gerda's wealth, and her duplicity in offering Torunn a grave mound for a home. Gerda had wronged Torunn, had wanted to make things right, and had made Torunn both claimant and judge. Her judgment, she found, was not clouded by affection.

"You must go to Norway immediately, Gerda. I have heard many tales of bad people acting worse when they are dead, and I don't trust this Bjarki and Boga to be patient all winter. I fear that we may come to harm should you not acquiesce to their demands.

Leave me payment and I will take care of the stead. It may be that I hire help, or it may be that I find I can manage on my own here."

Torunn felt satisfaction at using Gerda's hypothetical phrases to set in motion a fixed and secret plan.

Gerda protested and a disagreement arose between them for several days. The matter was decided only when they were eating one evening and a heavy pot fell off its wall hook and glanced Gerda's shoulder. Thinly they heard the sound of Boga's laughter.

"I see these scoundrels mean to chase me out. I will do as you advise, Torunn, though it gives me no pleasure to leave you."

It was a rainy and cool morning when Gerda set off on her voyage. She handed Torunn a few silver beads and a torc with open-mouthed wolves chasing each other through golden ribbons. These treasures, Torunn knew, were worth far more than a year of her labor at any farm in Iceland. She wondered where Gerda had been hiding them. Then Gerda handed her a silver coin with unfamiliar markings.

"This silver coin, Torunn, is a dirham from the far, hot east lands, a place called Syria. It is worth a great deal. I am told the markings on the front spell out the name of their king and a verse to "Allah," is their chief god. I am told that if the bearer says Allah's name while carrying a dirham, it will protect as well as any weapon. I cannot confirm that rumor, for I have always called on Freya for help, but I do know this coin will give you freedom to live as you choose in my absence."

As they stared down at the shiny coin, Torunn felt the cold wind moving around her legs, rustling her skirt. Both women knew Gerda had given Torunn passage wherever she wanted.

"Still I hope," Gerda said, "to find you here on my return, and share this stead with you."

Torunn rubbed the coin's strange lettering, opaque to her as runes. Nevertheless, the markings were familiar as a plea to a god for help, protection, revenge, adventure. How many times throughout her life had she almost uttered those prayers, then swallowed them for fear of disappointment? She turned over the coin and saw a galloping horse, its mane wild, its haunches strong and pliant like her own. She said,

"I hope also to see you again, and I would not be unhappy if it came to pass that we should live in the same stead again. May Freya give you safe passage and return."

As Gerda turned away, Torunn saw her face crumple. She watched Gerda's figure, stooped under her travelling bags, disappear over the rim of the cliff. Torunn then spent a week in the stead, and things went mostly as she expected, apart from the animals. Boga had stayed behind. Torunn was prepared for this, knowing Boga would not leave her hearthside unwatched. Boga rattled around on the roof from time to time, and sometimes tugged at Torunn or prodded her towards a leak in the roof, or a rotting beam. One evening Torunn even thought she saw the dim outline of Boga's lumpy body hunched beside the fire, stretching her hands out to its warmth. Boga was, Torunn mused, a better housemistress than most living ones she had worked for over the years, but still Torunn had no intention of keeping house for the dead.

On a fine evening when Boga was quiet or off on her own business, Torunn gathered her belongings in her sack and dumped this outside. She grabbed Bjarki's old spear, still savagely sharp. It would double as a walking stick. Then she let the goat and sheep out to pasture, hitting them on their rumps to encourage them to move off down the valley. They lingered stubbornly. The chickens, too, pecked around the yard in ignorance.

The next task needed to be accomplished quickly before Boga could interfere. Torunn grabbed a swatch of kindling and thrust it into the fire. Next she darted about the house setting small fires. The flames would swallow the house and roof and the stead would collapse in on itself. The lintel and its runes would crash down scorched and meaningless. Bjarki had been wrong about words. Torunn then dashed outside, grabbing her bag and spear. As she ran swiftly up the valley, she looked back to make sure the animals had cleared the area. The wet moss would stop the fire from spreading far, but what would become of the animals, she did not know.

On top of the cliff, Torunn paused to watch the burning. Already the stead was yielding to the angry orange fingers and black smoke. Boga cuffed her shoulder and hissed in her ear,

"Curses be upon you, Torunn Svanadóttir. You have taken my home and my resting place. May you never again live under a dry roof, and may your grave be a den for wild animals."

"Your curses are no more than a snivel to me, Boga the Forever Unhoused. No longer do I intend to be bound by others' words. You may as well return to Gerda and tell her where you want your salt-caked bones buried."

And that was the last Torunn heard from Boga, for Torunn was of no use to her now.

Torunn had her small hoard and a tiny steed that would give her passage wherever she chose. Perhaps she would buy her own farm somewhere. First she would sail across the ocean and see the cities of Norway or even of Europe. She'd like to roam through land so large it could not be taken away from her.

# WHAT A MISERABLE DRINK,
# — AND WHAT A TERRIBLE PLACE —
## Alex Kreis

*Hrolf the Hunter*

I t is said that four pillars support the state: a judge without reproach, a head of police who defends the weak, a minister of taxation who does not oppress the poor, and a master of the post to inform on the other three. Ibn Kurradadh had been that fourth pillar for much longer than most citizens of Baghdad, and even the Khalifa himself, had been alive. As master of the Barid[3], he directed the couriers who carried messages from city to city, heedless of weather or darkness. It was he who knew what the emirs of each town and city were doing, whether they were loyal or not, corrupt or not, competent or not. And further, he watched

---

[3] Postal Service

the Romani, the Firanji, the Samanids, and all the other nations near and distant.

Sallam the Interpreter had served Ibn Kurradadh many times: translating from Hellenic, Persian, Saqalib[4], and dozens of other languages; carrying urgent messages through the night; reviewing the tax rolls of city officials. Yet no mission had brought him even a tenth as far from Baghdad as this, two thousand miles and more than a year away, at the muddy and stinking court of an infidel king in the frozen north. No, not infidel, he corrected himself. He had accepted the word of God and was now a true believer. But somehow, as he looked around at the gathered assembly dressed in skins and furs, it was hard to remember.

Sallam withdrew the Khalifa's letter from his case. "These are the words of the Commander of the Faithful." He looked around at the gathered court. When he and the other members of the embassy had arrived, they were nonplussed to discover that Almish, the King of the Bulgars, was hosting delegations from many lands: Khazars, Saqaliba, even Romani from Christian Byzantium, and a strange and filthy race from even further north called the Rus. The Bulgars, even the king and queen, dressed in animal skins. The Rus stood above the crowd like ragged trees. Only the Romani were dressed in fine silks, looking oddly at ease as if they were at court in Constantine's city. The King had entertained the assembled guests with meat charred over a fire and drinks of sour honeyed milk.

Finally, it was time for Sallam to present the words of the Khalifa. He stood and paused. The first moments of an embassy were key. He had bad news to deliver, and appearing weak before the Bulgar King, not to mention the rival kingdoms, would doom the embassy before it even began.

---

[4] Slavic

"Stand!" he bellowed. "You are to hear the words of the great Khalifa of all true believers. It is not proper to sit. When I speak his words, it is as though he stands here before you."

King Almish looked from side to side at his advisors and countrymen, and then labored to his feet, his large paunch hanging down. Those of his court that had been sitting quickly stood to follow.

Sallam read the letter from the Khalifa aloud in Bulgar, which he had learned on the trip from Bors, one of the ghulam[5] soldiers of the embassy. It began with the customary praise of a brother king. King Almish was pleased with the accompanying gifts: a richly appointed saddle; robes and silks in black, the color of the Abbasid Dynasty; a leather-bound Qur'an. He grinned widely when Sallam read the words of the Khalifa promising four thousand dinars for the construction of a great wall to defend the Bulgars, but his smile fell as no accompanying chest of coins was presented.

When the letter was done, the king demanded the letter and then hurled it to the ground. "You say that the Khalifa answers my request, but you lie! Does this letter not promise four thousand dinars?"

Sallam clasped his hands behind his back. "It is so, king."

"And where are these dinars?"

"We were unable to obtain the funds due to unfortunate events in Bukhara. A future embassy will honor your request."

The king's eyes grew even wider, and the pulse on his neck throbbed visibly. "Unfortunate? You speak to me of fortune? Your lies and failure will cause the blood of the faithful to run in rivers!"

Sallam began to answer, but the king held up a hand imperiously. "Enough lies!" He spoke to his adviser in words Sallam could not hear. "You will be shown the evidence of your foolishness!" He strode from the room.

---

[5] Slave

The embassy looked at each other, unsure whether they had been dismissed. The adviser, a man about the king's age, sharing his look and color—perhaps a relative—spoke in a formal tone. "The king requests that the ambassador accompany his men on a journey at dawn." He paused and appeared to take some mercy of the stunned embassy. "You may go."

As Sallam turned to leave he noticed the eyes of a Rus and the Romani[6] on him. The Rus man seemed only genuinely curious, but the two Romani seemed amused at some private joke.

Sallam thought back to that morning in Baghdad so long ago when ibn Kurradadh assigned this task to him. The two men sat in the courtyard of the palace and sipped tea. Ibn Kurradadh had asked him how he fared.

For a moment, Sallam had been overcome by this smallest sign of compassion. "Fine. It has been...quiet. We donated Ahmad's possessions to charity, praise be to God."

Ibn Kurradadh had spread his hands. "A noble act. God is pleased. You will meet your brother again in Paradise."

"Inshallah. But everywhere I go in the City of Peace I am reminded of his absence."

"Ah," ibn Kurradadh had said, somehow showing both kindness and as if he had seen some opportunity. "Then my request of you may be a blessing."

"Request?"

"The Khalifa has dreamed of the distant north. Do you know the words of the Eighteenth Surah? *We have prepared for the unjust a Fire.*"

---

[6] Roman. The Byzantines or the Eastern Roman Empire's self-designation for itself.

Sallam had felt a chill that had nothing to do with the morning air and tried to bring the words to mind. "The verse with the giants that come at the end of the world? *They will be relieved with water like molten brass. What a miserable drink, and what a terrible place!"*

Ibn Kurradadh nodded. "He saw those events come about. He wishes someone to investigate to see if it is a true vision."

"You wish me to travel thousands of miles for a dream?"

The old man smiled. "Well, while you are on the Khalifa's business, there is a small matter you can perform for me. The King of the Bulgars has broken from his masters the Khazars, and all manners of other kingdoms are circling like desert vultures. You can carry the words of the Khalifa of friendship, and report."

Sallam had laughed. "As you always say: behind every tale is another truth."

Ibn Kurradadh had wagged a finger. "You listened, but not well enough. Behind every *truth* is another truth. Perhaps the dream is true. Perhaps you will learn of the end of the world and return to us with happy news that we will all meet again in Paradise sooner than we thought. But in the meantime, we must still wake every morning and begin again."

Sallam and the others walked to their tents, speaking quietly of the King's reaction.

"Do you think he has been manipulated by others?" asked Tikin, the second ghulam. "Do they plan to kill us?"

Sallam looked at Sawsan, a eunuch who had served at the Khalifa's court for many years and had seen countless intrigues and plots. "It's possible," he said. "Or perhaps it is some plot by others to embarrass us so that the King allies with someone else. We do not know nearly enough. Perhaps it is just the way of these strange peoples, or perhaps it is an opportunity for us to prove ourselves."

Bors scowled. "What could the King want to show you?"

Before anyone could speculate, Tikin sliced his hand through the air to silence them, then silently nodded to a stand of trees ahead of them. Sallam saw nothing at first, then spied a silken hem behind a trunk. As they approached closer, the two Romani, a man and a woman, casually walked from behind the trees and came toward them as if they had intended to meet all along. Perhaps they had.

"Mine, ah, bright embassy town man," the man said in terrible Arabic. "Peace be on your head."

Sallam failed to suppress a grin but hid it by bowing, his hand on his heart. "And upon you be peace," he replied in Hellenic. "You are dedicated servants of the Christian Emperor to travel so far from Constantinople."

The man's eyebrows raised elegantly, and he bowed in return. He answered in Hellenic. "I am Licinius Theophylactos. This is my wife Epiphania. We are servants of Emperor Romanos."

Tikin bristled beside Sallam. He had fought the Byzantines at Qaliqala and had no love for them.

Sallam's head ached from the court presentation and he had no wish to fence words with these Romani. "It is an honor to meet you. But you must excuse me; I must retire to prepare for my ride with the King's men tomorrow." He wondered then if they had intelligence he could extract. "Have you seen...it?"

The two Romani looked at each other for a brief second. Licinius said, "I have no idea what the King wishes to show you. Perhaps you will join us after you return and tell us the tale?" But Sallam noticed the lady Epiphania wince almost imperceptibly. Ibn Kurradadh always said that a Romani knew twice as much as he said and lied about half of it. They knew something of what was afoot, and Sallam would swear that they feared it.

The next morning, Sallam stepped from the cabin and wrapped the fur cloak more tightly around himself. The rough-hewn logs had done little to stop the wind from entering at night. In the open it was even colder. At least the sun shone brightly; he did not miss the interminable sunless days of snow on their journey north.

The King had sent word that only Sallam would travel with the Bulgar King's guards to see this mysterious sight. At the gate of the rough wooden stockade that surrounded the city, two men armed with spears and the King's advisor from the court waited with four saddled horses.

"Greetings, Lord Sallam," the advisor said. "I am Kubrat, the King's cousin. Please, ride with us."

Sallam had only just swung his leg over his horse's saddle when another man rode up. It was the watchful Rus man Sallam had noticed at court. He was of middle years, Sallam judged, though strong, and had straw-colored hair and beard. Behind him, an unstrung bow and quiver of arrows was tied to his saddle. "I thought I would go hunting today," he said with a smile. And yet he made no effort to pass them or exit the open gate of the stockade.

Kubrat looked displeased but said nothing, perhaps warned by the King to not offend any of the guests. "Very well," he said, and motioned the two guards to ride out.

As they rode out onto a wide path across the fields outside the settlement, the Rus rode up alongside Sallam and spoke in halting Bulgar. "I speak little Bulgar. Do you know the tongue of the Byzantines?" He switched to Hellenic. "I have some from my time with the Varangians in Miklagard."

Sallam bowed as best he could while mounted and answered in the same tongue. "Your Hellenic is quite good." He switched tongues. "But perhaps Slavic would be more comfortable?"

The Rus' eyes widened and he laughed in a booming shout that startled a flock of birds from one of the few trees on the plain into flight. "And I thought to impress you with my Hellenic! Well played, Caliph's man. I am Hrolf, called the Hunter."

"And I am Sallam, called the Interpreter."

"A suitable name!"

They entered a wooded area as suddenly as passing through a curtain. Below the leafy canopy, it was much darker and Sallam's eyes strained to adjust.

"I had not heard of your people before," Sallam admitted. "From where do you come?"

"There are people from many tribes in our camp. We traveled for many months to get here: on boats through the sea, over land to the source of the river, then many weeks of river travel to this place."

Sallam shook his head in wonder at the breadth of God's creation. Who could have believed that he could travel two thousand miles only to meet a man who had traveled as far from the other direction? "Far indeed!"

Hrolf laughed. "I come from farther yet, across another ocean to an island called Iceland. My steading is called Nastrond."

"Is that not your tongue for the land of the dead?"

He raised his eyebrows. "Your mastery of languages truly is impressive."

Sallam ducked to avoid a branch that crossed the path. "Do you know what the king's men seek to show me?" Sallam asked.

Hrolf shook his head. "No, but I was too curious to wait to hear the tale. My people have a saying: *Every man is the smith of his own fortune.*" He grinned again. "So here I am!"

Sallam laughed, finding himself liking this strange barbarian. He reflected that he could not remember the last time he had laughed so. He began to answer when Kubrat turned from his horse in the lead to hush them. "We approach it now."

Sallam and Hrolf rode ahead to where Kubrat and the soldiers waited. In a long trough dug into the ground not far from the path lay a body of a man. But not a man as Sallam had ever seen. It was at least as long as two men; its head was the size of a beehive, its chest a barrel. Sallam grew unreasonably frightened. From the quickened breaths of the other men, it seemed it had the same effect. "In the name of God. What manner of creature is that?" he whispered.

Kubrat's horse danced nervously and he pulled on the reins to try to control it. "The tribes to the north call them Gog and Magog. They live beyond a great wall to the north."

Sallam's heart beat faster and the hair on the back of his neck rose. Yajuj and Majuj, foretold by the words of the Prophet as appearing at the end of days. He had told no one of the Khalifa's dream, and yet he had been led here to see this.

Hrolf said, "In my land we call them Jotun and Muspel. At the end of the world, the Muspel will release fires from the earth."

"Now do you see why the King is so eager for the funds promised by the Khalifa? If these giants are released, he needs better defenses or we will be destroyed."

Sallam shook his head. "If the giants are released, no wall will suffice."

The sun had not yet risen when Bors slipped back into the tent. He waited while Sallam finished his prayers, then spoke. "There is news. One of the Rus lords has died. The King put a halt to the embassies until after their funeral rites."

Upon his return last night, Sallam had recounted the tale of the giant in the woods to Sawsan and the two ghulam but was unable to convey the visceral fear the sight had caused. Bors and Tikin, who were not as lettered as the eunuch, had listened to Sawsan recount the tale of Yajuj and Majuj, the giants foretold by the Prophet that God would release on the world at the end of days. The four men spoke late into the night but came to no conclusions on how to proceed. Finally, Sallam had put an end to it and ordered all to bed. "We must find a way to convince King Almish to accept the alliance. I fear the machinations of the Romani; in their hands, this kingdom would be yet another knife pressed to the Khalifat. And if it is true that the day of fire draws near, true believers must stand against the giants."

And yet the news that morning did nothing to show the path forward. Sallam wondered if the King's halt was a further setback or an opportunity. He washed and went to see what he could learn.

Down at the river shore, a group of Rus men stood knee-deep in the water around a ship. Sallam tried to watch as the wind drove knife-sharp flecks of ice into his face. He winced and shielded his eyes with his hands. Nearby, Hrolf laughed. "All-father greets Halfdan with a pleasant breeze."

"What are they doing?" Sallam asked.

"They bring the ship onto land for Halfdan's death-pyre."

Sallam was not sure he had understood Hrolf's language. "His what?"

"His body will be placed in the ship, along with his arms and treasures. Then they will burn the ship to send his spirit to Valhalla."

Sallam watched the Rus strain to lift the oddly-shaped ship onto the land. "In my land we bury the dead in the earth."

Hrolf spat on the ground. Sallam would never get used to the disgusting ways of the Rus. "I have heard that. What a stupid idea! Do you truly love your dead if you leave them in a hole in the ground to be devoured by worms?"

"God sent a crow to dig a hole in the ground to show Cain how to bury..." Sallam took a deep breath, overcome by a sudden stab of grief. "...his brother."

If Hrolf noticed the pause, he said nothing. "Crows! They can be tricksters."

The strange Rus funeral proceedings continued throughout the day. The King turned away requests from the embassy to meet. The Romani, however, were eager to host Sallam and Sawsan to supper, and although Sallam wanted nothing less, he knew it was his duty to ibn Kurradadh to learn what he could.

He was dressing for dinner when a cacophony came from outside. He sent Bors to investigate, but then, too alarmed to wait, followed a moment later. The Rus, gathered around the ship, were beating their weapons against their shields and shouting. At their feet, the frozen ground was covered in blood. Aghast, he shouted for Tikin. The ghulam ran up, sword in hand, but it was soon clear that there was no immediate threat. The Rus merely stood and shouted, making their unholy racket. Sallam shook his head. This was a land of madmen.

At a long and tedious dinner with Licinius and Epiphania, he learned nothing of King Almish or the Romani's plans. However, they were more forthcoming in describing the day's events. The Rus had sacrificed cattle, horses, and fowl. The shouting, Licinius explained with a mix of gleeful horror, was to celebrate a slave girl who had volunteered to be killed and burned along Halfdan. Epiphania looked down at the table while he recounted this.

Sallam was disgusted, in equal parts with the Rus and the Romani. He soon made his excuses and returned to the embassy's tents for the evening prayer.

Shouts and screams woke Sallam the next day. For a confused moment he thought it was the call to prayer. He came to his feet and hurriedly pulled on the thick furs before heading out of the tent.

The sky was just barely lit. Down by the river, where the angry voices came from, torches lit the planks of the beached ship.

Sallam carefully picked his way down and saw Hrolf standing apart, chewing his long blond mustache.

"What has happened?" he asked Hrolf.

Hrolf turned to see Sallam. "Dark news, my friend. Thyra, the girl who was to die for Halfdan, has been slain."

Sallam frowned. "Is that not what you wanted?"

Hrolf made a strange warding-away gesture. "Gods forbid. She should have been killed by the Angel of Death after she was prepared. Only so could her spirit accompany Halfdan. This...this is some foul murder. Halfdan's funeral is polluted. I do not even know if his spirit will go to Valhalla now." Hrolf looked as if he would weep.

Sallam felt for the man's obvious distress, but honestly could not fathom it. First, these infidels were planning on performing human sacrifice to their idols, and now they were upset that the girl had died. He prayed that the Prophet's words would come to these benighted people soon. And yet he still felt sorrow for this man.

"Are you well?" he asked, knowing the fatuousness of the question.

Hrolf shook his head wordlessly, then took a deep breath and expelled it loudly. "How do we go on?"

Sallam considered and thought of the well-meaning sympathy and useless advice he had received in Baghdad after his brother's death. "You wake in the morning, and begin again."

As if the thought of distant Baghdad summoned the spirit of ibn Kurradadh, Sallam found himself considering the political situation. They could make no progress with the King until the Rus funeral rites were complete, and yet now it appeared that they could not be.

"What would it take to complete the ceremony?" he asked Hrolf.

Hrolf cocked his head, much like a bird of prey, and narrowed his eyes. Sallam was certain the Rus had perceived Sallam's own calculations. He considered that he should not underestimate this man merely because he was ignorant of God's word.

Hrolf considered. "If we find Thyla's killer, her spirit will be free to accompany Halfdan."

Sallam nodded. "Then let us find him. You are a Hunter, are you not? Let us hunt."

Sallam cornered Kubrat and impressed upon him the risks to the Bulgars of continued chaos. At last before the king, Sallam offered his services to investigate the murder. "If I do so, King, will you accept the protection of the Khalifa? Only by standing with the true believers can you hope to avoid the flames that will come with the day of judgment."

The king appeared torn between annoyance and fear. "I hardly see what your word is worth, but perhaps you can prove yourself. If you can find the guilty by dawn two days hence, you will have shown me that indeed your nation is wise and powerful. Otherwise, you must return to your city and I will accept no further embassies from your Khalifa without eight thousand dinars."

Sallam bowed, his hand to his heart. "It will be as you say, King."

He quickly informed Sawsan, Tikin, and Bors. Sawsan was horrified. "We have as good as failed. How can we find a barbarian who killed another barbarian?"

"I will get one of the Rus, the man called Hrolf, to assist me. He will know their ways."

Sawsan seemed skeptical but did not argue. "In either case it will be time for us to leave. Good riddance to this horrid land."

Sallam hurried to find Hrolf. He had already spent half the day pursuing Kubrat and the King.

Hrolf was pleased to hear that the King had agreed to let them investigate. "Let me show you the body. We are lucky in that the others fear it cursed and so have not touched it. Bring a lantern."

He brought Sallam to the beached ship and led him onto the deck. An opening led down into the dark hold.

"She's down there?" asked Sallam.

"Yes. Halfdan is there in his armor and with his gold as well. She was to spend the night and then she would be slain by the Angel of Death, but someone did the foul murder first."

Sallam shook his head at the strangeness of it, but had no time to argue. "Let us see." He lit the lantern, placed it on the deck, and carefully lowered himself into the hold. Hrolf handed down the lantern and then jumped down, landing easily.

The stench of blood and death was nearly overpowering. As Sallam shone the lantern around, gold shone and reflected brightly, while blood pooled on the ground like black oil. The girl lay on the floor, arms outstretched. A light tunic was soaked in blood. Sallam inspected the cloth; five cuts to the chest. He touched the blood; it was still damp. He held a rag to it and it slowly grew dark with absorbed blood.

"What can you tell?" Hrolf asked.

"It was done with a dagger. Each strike is true, so she did not fight or attempt to flee."

They looked around; many different footsteps tracked the blood through the hold. "I thought you said she had been left undisturbed," Sallam said.

"Her body wasn't touched. But she was discovered by the old woman who was to strangle her, and the three men who would do the deed. And then many others came to see."

Sallam stood. "I fear there is little else to learn here."

Hrolf sighed. "We will need the aid of the gods to find the killer."

"I would recommend praying to the one true God for assistance instead," admonished Sallam.

Hrolf pulled himself up through the hatchway and then reached back and grasped Sallam's hand. "I was not talking of prayer," he said, pulling him up, "but something more direct."

Sallam had been horrified by Hrolf's plan; he had no interest in trafficking in heathen gods or black magic. But Hrolf was intent on pursuing it, and in the end Sallam's duty to act as ibn Kurradadh's eyes had overcome his reluctance. It had taken the rest of the day and the night to make the arrangements, but by noon the next day they were ready to begin.

The slave girl—Thyra—lay on the bare earth near the ship, her bloody clothes replaced by a clean tunic. Sallam and Sawsan sat near her feet. Hrolf, four other Rus men, and two Rus women warriors, nearly as tall and strong as the men, sat or knelt around her. At her head sat an ancient Rus woman, her eyes nearly lost in the wrinkles and folds of her face.

Sallam had seen many dead bodies: men, women, children, dead of disease or violence or age; taken unawares or at the end of a long twilight struggle. The old Khalifa, draped in his golden robes. A soldier who took a blade intended for Sallam. Sallam's brother, skin sallow and sunken, gone and still beloved. In the bright noonday sun, the murdered slave girl was unlike any; at once she seemed both more dead, and yet alive.

The ancient Rus woman held the dead girl's hand in her own; with her other hand, she dropped bits of a plant into an iron pot. The flowers had red-veined yellow petals, and the leaves were thick and hairy. From the pot rose an acrid smoke, which the woman inhaled deeply.

Her mouth was slightly parted, and from it came a voice in a croak that sounded as though it came up from fathomless caverns. "The dwellings reddened with ruddy gore." Sallam felt the hackles on his neck rise, and saw Hrolf, who at daybreak raged in impatience to begin, mutter and put his hand to his blade. At the crest of the hill, near a cluster of shrubs, the two Romani watched.

The ancient woman's hand tightened on Thyla's. "Sun-beams turn black the following summers, the stars scatter."

Hrolf visibly gritted his teeth, even more disturbed by these odd words than Sallam would have guessed. He leaned forward. "Baby girl, entombed alive, for what crime were you killed? Who did the deed?"

Sawsan grabbed Sallam's arm and squeezed painfully. "He speaks the words of the Prophet!" he hissed.

Sallam's blood ran cold. He was right—the images had seemed familiar, but the Slavic words had not immediately connected in his mind with the Arabic words of the revelation. But it was true, Hrolf and the ancient woman—or the slave girl's spirit, risen through Northern magic—were reciting the words of the eighty-first Surah, describing the end of days.

"What does it mean?" Sawsan asked urgently, but Sallam had no time to answer before the old woman spoke again.

"Steam spurts up, flame flies high against heaven itself."

Hrolf, his hand now clenched into a fist, nearly growled. "Tell me what I need to know, spirit!"

The old woman turned to face Hrolf, smoke curling around her. As she still gripped Thyla's hand, the slave girl's body shifted and it seemed as though she rolled to face Hrolf as well. "A hall I saw, far from the sun, on Nastrond it stands, and the doors face north. Venom drops through the smoke-vent down."

Hrolf swore and stood. "False woman! These lies are the words of the trickster." He met Sallam's eyes. "You were right, friend. This idea was foolish beyond measure." He stalked away. The old woman's head went down, as if she were asleep, and she spoke no more.

The sun had sunk below the horizon by the time Sallam found Hrolf. He sat on the ridge, in much the same place as the Romani had stood watching the grotesque ceremony. Sallam wondered what they thought of it and what they had concluded.

Sallam sat down next to him and waited. He watched clouds slowly move and twist, glowing with the reflected light of the sun.

"They were just lies from the mouth of the trickster," said Hrolf.

Sallam let out a deep sigh. "I fear not, my friend. She spoke the words of the Prophet. They are true words, revealed by God."

Hrolf turned to look Sallam in the face. His face was even paler than its usual unhealthy white. "She spoke of my home, in flames."

Sallam nodded. "I know. It is strange, all the things we have seen and heard here." He thought back, wondering how long ago God had set him on this path. "Even a year ago, the Khalifa dreamed of the end of the world."

"What does it mean? Shall I and my home burn? Are we truly the smiths of our own fortune, or have the gods foreordained our path?"

"The words of the Prophet are true, but men have argued their meaning for centuries. This is what I believe: a world will end, but perhaps not for all men or all nations. You have been told this not as a punishment but as a warning: the land of your home will erupt in fire; ash will cover the sky. But I believe your people are right, you may still forge your fate. Return home, move your family, find a home away from the land of the dead. Begin again."

Hrolf said nothing but Sallam thought perhaps he was more at peace.

Sallam looked up. The clouds' motion was stronger now, and Sallam realized that they were to the north, not west, and it could not be the sun's light they gave off. Sallam's hand went to his heart. "God preserve us! What is that?"

Hrolf laughed. "It is a battle among spirits, or so the Bulgars say. To me it just looks like glowing clouds."

Waves of green and dark purple rose and fell. It was possible that they were waves of djinn clashing against each other, he supposed.

"You have seen it before?"

"Oh yes, many times. The farther south I travel the rarer it is."

They sat in silence, watching the battle, if it was such. Odd, thought Sallam, that such a clash should be so quiet. There should be a great din, or screaming, or something to mark this celestial conflagration; but instead, only the silence of the night.

Or not quite silence; Sallam heard the slightest crunch, as though an animal stepped on the frozen ground, coming from a cluster of low shrubs.

"What do you call that shape?" Hrolf asked suddenly, gesturing at a constellation.

Sallam looked. "That is the Great Bear."

Hrolf gave his big booming laugh. "I see it! That sounds like a name that my people would give a star-shape. But to us, it is the Wagon."

Sallam smiled, although Hrolf would be unable to see it in the darkness. "And that sounds like my people."

"Yes! My thought exactly!" Hrolf responded, and Sallam *could* hear the smile in his voice. "Perhaps you will ride such a wagon home. May it remind you of your time among us here."

Sallam was oddly moved by this strange and filthy barbarian's wish. "I will indeed. And if you see a Great Bear in the north when you return, think of us as well."

The booming laugh again. "I promise I will not forget. I am sorry that you must leave with Thyra's death unsolved."

"Oh, no," said Sallam. "I have quite determined how to reveal the murderer. Tomorrow I will do so before the King."

Hrolf was astonished. "But how? We have found nothing that proves the guilt of anyone."

"Not so," said Sallam. "In the House of Wisdom, I read of an infallible way to determine the identity of a murderer in such a situation. She was stabbed in the chest multiple times; her blood must have coated the hands and arms of the murderer."

Hrolf grunted. "It is certainly so, but they would have cleansed the blood from themselves as soon as the deed was done."

"True. But blood leaves a trace that does not wash so easily. You saw that I took some of her blood on a cloth. By mixing it with a compound discovered by our wisest alchemists, it will blaze in the presence of traces of her blood. At the assembly tomorrow, I will place the cloth on the hands of all present; God willing, the one who killed her will be burned. And so their guilt will be revealed to all."

Again, the faint crunch. Hrolf narrowed his eyes and considered Sallam thoughtfully.

Sallam stood and brushed at his knees. "Good night. I must go to prayers. I will see you in the morning."

In the morning they gathered at the King's hall, breath blowing steam in the cold air. As Sallam had expected, the Romani had departed in the night. He thought back to ibn Kurradadh's words. Behind every truth is another truth. Sallam wondered if striking at the Romani had been his true goal, behind this embassy, itself behind a quest to follow a young king's dream.

"Praise to God. Their cowardice reveals their guilt," he announced to the King. "They slew the slave girl to make you look weak and to frustrate the Rus. But thanks to your greatness and wisdom, they failed." At the edge of his vision, Sawsan rolled his eyes, but the King appeared to enjoy the flattery.

"We are glad our friends from the Khalifat were here," the King said. "Please return with gifts for the Great Khalifa." His eyes sharpened. "And send eight thousand dinars before the season turns."

—⟨ ✳ ⟩—

At the gate, as the members of the embassy scurried about arranging their materials and gifts from the King to the Khalifa on the horses and mules, Hrolf arrived to bid them farewell.

He gripped Sallam's arm with one hand and placed his other on his shoulder. "Thank you, brother. I believe the gods sent you to me to interpret my path. When I return to Iceland, I will move my steading far from Nostrand. If it is true that the earth fires will come, I will be safely away. And if it is the end of the world, one place is as good as another." A horse whinnied unhappily at his burden and sidestepped into the path. Bors cursed at him and dragged him back.

Sallam smiled at this strange heathen who called him brother. He thought of Ahmad, and for the first time the terrible pain in his heart was only an ache. "I do not believe in your gods, but I do believe that the One God has placed you in my path. God has told us that the world will end, and on that day all will be judged. And yet I do not think that time has come yet."

Hrolf grinned. "The world ends every day when the night falls. In the morning, we wake and begin again."

Around them, horses whinnied and stamped, and men and women shouted, and yet to Sallam it felt as though he stood in the mosque at prayer. Could it be so? Perhaps he would return to tell the Khalifa that his dream was true: the world was indeed about to end. And it had! Men and women had died, alliances were broken, fires went out, the sun went down. And then morning came and we woke and began again.

# — THE SAGA OF AUD THE SEERESS —
## Siobhán Clark

*Aud the Seeress*

## 1 - Thorgeir Hǫggvinkinni

There was a man named Thorgeir Einarsson, son of Einar *inn Sterki* the Strong, who was the son of Kráka Freki of Sogn. When Thorgeir was still young, there was a great dearth in Sogn, at this time many perished and among them was Einar. Thorgeir was black haired, intelligent, and of handsome but fierce appearance. When the time came, he took a wife, her name was Uksákká, she was of the Sámi that lived in the far north and herded reindeer. For a time Thorgeir and Uksákka lived well, she gave him a daughter named Aud. One night while he was sleeping, Uksákká left their *lavvu* and walked out into the snow, never to be seen again. After that, Thorgeir became *hryggr* such was the pain that afflicted his heart. This was in the time before Harald Hárfagri united the petty kingdoms and thus became the sole ruler of Norway. For his King,

Thorgeir took up his sword and cut many men in two, slaking his thirst with blood and feasting in halls he later burned to the ground.

A man named Hrolf Geirsson was dispatched by his Chieftain to murder Thorgeir Einarsson. Hrolf was a man of dubious character and his heart was filled with vengeance since it was Thorgeir who had slain his brother. He befriended his target, using deception and falsehoods to win the praise of those surrounding Thorgeir. There came a night, as the battle-weary slept on a heath by an open fire, when Hrolf seized his opportunity and crawled on his belly to the slumbering warrior's side. Lifting his treacherous hand, fingers wrapped around the hilt of a dagger, Hrolf chose to first maim Thorgeir by slashing him across the cheek. Thorgeir sprang from his furs and thrust his fist into the face of the attacker: Hrolf howled as bone and flesh were broken and torn. As blood seeped from the man's face, Thorgeir retrieved the blade and drove it deep into the throat of the traitor. Hrolf lay defeated, his blood seeping into the earth, and no man among them buried the corpse. After the attack, the son of Einar became Thorgeir Hǫggvinkinni, or cut-cheek.

Thorgeir left for the Hebrides at the behest of Hárfagri. He took his daughter Aud from the Sámi, so that she might live with him, though he had scarcely been a father to her. His blade pacified the rivalries between the Jarls and their *bændr* freemen, and he amassed much wealth in his time there. When the summer was swept away by increasing winds from the west, Thorgeir sensed change was coming to the Hebrides. Harald Hárfagri had sent more of his men, though some had been unwilling at first, and old rivalries were stirred once more. A ship was made ready, but when Thorgeir boarded the vessel his gaze was drawn back to the land. In the winter he was wed to Aldïs *in Bareyska* from the Hebrides, a wan and taciturn woman with storm-filled eyes and a reserved nature. Many remarked Aldïs often hid in her husband's shadow. Their days together were few, but Aldïs gave him one more daughter, before taking her own life.

Aldïs had little love in her heart for Aud Thorgeirsdottir, she said, "This child possesses too much of her mother in her tongue, and the fury of her father in her eyes." Thorgeir replied, "You see my dead wife in her, I don't care for that memory, send her away if it pleases you." When Aud was still young, Aldïs sent her to foster in the house of a woman who lived apart from all others on the islands. By the time Aud returned, knowing such things that would serve her well from here on in, her sister Sigrid was able to stand while clutching the apron of her mother. As the years passed, Aldïs became bitter and resentful of Aud, often mumbling curses by the fireside, and criticizing her husband's daughter in every way. There came a day when a wealthy man and his son arrived at Thorgeir's house looking for Aud. The girl hid in the shadows while Aldïs furiously denied them entry, she said, "Though I wish her gone, your offer serves only to insult Thorgeir, in his stead I turn you away. She is ill-fated, and I will not be known for cursing another family!" Aud knew then her father's wife would never allow her any chance of securing an agreeable future. A short time later, Aldïs suffered from a peculiar sickness, but refused Aud's healing knowledge, and gathered her cloak one night before walking into the sea. When Thorgeir heard the news, he resolved to depart the Hebrides for Iceland. He said, "It seems to me a curse has been placed upon my head, so I will go where ill-will is least likely to follow." The sisters knew well to remain close to one-another from that moment on.

## 2 - The betrothal of Sigrid

There was a man named Thorgils Grímsson, son of Grímr who was the son of Thorgest *inn Hávi*, an impressive and powerful *hersir* in life. Thorgils farmed with his father in Grímrfjörður, near the Drangajökull glacier; there the land was rich, fertile, and close to the sea. Hjalti was the name of Grímr's foster-son, a miserable lad with a sharp tongue and sullen wit. Grímr sold a tract of land to Thorgeir, a place that had been poorly cultivated and required a skilled hand. When Thorgeir placed the gold in Grímr's hand he said, "I want no man, or woman, to step foot on the place I now call Uksákkástaðr without my permission. You alone may seek me there Grímr, but only with good reason. I have with me the sword Dauði, and its blade hungers for *raven-wine*."

All this happened in the summer. When winter arrived, Grímr's wife worried for she knew Thorgeir had two daughters. She begged her husband to go to Uksákkástaðr with such things as the family might need. Grímr agreed with his wife but was not happy about the task, so he took his son Thorgils with him. Each rode a horse to the land bordering Grímrfjörður, and Grímr knew when he had reached it for Thorgeir's boundary stone marked the place.

Snow began to fall and Grímr felt increasingly uneasy, he looked at his son and said, "Son, you must go the house of Thorgeir Hǫggvinkinni and give him this sack. You are only a boy, and as I see it, no threat to him." The boy went, finding the entrance of a dwelling cut into the hillside, with smoke rising up through a turf roof. As he stood, something in the mist drew his eyes toward a large rock, as images of unfamiliar shapes appeared on the surface of the *sieidi* sacred stone. Fear overtook his senses at the unnerving silence hanging in the gloom. He dropped the sack and turned to flee, but a voice from behind stopped him in his tracks. "Thank you," was all the voice said. Thorgils turned to see the face of a girl his own age, he thought her beautiful and found the urge to run had left him. A shadow passed behind the girl, a pale hand reached out from the dark doorway startling Thorgils, and the face of an older girl appeared. At this, the boy turned and fled.

Grímr had been much relieved to have his son return safely from the farm at Uksákkástaðr. Thorgils told his father what had happened and Grímr forbade him to return ever again. Seasons passed and Thorgils became a strong, intelligent, and thoughtful man. Grímr was proud and boastful of his son's skills in farming, fishing, and the wealth they accumulated in the trade of walrus ivory. Grímr ignored the warnings of his wife, she told him all could be lost as quickly as it was gained, and Thorgils was yet to marry; she had no desire for a match made without some hope of happiness. "If our son is unhappy in his marriage, his work will suffer, and we will lose the life we have become accustomed to." Grímr's wife said, and he knew she had the right of it. Grímr approached his son, "The time draws nigh for you to take a wife, what do you think about this?" Thorgils replied "I've seen the woman I want." Grímr asked, "Who is this woman?" Thorgils said, "Thorgeir's daughter, the one with golden hair, her name is Sigrid and we have met often on the shore when her sister takes her fishing. Her father knows nothing of this, Thorgeir would have been opposed in the past, but I have made us wealthy and can offer Sigrid a good life." Grímr was shocked by the duplicity of his son, and fearful when he recalled the threat of Thorgeir. He struck his son on the chin and said, "All this was for Sigrid? Would you have worked as hard if you had never met?" Thorgils became enraged, he was a head taller and a foot broader than his father. "A man needs a purpose in life, you made yours by sitting on your backside while your son worked his fingers to the bone. You will not strike me again, if you do and deny me what I desire with Sigrid, Thorgeir's threat will be the least of your worries!"

Thorgeir met with Grímr and his son by the boundary stone, he listened in silence as his daughter's suitor proposed terms for Sigrid's hand. At this time, Thorgeir was advancing in years, his black hair was now as white as frost and his temperament had thawed a little. He said, "Sigrid is free to marry the man she chooses, if she tells me it is you, then you shall have her under these terms; you will stay in Uksákkástaðr for a year and a day as man and wife, then live where you wish. Sigrid will not be parted from Aud, they are sisters and the bond is strong, where Sigrid goes so too does Aud. Lastly, no judgement will be made about Aud or Sigrid, they are women with strong hearts and minds, I have made them who they are and no man will change what is deep-rooted." For a moment Thorgils considered the terms, but this was too long for Thorgeir, who said "No wedding feast will there be, no merriment in any hall, if you do it will curse your future happiness." Grímr became angry and entered into harsh words with Thorgeir, but Thorgils was pleased by the demands as his father would not have the opportunity to flaunt the wealth he had amassed.

Thorgils and Sigrid were wed. Grímr never lost the enmity he felt towards his son, Thorgeir, or Sigrid. Thorgils lived well with his wife for never had he known such contentment. He entered into a deep friendship with Thorgeir, who revealed his long and unfortunate story, in the evenings when the women worked at weaving. He learned Aud was *in draumspaka* a dream-reader, and skilled in arts unknown to him, but akin to healing, ritual work and *seiðr*. Few had such knowledge and so it was greatly valued. Aud refused to marry and neither Thorgeir, nor Thorgils, or Sigrid would change her mind from it. In the first winter following Thorgils marriage, a storm ravaged Iceland, and many cattle were lost. Grímr died, as did his wife, and their farm was left in the hands of their foster-son Hjalti while Thorgils remained in Uksákkástaðr.

## 3 - The death of Thorgils

One winter's day, Aud was sitting alone in the house she shared with her father in Uksákkástaðr. The door opened and Thorgeir Hǫggvinkinni entered, 'I have seen something while I was out in the field, I don't know what to make of it.' Aud laid down her spindle whorl and said, "Tell me." Thorgeir sat on the bench by the fireside and tugged his beard, "I saw myself, as a young man, though it was no more than a shadow or a memory of what has been." Aud nodded sadly, "When Oðinn's shield-tree earned the claim of war arms, he yearned only for the mead of one-eye's hall. Now, fewer are his steps to Uksákká in Fólkvangr, where she waits for Hǫggvinkinni." Thorgeir agreed and walked to the other side of the room where he pulled a bundle from beneath the furs on his pallet. Untying the bindings from the worn cloth he revealed Dauði, the sword that craved blood. He said to his daughter, "When I die you will be alone, I fear there will be none to protect you, as I fear there is doom upon Thorgils and Sigrid; our kin can never know true joy. Fate stole your mother from me, nights before she disappeared, she told me wolves were at the door of our *lavvu*, but there were never any marks in the snow. I see now what she meant; we cannot escape the past, though I believe we must try to live despite it. Here, take Dauði, but I forewarn you daughter, that sword is cursed. First Dauði will take from you, then it will give you everything you desire, though I had few to share it with." Aud could only whisper as she gazed upon the sword, "I dream of a black horse roaming the heath of Uksákkástaðr, it seeks to claim Hǫggvinkinni's daughter. There is a curse upon me already, one that Dauði cannot change." That night Thorgeir slipped out into the night, his body never was found, and no bones rest within a mound. Not long after this, Aud resolved to bear the pain no longer, she gathered her meagre belongings and burned her father's house to ashes.

When Hjalti learned of Thorgeir's death, he took a horse and rode to Thorgils house in Uksákkástaðr. Sigrid was not at home as she had gone in search of Aud who had left the dwelling at daybreak. She feared her sister was becoming *hryggr*, as afflicted by grief as her father had been. Thorgils was in the house when

Hjalti arrived, he welcomed his foster-brother inside and they each took a seat by the fire.

"You have been long in coming to my home," said Thorgils.

"You did not come when our father died, or mother, I buried them alone. Though I saw you left a marker by their graves." Hjalti replied.

"There was nothing left for me inside that house, but I would have come if you had sent for me, foster-brother." Thorgils said, not disguising the roiling anger he felt inside.

"Will you not offer your brother a drink? I have not come to argue." Hjalti replied.

Thorgils stood and left the fireside. Hjalti spied something hidden under the seat on which he sat. It was Dauði, the sword Thorgeir Hǫggvinkinni had given to Aud his daughter. When Thorgils returned he gave Hjalti a horn of ale and sat across from him once more. "Drink foster-brother, then return to Grímr's house, take your belongings and leave. Go to your own father, unless he does not want you back?" said Thorgils. At that moment Hjalti stood, revealed Dauði in his grip and thrust it into Thorgils chest. So deep was the blade that Hjalti struggled to pull it from the body of his foster-brother. Staring at Thorgils corpse, an unrelenting grief racked his body so that every bone shook. Tears of regret flowed from his eyes as he tore at his hair, scratching his face and groaning in anguish. After a time, he stood and left the farmhouse, intending to return to Grímrfjörður, but he paused to cut turf from the ground and concealed Dauði beneath the sod.

What happened next was this; Sigrid returned to find Hjalti leaning against his horse, seeing his face she gasped in horror, and soon discovered Thorgils dead inside the dwelling. "What happened!" She cried. "Where is Aud?' Hjalti said, for he now planned to kill both sisters and burn the house. "I cannot find her," Sigrid wept. Hjalti paused. He formed a plan; he would accuse Aud of murder, take Sigrid for wife and claim the wealth of both

Grímrfjörður and Uksákkástaðr. "It was your sister," he said, "I walked in as she cast her vile incantations over Thorgils and slew him with a sword. See what she did to my face when I tried to stop her! I have always loved you Sigrid, take my hand, in time you will see me as more."

Hjalti pulled Sigrid from Thorgils body and placed her on the back of his horse. He gathered men in Grímrfjörður who searched long into the evening for Aud. When she was found they bound her hands and presented her to Agnar Goði. "Why is there cloth in her mouth?" Agnar Goði asked the men in his hall. Hjalti replied, "To prevent her sly tongue, she is known for her spells and incantations."

At this time, there was no wiser man in this quarter of Iceland than Agnar Goði, he was shrewd and swift in his judgements. He advised Hjalti the vengeance lay with Sigrid. Hjalti claimed she had turned the matter over to him, but no man would vouch that this was true. Aud was sentenced to outlawry, so that no man, woman, or child in Iceland could aid her. Hjalti removed her shoes and cloak, he took her brooches, necklaces and charms. He then pushed her into the snow and sent her on her way, to where he cared not, so long as she cast no eye upon her sister Sigrid or shadow upon his lands. When Sigrid heard of Aud's fate she fell into a state of utter despair and silence.

## 4 - Aud the Seeress

There was a man named Gerðarr Hauknefr, the son of a merchant and *farmaðr* sea-farer. He owned a sturdy knarr, commanding a loyal crew of no less than twenty men. The snow that fell that winter had taken Gerðarr and his crew by surprise, the ship that now waited for a break in the ice, was packed from stem to stern with goods such as walrus ivory which was much appreciated in foreign lands. The night Aud came upon them, the men had made camp on the shoreline, huddled around fires and wrapped in thick furs. Gerðarr Hauknefr was *víðförli*; a far-travelled man, quick of wit, and sure in all his dealings with other men.

Despite her misery Aud did not let the arduous walk from the hall of Agnar Goði break her will. Though her heart was for now beyond repair, she had foreseen the suffering of Sigrid, as she had seen her own, and fate could not be escaped. Since long ago, she understood her visions of figures still unknown had a role to play in her vengeance against Hjalti. She possessed no weapon and felt fresh sorrow at the loss of Dauði; her father's sword. All the things representing Aud's status and wealth, were taken from her by Hjalti, who had returned to Sigrid though she staunchly refused him everything he desired.

The next thing to be told is this; Gerðarr Hauknefr had taken his post as watchman on land, as two men guarded the ship. The snow that had fallen all day and night lessened, so the men could clearly see one another by the light of their lanterns. There was a man called Arni Øxnamegin, or Ox-might, a hulking brute whose fists were as large as a man's head and shoulders as broad as two men standing arm to arm. His temper was slow to fire, his sharp pale cobalt eyes as cold as glaciers, and many a tale claimed he had been a *berserkr* of the most terrifying kind. It was also said that Gerðarr had known Arni in those days and had been wise to keep him as his man onboard the knarr. It was Arni who shouted to his captain when he caught sight of a form in the distance, one that staggered and dropped onto the snow-laden ground more than once. The men left their posts, charging with lanterns and axes in their hands, for there had been tales of *draugrs* or the undead in these parts. Such was their shock at finding a woman with no shoes or cloak that they tore off their furs, wrapping them about her. They carried Aud to the camp, placing her next to the fire, and rubbed her skin until the blood flowed warmly in limbs.

"I know your face, how is that so?" Said Gerðarr in astonishment, for her eyes were the color of *Freyja's tears*, glittering as the *bane of wood* danced in her gaze.

"I am Aud, daughter of Thorgeir Hǫggvinkinni and Uksákká. My sister is Sigrid, the murder of her husband Thorgils made me an outlaw. I am *in draumspaka*, I am a seeress, but not a slayer of men."

"If what you say is true, then tell me what I dreamt last night."

"A woman, and a sleek fox. But it was no more than a *hamrammr* shape-shifting man. You saw me chasing after it, running through the snow with my hands gripping my father's sword, Dauði. I followed the trickster onto a frozen lake, where mist began to grow thick and blinding. A woman's scream rang out from the gloom. When you awoke there was a scent, it was the *haar*; a sea-fog that rolls over the Hebrides, it clings to skin and hair as if it were smoke from a fire." Aud said this with such conviction that Gerðarr took a moment to reply.

"You will sail with us," he said at last. "I'm an honest man so will make my motives clear. You possess knowledge that will serve me well, in return I offer you safety, and perhaps one day you will have your vengeance against the fox." Gerðarr then told his men to make the ship ready. At daybreak they would sail for lands anew, to *Holmgarðr*.

## 5 - The Journey to Itil

The sail strained as the ship plunged and tore through the glacier strewn seas from Iceland to Norway. From there they made haste to Finland, cramming their stores with furs that promised overflowing purses of silver. Wind tore at their cloaks, rain soaked their *hudfat* sleeping skins, salt parched their lips and deepened the creases on their weather-beaten faces. Yet the ship did not stop, its prow slicing the frigid waters as Gerðarr stood pointing the way to *Holmgarðr*, or Novgorod. The men sang and goaded the wild temperament of the sea, they prayed to the gods Njörðr, and Oðinn, as they heaved oars and bailed seawater. Aud endured the crossing, withstood the waking visions, and tolerated the guarded glances. No man aboard said a word against her though she knew they were unsure. Afterall, she was a seeress, and not at all like the women they had left behind.

There was a man awaiting the arrival of Gerðarr in Novgorod, his name was Āraš Mosāfer, he was a scholar, a poet, and a cartographer. He knew the constellations of the heavens touched by the gods of men, the vast deserts of salt and sand that swallowed unwitting wanderers whole, the roads of silk and silver that spanned in every direction from his homeland of Persia, and the dark stains men could not expunge from their souls. Āraš Mosāfer was a man seeking knowledge, secure in his faith and path, he observed all men with tolerance. When his eyes fell upon Aud the Seeress, he felt sure their fates had met for a purpose.

"Your time here has come to an end, Āraš?" Gerðarr asked as his eyes drifted across the hall belonging to the richest, most trustworthy, chieftain in Novgorod.

Āraš replied, "Yes, my friend, this place has revealed all of its secrets. Yet, it would seem, you have brought a mystery to me." To Aud he said, "I am Āraš Mosāfer *the traveller*, none need know more than that. If there should be any who ask, I beg of you to tell me." Aud regarded the man; he stood shoulder to shoulder with Gerðarr, at first his clothing appeared simple and well made, but beneath a woolen cloak he wore an intricately stitched tunic unlike any she had seen before. He had a strong proud face, bearing the lines of a life consumed by thought, laughter, and sorrow. His hair was as dark as burnt timber broken with fine strands akin to ash. She was wary of the shadows behind his flint-grey eyes until the light of an oil lamp passed between them. In the gleaming reflection of his gaze she saw the *Leiðarstjarna*; the brightest star in the night sky. Aud then understood the journey he was on and said, "It will not happen that way."

"I pray it does not happen at all." He returned, knowing well the meaning in her words.

It must be told no man questioned Gerðarr's decision to journey the Volga, for they knew Āraš guided their captain in all matters regarding the land of the Khazars, and the city of Itil. When the weather was favorable, they departed. There came a night when stillness crept upon the water surrounding them. It was accompanied by a dense fog, and such an unnatural stench, that fear began to grip the innards of hardiest of men. Gerðarr called for Aud to join him, as Āraš was already by his side. He said, "Our ships are prey for tribes who prowl the waterways. Advise me now, are we approaching danger, or has it already found us?" Āraš said, "Four things every person has more of than they know; sins, duties, years, and… foes." Aud said, "Death is upon the breeze and it is turning in our direction." The sail was lowered, the oars drawn in, the eyes of the crew sharper than the tip of a whale-bone needle.

After hours of waiting, Sól eventually rose to part the gloom before them. The vessel landed on the shoreline where they found evidence of bloodshed. An outpost, for it was little more than a makeshift camp, was littered with the dead. Smoldering bodies lay strewn across the blackened earth, their lifeless corpses still clawing for escape. A dank mist rolled in from the sea so that it was almost impossible for one man to see one another. Aud stood before Āraš, peering over his shoulder, searching for what was made unseen by mist, smoke, and things not of this realm. "This is a haunted place," said Gerðarr. The words had not long left his lips when a shrill cry pierced the gloom. The men flinched, hands tightening on the handles of axes, fingers gripping the shafts of spears, and sword-arms pulling glinting blades from belts. Aud, perceiving what was sailing on the wind, reached for the shoulder of Āraš. Grasping his cloak, she pulled with might and speed, turning him from the path of an arrow bound for his heart. "It will not happen that way," was all that Aud said when the man attempted to thank her. At Gerðarr's order the ship was returned to the river and onwards they pushed without pause to the harbor of Itil.

It is said, when Aud first caught sight of Itil, it had an overwhelming effect on her being. When urged to rest she refused and whispered, "Let this place have my breath, let it remain long after I have gone." Gerðarr had his ship moored on the banks of the Itil river. It gladdened Aud to see wooden dwellings not dissimilar to those she knew so well. Two crewmen disembarked and walked with Arni Øxnamegin to inspect the hall. They disappeared inside and when they were next seen, another figure was with them, who moved on peacefully with a wave of his arm. Āraš explained to Aud that Gerðarr owned this tract and in his absence the hall was maintained and kept in good order. "This is not a place many call home for long, not when the sea flows in Gerðarr's body instead of blood," said Āraš. Upon hearing his name, Gerðarr approached Aud, drawing her attention to a clearing beyond the hall. He said, "We are never far from the gods, in our hearts or in strange lands, there you see a place for offerings. But you must always have an escort, any crewman would be honored to guard your life, those who don't will die." Aud nodded and returned her gaze to the pillars in the distance. She could name the tallest wooden pillar from where she stood, and hoped her goddess was among the smaller carvings surrounding it. As night fell, torches were lit, and the walk was made to the clearing.

"Freyja, I have nothing to offer but my voice, *Fólkvangr er inn níundi, en þar Freyja ræðr sessa kostum í sal; halfan val hon kyss hverjan dag, en halfan Óðinn á.*" As Aud sang, every man there closed his eyes, all but the Persian. After this, when Aud and Āraš were left so that none could hear, he said, "You truly believe in the heaven called Fólkvangr, where Freyja awaits her share of the dead?" Aud replied, "It is where my mother awaits my father, and where I hope to go when my life is at its end." Āraš contemplated this and said, "You sang beautifully, I believe Freyja heard you. There will come a time when you shall know justice." For a moment Aud said nothing, then as she walked by his side she sang softly, *"Tíminn es eins ok vatnit."* For indeed, time does run like the river current.

The next day Aud watched from the doorway of the hall as the crew went to work unloading the cargo. She overheard Gerðarr calling for Āraš to join him, there were notable men in the district who had silver he wished to make his own. Āraš returned before Skoll, the wolf who chases Sól, had eaten the day completely. In his hands was a leather purse which he gave to Aud. Contained within were ornate brooches and strings of brightly colored glass beads, rings of precious metals to decorate her wrists and fingers, and one silver coin strung onto a necklace with the image of Freyja by its side.

"This is not the only Rús ship to visit Itil. Gerðarr is wealthy and knows many men, he has done far better than expected and believes it has something to do with you. As do I."

"How am I to repay you?" Aud asked as she felt the weight of the purse in her hands.

"Your foresight. You are *in draumspaka*, you are a seeress... and perhaps a saver of men," Āraš said plainly.

With a nod Aud accepted the gifts, it would have been ill-advised to refuse and besides this, her options were few. As Aud placed each item on her body, the weight of her heart grew so heavy she wondered if some enchantment had laid upon her.

"Now, I will show you the city of the Khazars, it has every kind of merchant willing to sell you anything you desire... even lives have a price."

"It seems a poor choice to favor the company of one woman over that of many wealthy men." Aud replied.

"It is better to leave while you have the freedom to do so and avoid difficult questions. A bad wound heals but a bad word does not," said Āraš Mosāfer, then, "Come, there is someone I would have you meet."

## 6 - Aud sings the *Varðlokkur*

The Khazar city of Itil was a rich mosaic of cultures and creeds. Here was a place for every man and his god, for there were courts to judge between the disputes of Christians, Muslims, Jews, and Pagans. Itil, where the Volga met the Caspian Sea, possessed a spirited heart of trade and tribute, drawing men from afar who envisaged wealth beyond their wildest imaginings. Furs, slaves, silk, and silver; this is what drew Gerðarr so far from his homeland, and here is where he first met Āraš. It was through the narrow pathways and marketplaces of this vibrant city, that Āraš now guided Aud.

It is now to be told that Aud and Āraš spoke of many things. One woman at sea with a crew of men had revealed much, but nothing was as curious to her than the Persian Āraš Mosāfer. Each day, whether aboard ship or on land, the man removed himself to pray more than once. When Aud queried this he said, "Allah is God, who has always been, and is without end. Muhammad was his prophet, before him were the prophets Adam, Ibrahim, Musa, Dawud, and Isa. As a man who is alone in this world, I pray only to one God, for Allah is everything, knows all things past and present, but gives me free will to do as I must. Allah is merciful and just, I believe my course to be true, for I do not seek retribution or vengeance. What I seek is an end to misery, death, and isolation." Aud said, "No man is ever truly alone, though he might wish it from time to time. What is it you desire from me?" As he led Aud along a narrow passage into a room within a diminutive structure, he replied, "Everything you have to give."

The air was thick with perfume and smoke, on the walls hung richly woven tapestries, oil lamps illuminated intricate depictions of battle, men and women, and creatures she could not name. In the center of the earth beaten floor was a small fire burning hot with coals. Before it sat the figure of a person, wrapped in swaths of black cloth, so that not one feature could be identified save for a hand. The form shifted slightly as the scarred misshapen limb beckoned the guests to sit. "This is the woman I spoke of earlier this evening. I believe she can see all that dwells in this world and the next, as you can. It was she who saved me from an arrow meant for my heart," said Āraš. The gnarled and twisted fingers of the form reached for Aud. She did not recoil as her hood was pushed away, but when the fingers held her jaw, she caught the scent of decay. Āraš spoke, "This is Farbod, he was once a *Sufi*, a vessel for wisdom. A lifetime ago, he angered a man by revealing unspeakable visions, he was punished by burning. Farbod survived though his body became crooked and misshapen, it is for his safety alone that his whereabouts remain unknown. By bringing you here I have risked much, please, do not let me regret my decision."

Aud said, "You have not brought me here to heal him, but this man suffers, are there none who care for his injuries?"

"There are," Āraš replied as he took the aged hand in his. "Forgive me. I am ashamed of my actions. I put myself before my oldest friend."

"You did as you should have." Replied Farbod. He turned to Aud, his voice was labored and thinner than an overstretched hide. "Fewer are his steps to Uksákká in Fólkvangr, where she waits for Hǫggvinkinni. Sing the *juoigos* of your mother's people, sing the *Varðlokkur* of your kin, sing for Dauði the sword that craves *raven-wine*."

Aud failed in hiding her surprise at hearing those words uttered by a stranger, and replied by saying, "What you ask is the most ancient of *seiðr*, taught to me as a fosterling long ago, and in the years when I was with my mother's Sámi kin. If you want me to do this, Āraš, you will tell me why? Farbod surpasses my skills, that much is clear."

Farbod said, "I am dying, you know this to be true, you can smell death's touch on my skin. Where we must go, I will not return from, only you can give Āraš the answers he seeks, perhaps you will learn what it is that haunts you so. Let me help you find the voices within."

Aud replied, "The loss of my father's sword, Dauði, haunts me. Finding it will give me the vengeance I'm due and free me from disgrace. My dreams are haunted by Sigrid's face, her agony over Thorgils death, and now she is a captive of Hjalti. He is the fox that must be slain, but I am without the means to do it, I am an outlaw from my homeland."

"If there is a way, seeress, Allah and Freyja will guide us. I swear to you now, do this thing for me and I will be forever in debt," said Āraš.

What is now to be told, can only truly be understood by those who were there. We must try to accept these happenings and preserve their fragile memory, as if they were all that had value in a world that has forgotten honor, loyalty, and love. Words were exchanged between the mystic and Āraš, who then turned to Aud and said, "*Rōšngar xwarišn*, the drink of illumination, it will allow you to journey with Farbod." Aud took the flask and drank the contents without argument. From within the dark robes of Farbod, his twisted hand appeared as he cast seeds upon the coals, and whispered to Aud in his thin broken voice, "Breathe." Aud removed her cloak, on her knees she bent over the coals, breathing in the wisps of smoke. For a moment silence fell upon the gathering before Aud's hand drifted up to her mouth, gently she pulled on her chin and as she did so the room filled with the voices of many. The chanting, of such depth and strength, filled Farbod's being with the will to sing. The room hung with tapestries grew dark. Above the heads of Aud and Farbod the night sky appeared, shining brightly with abundant and innumerable stars, yet only the coals of the fire lit the faces of mystic and seeress.

Āraš remained in the shadows, astonished by the images before him. He witnessed the gathering of forms surrounding Aud, drawn to the beauty of her singing, the likes of which he had never heard before. Āraš was unable to comprehend or distinguish between the faces of man, woman, and animal as they hung like vapor before him. Aud's chanting began to change, her voice bearing the weight of a heart in mourning, bringing tears to his eyes. Such was the power of Aud in that moment, he felt sure mountains would have fallen at her feet if she had commanded it. She fell forward, one hand before her as she leaned heavily on the compacted floor. Something moved toward her, leaving the swaths of Farbod's body, stretching out a limb without flesh and bone. With a nod of her head the singing ended, the spirits withdrew, the night sky faded becoming a solid rooftop once more.

"The *varðir* wardens heard my song, they carried it to my mother Uksakka's *gáccit*, a bird so beautiful it caused my heart to soar and my eyes to weep, they've shown me the hiding place of Dauði. Vengeance will be satisfied though it demands what I fear is impossible. Āraš... your friend, Farbod has left this life but together we found the answers you seek. A *jinn*, a terrible creature follows your family. I would have understood if you had told me." Aud whispered.

"If I had, I could never be sure of trusting your ability, I had to test what I thought to be true," said Āraš. "The truth is this; to use my true name is to call upon death, I am not yet ready for that. It was too long ago to know when, but my family made a grave mistake. Words were said in the heat of a fury most cruel. On the banks of the Volga you saved my life from an arrow surely meant for my heart. My father and his, died in this way. As shall I, as shall my sister's sons should I fail. Reciting the names of my forefathers who were murdered would take a lifetime, more than they had to live. We have searched endlessly for those who hide in the shadows, the mist, the darkness. My father searched all of Persia, and I search beyond it."

"Farbod," was all Aud said. She required time to think over all that had happened.

"I must prepare Farbod for burial, you should not remain here while I do so, but I won't send you away."

"Tell me what I can do."

"Pray to your gods, ask them to grant him the honor of a warrior's death," said Āraš with great sadness.

"A wise man has no need for a sword, he shapes the minds of men with words, wisdom lives forever... warriors do not." Aud replied.

It saddened Āraš that he neither had the time nor items necessary to prepare his friend's body for burial. Those who had secretly assisted Farbod would soon return. They would perform the *janazah* funeral rites; the body would be bathed and scented with *kafoor*, wrapped in a simple shroud, and prayers recited. When Farbod was laid in his final resting place, he must face *Qibla*, towards Mecca. After this, they would mourn his passing and their grief would find release.

Āraš prayed for Farbod's soul and laid his corpse in the correct position. He was still as Aud approached, she lowered onto her knees, in her hand was a feather quill. "What you hold in your hand is a *Huma* feather, or so he said. It is a sacred thing, it belonged to a bird reborn of its own flames. Rising from the ashes as Farbod did. It is said the *Huma's* shadow, should it fall upon you, offers great blessings for eternity. I don't know where this feather came from, he used it to write *yashts* about the ancients, on the finest papyrus that I would bring him when I could," said Āraš.

Silence fell between them, then Aud replied, "He should carry it with him in the afterlife. Fate must find someone to speak through, I thank the gods they chose Farbod." Aud laid the quill beside the body as she and Āraš rose to their feet. Footsteps and low murmuring voices echoed along the narrow passageway, signaling the time to depart had come. Quietly they disappeared behind the tapestries and out into the remains of the night. Itil was never still, the hum of music and clamor of men was ever present, and for this Āraš was glad. He had no desire to talk while his grief was as raw as an open wound.

## 7 - Vengeance at the Alþingi

Gerðarr, on occasion, was a patient man. This night however, he had news to share with his crew, but first he wished to speak with Aud. Many things had been said in his dealings while in Itil, there was a change upon the horizon, Iceland was calling them home. When at last, Aud and Āraš appeared, he ushered them to the fireside within the makeshift longhouse. His eyes moved between them as he listened to their tale. At last he said, "I believe the time for vengeance has arrived, seeress!" Āraš said, "How can you be so sure?" Gerðarr replied, "Some time ago a man called Úlfljótr was sent from Iceland to learn the laws of our Kings, he returned, and a site was decided upon to gather all four quarters of Iceland's most powerful men together, Þingvellir the fields of assembly where the Alþingi takes place. People came to claim land, they required governing, it was decided our own laws and edicts were the only way forward. If we judge our arrival well, then our chieftains and their men will be gathered in one place, at the Alþingi. Hjalti will not be in Grímrfjörður, Sigrid will most likely be alone, and if Dauði is still where it was concealed then there will be no one to stop us from retrieving it. Think, Aud, where better to expose Hjalti and reclaim your family's honor and lands? Women have owned land before, and they can do so again. Aside from this, there are more than enough reasons to leave Itil so soon. Time is bringing a change here too, there will be more ways to make silver, there are plans at work in my mind. We must push the ship hard, cut through the sea as though Thor's hammer Mjolnir were smashing the waves in search of the serpent *Jǫrmungandr*! I say this is the time Aud, time to take your vengeance!"

Aud said, "Why would you do this for me? Sigrid and I have no kin."

"Ah, but you have land, and your sister is without a husband."

"Hauknefr... hawk feathers again... a sign from Freyja?" Aud muttered to herself. Then she said, "I will not agree to what I think you are proposing, not when my sister has no knowledge of it, but I promise to speak in your favor, and I believe the outcome will be as you wish. But know this, my friend, the ire of a woman is a dangerous thing."

"The bond of Thorgeir's daughters is strong. You have my word, so long as it shall not be questioned again." Replied Gerðarr.

"It seems we are to forever aid one-another."

Gerðarr said, "Indeed, and now we sail."

The next thing to be told is this; the ship tore through the waves, the force of *Aegir's daughters* straining the planks and strakes of the vessel, the breath of Njörð swelling the sail. The crew held fast the oars, plunging, pulling and heaving the blades from the sea. Not one eye drooped, not one man slept, all were consumed by the desire to reach the shores of Iceland. Some say there was more than will at work, that songs filled the heads of the men, the songs of Aud.

The ship did not make land near Þingvellir, but continued as far north as Grímrfjörður, where the shore and Uksákkástaðr were separated by a jagged cliff. A sharp piercing cry from a bird of prey drew Aud's attention toward the cliff. Clasping her throat in horror she saw a woman standing on the edge of the precipice, it was Sigrid. The wind was high and swallowed Aud's cries of anguish. Āraš turned to Gerðarr, who turned to Arni; the great bear of a man grunted as he lifted his axe and with a roar threw it toward the woman who was surely about to plunge to her death. The axe flew through the air and landed between the feet of Sigrid. At once her sight fell upon the ship and the long hair of her sister blowing in the breeze. They met on the shoreline, they embraced and shed tears of mirth and sorrow.

"Let us flee, now, while all the men are gone!" Said Sigrid.

"We won't run, we must end this thing, I have men who will help us," replied Aud.

Sigrid stared at the figures of Āraš, Arni, and Gerðarr on whom her gaze lingered. "Who are they?"

"Friends we never had before and shall never again be without. Dauði is buried near where Thorgils fell, we will find it now, and then we will go to the assembly." Said Aud. And this is what was done.

With the might and force of Øxnamegin before them, Gerðarr, Āraš, and the crew of the ship, formed an unbreakable wall around Aud and Sigrid. Men parted before them, eyes drawn to the spectacle, silence remained unbroken in their wake as the group trod towards Hjalti and his men. Pale was the pallor of the cretinous face of Hjalti, fear swallowing his eyes with blackness, sweat slick on his brow. He reached for his axe only to find it in the hand of Agnar Goði, who said, "The vengeance lies with Sigrid." Sigrid emerged from the ring of men, and said, "The vengeance lies with Aud, for though I have suffered at the hands of Hjalti, she has borne the dishonor of it all."

Hjalti had known this day would come. On a heath in Grímrfjörður he had gone to the temple Grímr had erected so many years ago. *Tell me what I must do to make this right?* He had said. A voice replied, *A man who abandons his kin, can expect little in return.* The eyes of Hjalti swept the room and fell on the altar before him, there lay the blood-stained blade Dauði, edges dulled by the bones of Thorgils breast. *No! Dauði is in the ground, as cold as the bones it took life from. None will uncover my treachery, for it is my shame to keep, and mine alone!* Hjalti wept as he closed fast his eyes. But that did not stop the voice that spoke once more and said, *The doom upon you remains.* When Hjalti had at last opened his eyes, he saw the carvings had turned their faces away, and he knew then the gods had abandoned him.

Now Aud stood before Hjalti, staring into the eyes of the coward, her hands unbearably tight on the hilt of Dauði. "Thorgeir told me this sword would take from me and then grant me everything I wanted, I do not crave your blood, but *raven-wine* will be spilled." She handed Hjalti the sword. The man's lips quivered, Aud whispered in his ear, "No, Hjalti, all men here will fall deaf at the sound of your words. You will not be saved." As if entranced, the man took the blade and plunged it into his chest. No more need be told about Hjalti's death. Quietly, Aud turned and took Sigrid by the shoulder, their men followed. Not a word, save these, recount the deeds of that day.

Of the days, months, and years that followed, much has been well told. For this island is a guardian of legends, a keeper of folklore, a home to the men of land and sea, warriors, women, and outlaws that roam it still. The story of Aud does not end with the reclaiming of Dauði, or the marriage of Sigrid and Gerðarr, or the time she spent with Āraš in this most northern part of the realm. There is more to tell, and it begins in this way.

Dawn broke over the stillness of the bay. A ship was being readied, the crew eager to set sail and trade without adventure or mishap, though this was not to be. Two figures stood on the shoreline where once Aud had stumbled in the snow.

Aud turned to Āraš and said, "Tell me, why Āraš? Why that name?"

"Long ago, a war consumed my homeland, a war it lost. The foe was Turan, and the terms of peace were simple; one of Manūchehr's men was to fire an arrow, where the point of its tip entered the earth was to become the border of our lands. What a weight upon the shoulders of one man. The task fell to an archer named Āraš, he climbed Mount Damavand and declared *All I am is in this arrow*! For two days and nights it flew through the air until it fell. Turan was not the victor it had hoped to be. Far and wide does my homeland of Persia still reach, the deeds of Āraš are often told, but it is the arrow that is always foremost in my mind. With the release of the shot, Āraš had given his life so that others might live, though some say he simply disappeared. They also say his voice still echoes atop the mountain. So, it seemed to me, that when an unseen foe I had little hope in defeating, had its weapon of choice as an arrow; Āraš was a good name to take. My own has never served me well."

"Will you tell me your name?" Aud asked.

Āraš looked at Aud with a knowing laugh, "I believe you know it, seeress."

Aud, who kept much of what she thought unspoken, agreed with Āraš by way of a shared smile. Then, she said, "Gerðarr's ship is waiting, Āraš Mosāfer. The time has come to find the archer of the arrow seeking your heart."

"As well you know, seeress, my heart has found another place to call its home. But we shall go, though I must admit, I am not yet ready to tempt my soul from this body." Āraš paused, as a feather floating on the breeze landed at their feet.

"As I said, when first we met… it will not happen that way," said Aud the Seeress.

# — DRAGOSLAVA DREADKEEL —
## Giti Chandra

*Dragoslava Dreadkeel*

**B**iting down on her overshirt, a corner of her jittering brain registered the smooth wool texture. For the most part though, she concentrated on drawing quick, shallow, breaths as quietly as she could. Under the heavy cross-beams of the large oaken settee, her head crouched into her lap, silence was the only ally she was going to have against the killers. A ribbon, silken and broad, dripped spit from her clenched mouth, wetting the long braids coiled in her lap. Dry wool. Damp satin. Dry wool. Damp satin. Dry. Damp. Dry. Damp. Dry. *Not drip. Not slippery. Feet moving in silent choreography.* Dry mouth. Damp hands. Dry tongue. Damp fingers. Dry. Dry. *Not wet thud of blade! Not pooling splashes of red! Not the dance of shoes around falling heads.*

When she reached the woods, her eyes were dry, her hair was dry, her hands were dry. Not a lick of her mother's blood was on her skirts, not a sliver of the shattered skull of her father stuck to her sandals, not a sound could be found in her head, no echo of steel, no memory of screams. Nothing except silence, her one ally; a shield and a crown. And she wore both as she turned her dry face to the wind. "I am Dragoslava, Queen of Queens". And the wind carried her words beyond her lands, out to sea.

No one is as entirely alone as a deposed royal. She knew this, and turned over names and faces in her mind as she headed deeper into the forest towards the hills, knowing that she was leaving all names, all faces, behind her. The last light of the day pointed long shadows that guided her feet. Some small part of her silent heart saw other evenings, other walks, so many that she had not stopped to wonder if they would ever not be more, if there would ever come a day when racing to her little refuge from the castle would not be a thing of joy. But she entered the log cabin now with a mind sharpened by pain into a dagger, and it cut through grief and fear and longing and found the objects that it needed.

Taking the leather satchel down from its hook she folded into a small linen bag everything she was wearing—the fine tunic, the lovely loose trousers, the embroidered slippers, the jewels from her hair, ears, wrist, ankles, and throat. This bag she placed carefully at the very bottom. Then she added one extra set of plain trousers and tunic, a shawl, and headscarves. Next, she wrapped two wedges of hard cheese, some crusty bread, a string of seasoned sausages, and some dried fish into a large fold of wax paper, and put this in on top and around the linen bag.

Stepping barefoot around the cabin, she slipped on her sturdy pants, the thick tunic and overcoat, and belted herself into these. The knitted socks and long, sheepskin boots were cold when she put her feet into them but there was no time for fires and warming. From a pocket under the floorboards she pulled out her hunting knife, several small blades, and the dagger gifted to her on her last birthday by her fa—the silence clamped a damp hand on her dry heart, as she methodically tucked the knife and blades into their various sleeves and pockets in her tunic, pants, and boots. Finally, she stood before the polished metal of her mother's shield and allowed herself a moment of outward and inward reflection. Almost thirty, never very slender, shoulders too muscular to be thought feminine, her long-fingered hands and the fire in her eyes were seized upon by the court poets paid to sing ballads of praise to the princesses in the long winter evenings. Dragoslava grimaced, wound her braids cruelly tight about her head and reminded herself that she hated having her body constantly appraised by the world. She was not going to add to that by glaring at herself in the shield; she shouldered her bag, tucked a knife into her belt, and stepped out. She had taken too long already.

It was almost dark. The door was barred and locked as she swept the darkening shadows for the gem-bright gleam of wolf eyes. Whatever the priests may say, no land can change its gods in a day, a month, or even a Pope's lifetime. And whatever they may hang over their altars in the old temples and call them by a new religion's name, the spirits of the forests heard the call of the ancient ones.

And that is why the dispossessed and hunted heir to the crown knew that she would get to the harbor safe and in time to catch the night boat: Vukoslava would escort her there. Through the long night's march, the wolf's pacing followed the beat of her heart—into thickest byways and under heaviest boughs, through the loneliest paths and over the roughest terrain, Dragoslava knew that she was watched over on a route that only she knew. The little kingdom, curled in the arms of two rivers, swooped skywards and down through the hills and valleys that sloped through it, and the royal children grew in those woods and forests, mountains and dells, their heads blessed by the sun and their hearts filled with the ripple of swift waters. She knew her way.

Gaining passage on the boat was easier than she had thought. The ports bristled with boats headed to the Adriatic, and money stopped the too-enquiring glance. She remembered to keep her hooded head lowered, her knife hidden, her hands still, and her back slightly less straight. The dirt and grime of the night's trek covered her modest, workman's clothes, and she sank into a damp corner bench, grateful to have remembered to pack a rosary. They were magic, she thought wryly, these new accessories of the new religion—they seemed to render her immediately invisible. No one saw a not-young not-beautiful not-rich not-curious woman in a corner telling her beads. As she moved her lips in some semblance of silent prayer, Dragoslava's mind raced furiously through possibilities and options. She had a cousin in Constantinople that she was reasonably sure was not party to the coup against her parents. The killing had been swift, efficient, and silent. Not a word had been spoken. *Screams. No words. The thuds of bodies and the clatter of crowns but no words. The soft squelch of leather-soled sheepskin shoes stepping over her mother's satin-slippered feet but no words.* Nothing to give some hint of who was responsible.

She blinked. Cleared her mind. Followed again the route she would take from the Byzantine port to the imperial center of Constantinople. The glittering capital of an empire ruled by not one, not even two, but all of four emperors, and a new Patriarch of the Church—well, that was the place for a queen to hide in plain sight. She thought of the strange phenomenon of four emperors on a single throne—three of the names still odd to her determinedly pagan ears: Christopher, Stephen, Constantine. But the senior emperor, recently crowned, retained his Armenian name, Romanos. Son of a peasant who had rescued the emperor Basil I in battle and had been rewarded with a place in the Imperial Guard. Romanos, son of a peasant, now emperor. Dragoslava thought about that, her head bent over her beads, lips moving soundlessly; a world in which royalty was not divinity.

She closed her eyes and counted the strokes of the oarsmen, feeling the forward pull of sail and oar together. Yes, it would take her almost two weeks—maybe 10 days if the gods were kind and sent the winds she needed—to get to the Black Sea. And then maybe another day or so along the coast to the Byzantine capital. She considered and discarded the idea of travelling in a straighter line over land. She had shelter here and could buy the food she needed. Traveling by horse and on foot meant braving the coming winter and all the hazards of men and animals along the way. No, she was better here. If she could just keep her head down and behave as if she were used to being invisible instead of the centre of all eyes…

"You missed a bead." The voice was mild, but the Greek was perfect. Dragoslava fought the impulse to freeze, the lips hardly wavering in their repeated prayers. She stared pointedly at her lap, the fingers telling the beads one by one. Why was he speaking to her in a language only the educated aristocracy could be expected to know? Some rustling and scratching later, a small piece of paper slid gently into her view. In elegant handwriting, the paper on her lap informed her that a jeweled sleeve peeped from a hole at the bottom of her leather satchel and that the soft unblemished skin of an aristocrat shone from the gaps in the dirt on her hands and face.

Dragoslava rose, adopting the self-effacing, shrinking attitude of the women of the village, and walked slowly towards the women's toilet. The boat, an old retired *khelandion* now refitted as a passenger and cargo boat, had had to provide such amenities as women's toilets, and Dragoslava had blessed the old gods who had provided this vessel for her escape. She could not have afforded to wait longer for a convenient boat. Now she waited in the tiny space just outside the women's toilet, feeling the river breeze lift the hair on her neck. A few minutes later, she heard the man walk out to stand a little distance from her, staring out at the green waters of the Danube.

"It is at least ten days to the Istros. If the gods favor us with the winds on the Dunai." Her ears pricked at his choice of the Slavic name instead of the Roman or Greek; and his assumption that she would follow the river all the way to the Black Sea. He knew. "Allow me to help you. It will be an honor."

Her still downward bent gaze took in the embossed leather sandals, the rich weave on loose trousers gathered at the ankle, even as her ears had already registered the throaty consonants and the broad vowels still faintly discernible under the beautifully educated annunciation. Arabic; educated and prosperous, as most of those who travelled into these territories were; the flowing calligraphy and ready ink and paper marked him as a scholar, one of the many who traversed the known world, documenting cultures and peoples, acquiring and making copies of texts of literature and learning, spreading scientific knowledge and theories, and philosophies encompassing mysticism and spirituality. He waited in silence while she sized him up. When he felt she had arrived at her conclusions, he allowed himself a small smile and, bowing his head in a barely discernible gesture, introduced himself.

"Aḥmad ibn Faḍlān ibn al-ʿAbbās ibn Rāšid ibn Ḥammād." After the merest pause—"probably best shortened to Ibn Fadlan." After some thought, she looked up and acknowledged the self-deprecating twitch of his lips. She had meant to glance quickly and look away before she gave more of herself away to this strangest of strangers, but she found her eyes lingering on the hooked nose, the neatly trimmed beard, the intelligence in the brown eyes, and the gentleness about the mouth. Not much more than her own age— perhaps in his late forties at most—he had the air of self-effacing confidence that she recognized from the more pleasant among the ambassadors who regularly lined the hallways of her father's court. Had lined—her throat constricted and she looked away.

His eyes followed the turn of her head. "If you are she whom I think you might be—" he hesitated—"then you are in grave danger. Your majesty." She heard the tiny but significant pause before the "your majesty" and drew in her breath to protest against being anything but a rustic woman on her way to join her family downriver but his voice, dropped to a low whisper, continued. "Your skin, your hands, the lustrousness of your hair, all mark you, Your Highness. News of the...events...at the castle has swept abroad on the wind and it is whispered that the princess has escaped."

*The Queen's dark hair floats in red pools. Crimson ripples lift and drop the strands, the gloss already dulled by the crud of clotting blood. The shoe splashes through, strange markings on the killer's exposed ankles, black slashes of hair stuck to the diamond patterned sole. It is as if the breath has stuck in her throat and she remembers to breathe slowly through her nose, taking the strange metallic smell into her very bones, and she feels her bones patterned in sharp diamonds...*

"Perhaps I can be a guide for you—on your travels—or a fellow scholar—or apprentice."

"That will suit admirably, Your Grace. I am an emissary from Baghdad, secretary to the ambassador from the Abbasid Caliph al-Muqtadir to Almış, the iltäbär—the vassal-king under the Khazars—of the Volga Bulgaria. I serve as the Faqih to the group—the religious advisor and lead counselor for Islamic religious doctrine and law. I am to introduce his people to the principles and tenets of Islam." Ibn Fadlan spoke quickly, rapidly rehearsing his credentials and position. "In short, Your Highness, I can offer you some degree of security and protection. I can appoint you, in fact, to be my guide and fellow scholar for this region."

It was the work of a few minutes to decide on her appearance and their immediate course of action. Most of the passengers would leave the boat at the next port, half an hour away. Dragoslava would have enough time to slip into the women's toilet and subtly modify her demeanor; she scrubbed away some of the dirt from her hands and face, changing the modest peasant scarf about her head for one slightly more genteel but in the same russet shades. When they walked back to their seats, the boat had docked and the passengers had departed. As the new stream of passengers entered, they found a distinguished Arab scholar speaking in formal tones to his local guide, who produced some paper and ink and schooled him in the new, Cyrillic, script of her people.

Dragoslava would look back on those ten days as some of the most idyllic in her adult life. Highly educated, extremely well-read, she was not your average princess who had spent her life languishing on velvet couches—although, as she would often point out to Ibn Fadlan, some of her aunts would have much preferred that to be the case. Her parents had indulged her insatiable need to know and learn, and she made the most of the endless line of learned men and women who were welcomed at their court. But it was a newly discovered pleasure to teach and share her vast store of knowledge with someone else—especially someone whose command of languages, theological discourses, and scientific knowledge ran, perhaps, even deeper and stronger than her own. She, in turn, wondered at a religion that exhorted the study of the natural world, encouraging scientific enquiry, which scientists took inspiration from, and a system of mathematics and physics so far advanced from anything she had been taught. There were hours spent discussing philosophy and the strange mechanisms he kept in his bag, nights reciting poetry in their native tongues which the other did not understand. Long afternoons were devoted to examining the boat's features and wondering at the kinds of wood and systems of load-bearing that kept it so steady on the seas. Many animated discussions were given to predicting the weather based on calculations of various kinds, and indeed, they had discovered a storm due to hit almost as soon as they arrived at the Black Sea. Dragoslava covered sheets of paper in projections as to the height of waves which she insisted were likely to be higher than usual, and Ibn Fadlan, not really worried about the sturdy *khelandian*, nevertheless demonstrated the amount of water in her hold that it would take to tilt the boat far enough for it to capsize. On their walks through the boat, they found the hold and took measurements of volume and calculated the weight of water, laughing a little nervously at the tingle of danger. But the hold was very lightly filled with the meagre belongings of the passengers and a few supplies that would be dropped off at the next port. Such scientific, artistic, and practical conjectures kept them busy and a little giddy in each other's company, and the days passed gently. And then the idyll ended.

They had just reboarded the boat after a longer-than-usual stop at a tiny cove called Sulina. Almost at the mouth of the Black Sea, where the mighty Dunai met the Sea and was known by its old Roman name, Istros, the old *khelandian* found itself in need of stronger rope for its sails. The aftermath of the Bulgarian siege of Constantinople a few years before had left an uneasy sense of truce in the mixed population of the small fishing village. The two sets of men who boarded the boat had clearly not had an amicable few days. The Byzantine party seemed to be gloating over some sort of tavern-induced brawl with the Bulgarians—and there were many of them. Dragoslava pulled her shawl closer about her head and shoulders, drooping her shoulders just a little more into a more submissive posture even while she covertly evaluated the mood of the crowd and its chances of bursting its bounds in the couple of days it would take for them to reach Constantinople. Even if the boat hugged the coast, there would be little chance that any of them would be leaving the vessel before the Byzantine capital.

Then the hulk in front of her stumbled.

She stepped back.

Ibn Fadlan reached out to steady her.

The hulk turned.

Saw a Turkish looking man holding the shoulders of a Slavic-looking woman.

The hulk snarled.

Within moments the two were at the center of a circle of battle-hardened, bleary-eyed, slack-jawed mob. Their hostility set aside in the face of this mutual abomination, the men eyed the young man and woman hungrily. A growling of "Filthy foreigners!" and "Whore!" rumbled along the deck. The shuffle of worn shoes and the dragging of leather satchels grated along the wooden boards, closing in, caging, stinking. A long sword rasped out of its sheath.

"What is going on here?" The captain came pushing through the lumbering men. In the center of the circle he blinked at the two figures, familiar but unheeded over the last ten days. Now he eyed them warily, balancing their innocent but provocative position against the weapons and bloodlust of the crowd. He was late, off-schedule for his deliveries, his cargo not properly settled in the hold, a newly-incurred debt on his head thanks to the ragged ropes on his sails. These people were innocuous but dangerous, the foreigner ostentatiously influential but alone, the woman educated but unassuming. Whatever influence either had was far from their reach right now, while the clink of money bags and steel alike weighted the power of the crowd in its favor. But if delay and complications could be avoided that would be best. The captain threw his shoulders back and adopted a sterner tone than before.

"Unhand the lady. This is not how we conduct ourselves in these parts."

But the sword was out and damned if the man was going to sheathe it like a cringeling. Smaller than the others and with a weasel-like motion he stepped forward, thrusting the blade at Dragoslava.

"Kill the bitch! While the menfolk die to protect them these sluts fornicate with the enemy!"

The slide of metal rang in the air. Swords and knives flashed in the early-afternoon sun. Roars of "Hang him!" "Teach her a lesson!" swelled around him. The captain shifted uncertainly. "Drown her!" "She's a witch! I have seen her copying the devil's signs in her books!" A hush fell. Dragoslava knew now what would happen. Her mind raced.

"Yes drown me! Drop me here into the ocean if you dare!" she shouted out. Ibn Fadlan's fingers dug a warning into her shoulders but she shouted again. She had seen the Varangian ship set sail minutes before they boarded and she had felt their own boat weighed down on one side with the displaced cargo. She calculated the combined weight of the men with their luggage all on the same side of the deck. And she shouted out "Do it! Do it now or I shall turn you all into pigs!"

Ibn Fadlan thrust her from him in fear. "She has cast a spell on me which is now broken! Drop her here and she will swim in these shallow seas. Let us take her out and drop her into the deepest depths of the Black Sea!"

Fear stoked the rage in the crowd and in the din of their confusion and anger he spoke into her ear, pretending to curse. "There is a storm coming. Waves will be high. I will open the hatches to the small hold in the captain's room." It was enough.

They bound her but left her on the deck, tied to the mast. Ibn Fadlan ostentatiously celebrated his release from her clutches and the men, unused to Persians in general and to scholarly ambassadorial ones in particular, kept their distance from him. The boat changed course, heading out into the open sea; it would be a matter of hours. They could dump the witch and head back at full speed. The captain cast a worried eye at the horizon but was more concerned with keeping his head attached to his neck and his hand on the tiller of his own ship. The sooner he was rid of them all the better he would sleep.

Dragoslava kept her eye on the sails of the Varangian ship and calculated the angles of the waves. According to Ibn Fadlan's calculations, there would be a sudden and powerful squall close to sunset. She allowed herself a grim smile of satisfaction; it did help to spend your leisure hours calculating things like atmospheric pressure and angles of sun and the heights of river swells, to discover squalls that the most seasoned sailor might not expect. Just a little more out to sea and...

"Enough! Dump her now!" The captain cast a fearful eye at the dipping sun and the swelling seas. Dragoslava jerked to attention. She saw Ibn Fadlan slip away downstairs and knew he had gone towards the hold. They had calculated this in jest, and yet, now the reality had struck, she was filled with fear. She needed more time! He had not called her a witch. In all the cursing, he had not acknowledged this. She had heard enough stories at court and knew that it could be the end of a sailor's career if word got around that a witch had been on his ship—or worse, that a witch had been mistreated on his ship. Everyone would consider it cursed ever after.

"Captain!"

He swiveled towards her. She looked him straight in the eye.

"Turn the ship to face my home. And bring them all out to see me die. You owe me this."

The boat lifted onto a wave and the sky darkened suddenly overhead. He jerked his head in acknowledgement. "Alright all of you! You wanted to see her drown! Come and see the Black Sea take her!"

The restive crowd moved quickly towards him, eager to get this done before their bloodlust dissipated and the cheap liquor of the village taverns wore off. The captain set up a short plank and motioned to the helmsman to bring the boat about. Then he unbound Dragoslava from the mast and marched her to the edge, pushing her up the few makeshift steps. A gust of wind whipped the scarf off her head and she stood with her hair streaming as the long braids unwound in the wind. The fear in their guts blew like a disease into her nostrils and she breathed it in and took her courage from it.

The captain shoved her roughly out onto the plank. The boat swung about as a huge swell rose beneath it. The cargo rumbled in her hold and the crowd lurched and clung to the rails. She sent up a prayer to the old gods that Ibn Fadlan had opened the hatches releasing water into the hull. And leapt backwards onto the main deck.

The giant wave lifted the boat as the cargo and men weighed it down. The tilt began. Dragoslava landed on her feet and turned, lifted her bound hands and brought them down on the first drawn sword she saw. Ropes tied to sails hovered above her. She caught two and swung herself up, grabbing holds on dipping masts and tilting edges, clawing her way up the steep incline of the deck. Screams and clanging erupted about her but she sighted one foothold one handhold at a time, leaping and jumping her way up the capsizing boat. The keel was exposed now, horizontal, a meter above the rolling wave. Clinging to falling sails and masts for their very lives, terror and disbelief in their eyes, a hundred men saw her silhouette as she stood on the keel, wild as the storm that raged around her, a bellow of pure exultation screamed into the skies.

The lookout man perched high in his basket on the top of the mast of the Varangian ship shouted to his captain and the men transfixed by the drama unfolding on the old *khelandian*. "There's only one way a boat that size capsizes," muttered the captain, ordering his helmsman to turn the ship around. When they picked up the two swimming creatures the boat was slowly righting itself again and they left her to rescue her own people.

"Next time you expect to be rescued, lose the baggage!" huffed the tattooed arm that pulled her aboard. Ibn Fadlan had, of course, thought to discard anything billowy or heavy that might affect his chances of remaining afloat in rough seas. He stood shivering in leggings and tunic, barefoot and without any baggage except a greased leather sheath wrapped around his hip. Dragoslava shrugged her satchel closer to her hip; of course she too had had the foresight to wrap its contents in greased goatskin a few days ago when the first rains came, but it was true that her clothes and sandals had weighed her down, the loose trousers and long tunic billowing out in the sea and dragging against her body. Now she straightened up trying not to clutch herself for warmth in the raging wind. Forty men stood around in various attitudes of casual curiosity, busy guiding the ship through dangerous billows and whipping sails.

"Skarphéðinn Arinbjarnarson at your service my lady"—the captain bowed in mock obeisance. Like the rest of the men, he was taller than any man Dragoslava had seen, broader in the shoulder than most doorways, and more covered in swirling patterns than the intricately embroidered shawls of the noble ladies of the royal court. Even in the wind and the rain she could see the brightly braided hair and beards and the occasional flash of gold on fingers and ears.

She drew herself up and inclined her head towards him. She was a queen, and these were the men of the north, a special guard to Byzantine emperors, famed for their strength, their loyalty to the throne, and their beauty. "Dragoslava." She raised her chin. "Dragoslava of Serbia."

The ironically raised eyebrow rose in genuine admiration as realization dawned but the captain did not miss a beat. "I am honored to make your acquaintance, Dragoslava Dreadkeel,"—this time the bow was genuine—"from what I saw, you have earned the name."

She was given a tiny cabin near the kitchen—a pantry hastily cleared out, still smelling of cured shark and blood sausage preserved in vats of whey. But it was dry and well-sealed from the winds and for that she was grateful. She had judged these Volga Rus men correctly, she thought. Word of them had, of course, reached her father's court, but they were mercenaries, after all, and owed no man their fealty. Many had gone into the service of Byzantine emperors; if an emperor were killed or dethroned, their allegiance was immediately transferred to the new emperor. She and Ibn Fadlan had had little time to confer, but she knew that they were all headed to the Byzantine court. She had intended to find refuge in anonymity there under the name Milica Minic, a famous story-teller in the Serbian court. Now she would be dependent on the goodwill of the Varangian guards to keep her secret and she had earned their admiration but not their loyalty.

The squall died down sooner than anyone, except perhaps Ibn Fadlan, had expected. Dragoslava blew out the single candle she had been given, checked the lock on the door again, acknowledging gratefully the need to have a lock on food stores in ships, and settled in to stay awake for the few hours left to arrive on Byzantine shores. Adrenalin still claimed her body and she knew sleep would not be her companion tonight.

She sat on the makeshift bedding and clutched her knees, rocking rapidly back and forth, trying to keep her breathing steady. She had done it. Really capsized a *khelandion*. Luck had played a card in her favor of course—the crisis had distracted the captain from settling the cargo evenly through the hold and the locker need not have opened into the hull. Racing up the tilting deck could also have ended very badly for her, but here she allowed herself a fierce grin of satisfaction. She was not petite and fragile and girlish, no. She had trekked through the forests of her lands and dueled with the best of her father's soldiers, tamed the wildest of their horses and climbed the highest trees. All of that came to her aid; that, and the long hours spent bent over books, talking with scholars, learning, imbibing, knowing that knowledge was valuable both in itself and as a tool. Between Ibn Fadlan and herself, they had calculated everything from the prospect and intensity of the squall to the height of the waves and the weight of the men on the boat—even the amount of time it would stay on its side, giving them a fighting chance of swimming free.

The rocking slowed and the breathing steadied. Yes, luck had played its part—in her favor, this time—but she had done the rest. Dreadkeel. She spoke it softly under her breath and savored its contours. She had indeed earned it. Dragoslava Dreadkeel. It felt more her own name than Princess Dragoslava. She smiled.

A knock sounded on the pantry door. She jerked upright, clutching her still damp shawl about her.

"Who is it?" Even to her own ears her voice sounded somewhat less than 'dreadful', and she spoke again, firmer this time. "Who is it?"

"Geirhjörtur Rustíkusson. I have a message for you."

"From whom?"

"Your man friend."

She heard the sneer in the tone and closed her fingers on the heavy brass candle-holder. "Well! Give your message."

"He sends you food. With a message." The door thudded again, the light latch rattling. Dragoslava strained her ears to listen for any other activity in the area that might signal another human being close by but the kitchen was tucked away in a corner, the pantry even further within it, and the boat's timbers groaned in the dull roar of the sea. Another thud and the latch fell into the pantry. The man entered.

Like the others, he was big, and his bulk filled the tiny room barely big enough for one woman to lie down in. She remembered this one: the only man among them whose eyes had stayed upon her even as the others bent to the arduous work of manning the ship in the midst of the storm. Now his eyes fell on her still wet clothes, flicked to the satchel on the bedding, and then to her face. He smiled, gold flashing in his teeth. "Here is your message. My lady." Now she could see the sneer. "Choose another man-friend. And your secret is safe." She stood her ground. Annoyance and surprise flickered in his leering grin but he took a step in and caught her shoulder. "Or maybe you are worth good money to me one way or another!" The slap caught her backhanded as he caught her shawl and pulled, throwing her to the floor.

She tilted as she fell, landing on one shoulder and rolling to her feet. The tiny cabin filled with grunts and thuds as they locked in grim battle until he thrust her against the wall, forearm lodged like an iron bar across her shoulders cutting off the air in her throat.

"Oh I'm worth good money alright!" she rasped as she brought her knees up holding onto his shoulders. Swinging them tight against her, her feet pushed him back with explosive force. He crashed through the door and out onto the kitchen floor, the disbelief in his eyes making her laugh. He caught her tunic and pulled but she held onto the doorframe so that the material tore off her shoulders into his hands. She grabbed a knife and a large pot hanging from hooks on the ceiling. He leapt to his feet and lunged for her. She brought the pot down on his head but he merely roared with rage. Then her other hand plunged the knife into his side. He roared louder and grabbed her throat.

She took the knife out and plunged it in again, twisting in his hold and bending over so that his hand slid from her throat and snatched at her for a hold. But her tunic was gone and the thin woolen slip, soft and clinging, allowed him no handhold. She brought him over her back and on to the floor, crashing through the kitchen door onto the deck.

Dragoslava brought the knife to his throat and knelt on his chest, her trousers red from the blood seeping out of his sides. She looked into his wild eyes, her own blood pounding in her ears. Perhaps that is why she didn't hear it the first time.

"Kill him." When the voice broke through the throbbing in her head she registered the third repetition. Calm, decisive.

They stood about her in a cluster. Skarphéðinn Arinbjarnarson spoke again. "You have bested him in fair fight. It is your right."

Dragoslava rose, straightened her woolen shift, and dropped the knife away from both of them. "I will not have this malodorous beast's blood on my hands," she said. "Do with him what you will."

Geirhjörtur Rustíkusson leapt to the knife, his feet kicking her legs out from under her. Before anyone could react, she had swept up the knife and buried it in his neck. She thrust the twitching body from her and staggered to her feet, all her strength leaving her as water draining. The thudding began, first one then another then more until forty men stomped the wooden boards with their feet. She looked about her, focusing slowly on the wall of white, tattooed, muscle and sinew that faced her.

Skarphéðinn Arinbjarnarson gestured. One man disappeared into the ship; two more caught the still-stirring body and prepared to fling it over the edge.

"Stop! Please! Wait!!"

Dragoslava heard her own voice cry out in wonderment. But she had seen the shoes on the legs about to be consigned to the black waters. *Leather-soled sheepskin shoes with diamond patterns on the sole. Ankles tattooed in odd patterns. And there. Against all laws of nature and possibility. There. Embedded between the diamond shaped treads. Strands of dark hair. Crusted in between.* It was as if the old gods had given her the sight of the hawk.

"Wait please! It's him! He killed my mother and father. I saw his shoes. Look!" She pulled off his shoes and pointed to the crudded strands of hair.

Skarphéðinn Arinbjarnarson gestured once more and the men dropped his fellow Icelander, Geirhjörtur Rustíkusson at his feet. The Icelandic were rare recruits to the guard, and until now, the two men had stuck together. Now, he eyed him dispassionately for a moment and then gave his verdict. "He will live. Bind the wounds. Chain him. And since the lady will not exact her just revenge, we will take him to the Althingi. I am due there to settle some scores with a man to whom I owe much misery." He turned to Dragoslava waving the waiting man to her. He came, carrying in his arms armor, weapons, shoes, clothes, a small bag of coins, and a few other items. "His belongings are yours. We gift them to you and offer you a place as one of us in his stead, if you will accept it, Dragoslava Dreadkeel." He bowed.

She stood before them contemplating a fate too many-faced to look squarely upon and evaluate. More and more the plan she had settled on of living in disguise, slowly making allies at the court, always sifting and seeking information that would lead her to her father's and mother's killers, and then the impossible task of gathering a force strong enough and influential enough to restore her to the throne from which she had been exiled. All this began to look like the impossible mountain to climb that it had been from the very beginning. She saw, as she stared at the helmet and bracers and sword of the dishonored Viking guard, protection both for her body and for her bruised honor. In the green eyes of the rows of stalwart warriors she saw what looked like admiration and respect, perhaps even acceptance.

"What says the Queen, can she set aside monarchical aspirations? What says Dragoslava Dreadkeel? Can she accept a place among warriors and treat them as her equals?"

"What is this Althingi you speak of?"

# — THE GOLD OF ISKANDER —
## Nicholas Kotar

*Magnus the Sailor*

**T**here are many legends of the historical Prince Oleg of Kiev. One of the least known is perhaps the most likely in terms of actual history. Al-Masudi, the "Herodotus of the Arabs", wrote of a fleet of 500 Russian ships that attacked the Kerch Strait in 912 AD, led by two warriors he named "Al-Dir and Olvang," presumably, Oleg of Kiev. The Khan of the Khazar Khaganate allowed the Rus access through the Don River to the Volga, and from there into the Caspian Sea. In return, he was to receive half of their spoils of war. The goal of this adventure was the legendary riches of Persia itself. One of the results of this invasion was the almost complete destruction of Persian Azerbaijan. When the loot from "Persia" came back to the Khan, some of his Moslem mercenaries were so incensed at the deaths of their fellow Moslems in Azerbaijan that they decided to attack the Russians. The Khan of the Khazars didn't warn *his allies, and the chronicles claim that 30,000 Russians were killed in retaliation. Some historians believe that this was the most likely demise of Oleg of Kiev. The following story is a fictionalized account of this semi-legendary adventure.*

*Crimean Highlands, 912 AD*

The autumn of the year that Oleg the Rus came with his armies was unseasonably warm. That should have been enough of an omen.

But Yaropolk was young, then. Of course, he believed in omens—any self-respecting Rus living among the Khazars kept a wary eye for omens, naturally—but the warmth had been so pleasant, so unexpected. It had all the tell-tale signs of a year blessed by the gods. For Dazhbog's sake, the wheat was man-high in some places!

It would take an expert on the fickleness of the gods to determine that such a pleasant sign was actually a trick.

Yaropolk stopped in the fifth hour of scything wheat. He had reached that level of pleasant unconsciousness in work that was his haven. The one place where he could be free of his family, free of his Khazar neighbors with their inquisitive eyes and wagging tongues, free of the Moslem mercenaries who prowled the grasslands, looking for recruits for their endless wars of religion.

Ahead of him, the thin strip of his family's field was hemmed in by grasses that were bursting with wildflowers—most of them red like tongues of flame, some blue like fallen pieces of the sky that the nomad Pechenegs worshiped as the greatest god of all.

Beyond them all to the distant south, the mountains of the land he only knew as Persia shimmered in the heat, insubstantial as a mirage.

But they were real, Yaropolk knew. They spoke to him every night in fell voices, towering over him in dreams filled with grim, hooded shapes. They were the source of the earth's darkness, the place where every soul wanted, but feared, to go. The place of infinite potential, but infinite chaos.

They were the lands that hid Iskander's lost gold.

The local Khazar grannies spoke of it only in hushed voices. "Gold tainted by blood and the dark arts," they said.

Yaropolk had heard the stories, told by half-drunk storytellers picking at their stringed instruments with dirty nails. Iskander, that great king of the Greeks, had become a priest of the foreign Eastern god Ahura Mazda. But he had not believed in Ahura Mazda, performing the rituals merely to placate the locals. All he wanted was the legendary gold of Persia.

But in his pride was his fall. He disregarded Ahura Mazda, and so Ahura Mazda ignored him, abandoning him to the demon-god Angra Mainyu. That dark god accepted Iskander's worship—the blood of the warriors of the greatest king the world had ever seen— in Ahura Mazda's stead. Iskander expected the gold of Persia as a reward. But Angra Mainyu's favorite gift is plague. Iskander rotted from within, dying under a bleak, foreign sun.

Yaropolk turned away from the mountains, thrilled by the stories but terrified as well. Terrified, because he craved that darkness sometimes.

As he turned, he didn't look at the yurts lining the river, not at the multi-tier wooden palace of the Khan leering over the yurts on its lone hillock, nor at the merchant caravans lining the road by the river—the Silk Road that led both to darkness and to the trade and wealth of silks from the Far East.

Yaropolk saw all of that, but he looked at none of it. His gaze caught a strange plume of dust coming from the western road. He thought he smelled leather, mixed with dust, on the faint breeze.

Horsemen. It had to be. Nothing else made that telltale plume. And they were coming fast, faster than any courier mounts. They must be war mounts, as good as the Arabians, except they were coming from the wrong direction.

*Who could it be? Nomad raiders?*

He never expected it to be his own people.

But as they approached, there could be no mistaking it. Rus warriors, riding in groups of four, perfectly spaced as though they routinely practiced marching on Sunday afternoons. Their spears sparked like fire, the peaks of their helmets glimmered like stars in a moonless sky. And their faces—Yaropolk had forgotten how noble the Western Rus looked. Next to the farmers of his own transplanted Eastern Rus, they looked like sons of gods.

Yaropolk couldn't help it—though his back was hunched after hours at the scythe, he stood proud and tall in their wake, the tiredness evaporating off him with his sweat.

Unbidden, the tales of his people came back to him. Tales of talking wolves, of hags riding giant mortars, of villains with names like "the deathless" who kept dying in every story. There was a darkness in those stories, too, but it was different than the brooding of the mountains. This darkness had an edge of mischief to it, but the mischief was joyful at heart. No matter how shadowy the path of the hero, he always found the firebird, the princess, and the kingdom at the end.

As he watched those proud riders of the Rus, Yaropolk felt a glimmer of hope, poignant as grief fluttering in his chest. It felt like the ice of the mountain-darkness was melting under the scarlet sun of the Russian steppes.

"I'd close your mouth, Yaropolk," said Gleb, his thirteen-year-old brother. "They might think you're a wizard uttering foul spells."

Yaropolk's peace shattered like glass. He smacked Gleb hard across his head. Gleb only laughed and continued to scythe. Even at thirteen, he could outwork Yaropolk with one hand tied behind his back. It irked Yaropolk, though he knew it shouldn't. The Rus considered it dishonorable to envy one's lessers.

But the darkness of the mountains often told Yaropolk that he wasn't an honorable man. And father made sure to remind him of it every evening at dinner.

Yaropolk's jaw ached from his teeth clenching; his scythe shook in his hand. He spit on the ground, disgusted with himself for showing the emotion without realizing it. How far he had to go yet, before he would be like one of those god-men.

With a dull ache in his head, he resumed scything, trying not to look up. But the hoofbeats continued drumming, beating so loudly they seemed to be inside his chest, pounding his head from within. He only remembered to breathe after the dust settled and a ghostly silence rose. Then came the noise: the scarfed old Khazar women chittered and gestured excitedly, sitting by their yurts, their brown prune-feet baking in the sun.

He hated them in that moment. But he hated himself more.

"You know what I heard?" Gleb said at dinner, without even bothering to ask if he could speak, as any youngest son of a Rus household should. Yaropolk hated that their household was slowly assuming Khazar customs.

"What's that, my boy?" Father answered, smiling at the left corner of his mouth. Why he never rebuked Gleb, Yaropolk couldn't fathom.

"Prince Oleg of Novgorod is gathering warriors for an expedition."

"Gathering them?" said mother, her fat belly already taut in expectation of the rolling laugh that always made her look like a mountain about to topple over. "Hasn't he enough already?"

"Not for *this expedition*," said Gleb in that hateful, secret way he had about him. He even tapped his nose conspiratorially.

"Well, out with it!" said Yaropolk.

Father's eyes were rebuke incarnate. For once, Yaropolk didn't look away. It gave him a momentary rush of elation when father's eyes retreated first.

"The fabled gold of Persia!" announced Gleb. "Iskander's own riches!"

The darkness filled Yaropolk's chest with hot anguish. His heart beat feverishly.

*It's time*, he said to himself.

Or was it the darkness of the mountains speaking inside him?

"I'm going to join up!" said Gleb, then laughed. *That* jibe was meant for Yaropolk, no doubt about it.

"Oh no, you're not," said father, looking at Yaropolk. "None of you are, so don't get any ideas. This harvest is going to be the best one in ten years. I need both my men with me. And what would you do with a sword? Chop down wheat?"

Then mother *did* laugh. Everyone laughed.

Everyone except Yaropolk.

He was up the next morning before the sun had even thought of showing up over the horizon. As usual, Gleb slept with his mouth open, snoring loudly. For once, the noise was welcome. It distracted from that buzzing in the head that accompanies a bad night.

All night, Yaropolk wanted to scream. He felt a tension like a hardboiled egg pushing out of his right temple. It throbbed, to boot. He tried the usual things—breathe slowly, try to find gratitude in your situation—but it didn't work.

He simply had to join Oleg's campaign. He could run away, of course. But father was mule-stubborn. Surely he would invoke some ancient Khazar law that would bind him like a slave to the land.

For a moment, the buzzing in his head produced an unusually clear thought, as if spoken from outside him in the second person. *Kill your parents. Blame Gleb.*

Yaropolk actually considered it. But Gleb snored again, and the vision of his dead parents crumbled. No, he would simply remain a drudge for his family until some gracious deity ended his miserable existence.

He walked out into the gloaming. The Persian mountains seemed to be simmering with orange flames.

It was a bad omen. With it came a sinking feeling of inevitability. A rush, similar to standing on the edge of the precipice, looking down at clouds *underneath* you.

"Up so early?" Naturally, it was Gleb, who always seemed to get up at the crack of dawn as though he had slept twelve hours. "Unusual for your lazy bones, eh?"

It was too much. That casual, glib self-satisfaction. He was *lesser* to Yaropolk. The *bogatyr* of the ancient tales, the superman who even challenged death itself to a duel, would never have stood it.

Gleb must be humbled. It was the right thing to do.

Yaropolk said nothing, but swung hard at Gleb. His brother never saw it coming.

The blow was a good one: right across the head. The spike of pain jabbing all the way to Yaropolk's elbow like lightning was a savage pleasure.

Gleb's head struck something as he fell. Something hard, judging by the hard thunk.

"Come now, brother, I didn't hit you that hard."

Dark liquid pooled out from under Gleb's head. Then Yaropolk noticed two things. The first was that Gleb's eyes were slightly open, but his eyes were unfocused, slightly crossed. The second was how his upper body twisted over his legs. It was not natural.

And he knew, with the strange calmness of utter panic.

He had killed his brother.

The sun rose above the Persian mountains, and the orange sky turned blood crimson. Yaropolk thought he heard laughter coming from the mountains. The cackle of the demon Angra Mainyu.

But no. It was the shrieking of his mother.

Yaropolk ran and didn't look back.

For the next two weeks, the combined armies of the Rus and the Khazars had seen nothing but grasslands day and night. Hardly a dip or a rise, only the grasses bowing to them, as though already giving them homage for the glory they would doubtless receive. But there was no monotony for Yaropolk. It was like riding through gold.

Yaropolk had to continually pinch himself that this was really happening. He, little runt Yaropolk, who would never amount to anything, the one great regret of his father's life, was riding astride a nomad steed, armed with borrowed mail, his own father's sword at his side. The mail had been a god-send, as was his new friend, the dour Icelander named Magnus.

He was a strange one, this Magnus. Taller than anyone Yaropolk had ever seen, he dressed almost all in dark browns and blacks, disdaining the bright colors of both Khazars and Rus. He was bald, though not from age. He couldn't have been more than twenty-five or thirty years old. With a forked beard tied into a knot that he fingered every time he was lost in thought—which was often—he was a strange contrast to the boisterous army camp of young men and renegades out to make their fortune.

But for all his strangeness, it was he who had saved Yaropolk from certain death. Now that he remembered it, Yaropolk didn't know whether to laugh or to cry. What a backwoods rustic he must have looked, when he came into the Novgorodians' camp that morning, begging for sanctuary. As fate would have it, Yaropolk had blundered into Oleg's own tent at the moment the Rus war-leader and his captains sat at meal. The great Oleg had eyes that would have forced even Yaropolk's father to look away. Those eyes looked about ready to skewer Yaropolk alive at his impudence. The warrior at Oleg's right was already drawing his sword, suspecting sabotage.

But then Magnus had laughed. He sat at Oleg's left hand, and even so, he towered over everyone else. In the wake of his laughter, something snapped in the air. The darkness receded, and everyone laughed with Magnus. Oleg's eyes changed at that moment, and he invited Yaropolk to the table.

Yaropolk had noticed something else: Magnus had looked at him with recognition. At that moment, Yaropolk knew the sympathy felt only by men who have killed. But strangely enough, the look in Magnus's eyes was one of deep sadness.

When the Khan's men had come into Oleg's camp demanding that Yaropolk be handed over for the murder of his brother, it was Magnus who spoke to Oleg. And Oleg had paid the blood price to the Khan directly, with a handsome addition for the purchase of two of the Khan's own horses. Afterward, Oleg himself had handed a set of mail to Yaropolk.

"Now you belong to me," he had said, with a cryptic smile.

It was a moment Yaropolk would never forget, he was sure of it.

Even endless grasses come to an end at some point. That evening, Oleg's army came within sight of a great lake. It was long and sinuous—almost like a river that had swollen beyond its banks. On the nearest shore, several hundred longboats sat moored, dipping gently up and down. The far bank of the lake ended in a silver river that reached like a crooked finger into a narrow gap between the foothills of the mountains, which now towered black in the fading light.

After they had decamped, Yaropolk sat with Magnus, as he often did.

"I didn't know we would be traveling by boat," Yaropolk said.

"We need to get off the road, if there's any chance at all of us coming into Persia without the entire countryside knowing of it in advance."

"I see," said Yaropolk, though really he didn't. He felt very rustic indeed.

"Scared?" asked Magnus, grinning slightly as he poked at the edges of his just-lit campfire.

"Aren't you?"

Magnus rumbled, which was as close to a laugh as he ever seemed to get.

"You didn't know?" he finally said. "I'm leading this little armada."

"You?"

"I'm a shipwright and navigator, you silly child! Why else would Oleg have hired an Icelander for this little expedition of his?"

Yaropolk had had no idea. But nothing surprised him about Magnus. If he had instead told him that he was secretly the descendant of Iskander himself, come to reclaim his rightful inheritance, he would have believed him.

"Magnus, tell me. What was it you said to Oleg when the Khan's men wanted to take me?"

Magnus stopped prodding the fire and looked at Yaropolk directly. Yaropolk's heart danced inside him again, warming to the sympathy he had felt at their first encounter.

"Do you think that killing your brother was an accident?" Magnus said.

Yaropolk felt blood rush to his face. He looked away and managed a lame half-shrug.

"It wasn't. You know the old tales as well as I do. My people's stories are not that different from yours. We come from the same Viking stock. And what do those tales tell us?"

Yaropolk felt like a child. He wanted to impress Magnus, but he feared that his answer would be foolish.

"There is no such thing as an accident," he mumbled.

Magnus smiled. It lit his face like a sunrise, but there was an edge of darkness to it as well.

"Oleg is no fool. He knows that we go into the heart of a very powerful darkness. He also understands omens. You told me that Gleb was an arrogant boy, yes? Well, that upsets the natural order. Odin… or Dazhbog, I suppose you call him… he restored it, through your mighty arm. You brought the natural will of the gods into being. And you did it on the eve of our journey. That is a good omen. Omens come through very special men. Men who are transparent to Valhalla."

"Are you such a man?" Yaropolk asked. Immediately, he wished he hadn't. It was the sort of thing father always rebuked him for.

"We shall see," Magnus answered, and returned to prodding the fire and fingering his beard with his other hand. They could have been talking about the weather, for all the emotion that now showed.

Magnus seemed to do everything without excessive emotion, in complete control of himself. Yaropolk, who endured every emotion like it was a bucking horse, almost worshipped Magnus for his self-control.

The next morning was shrouded in fog that was darker than any fog Yaropolk had ever seen. It was almost like darkness itself had coalesced around them into shapes resembling cloud and mist. A creeping dread wrapped itself around Yaropolk. For the first time since they left, he wondered if he had made a mistake.

"This is the gateway," said Magnus. "Here, the power of Angra Mainyu dominates. Natural to feel a bit jittery."

Magnus chose ten warriors to man the first boat with him, Yaropolk among them. Oleg, himself no slouch when it came to boats, manned the second.

"Don't be too proud," said Magnus to Yaropolk. "It's like the cup-bearers, you know. First to die if something's wrong."

Yaropolk's first thought on stepping onto the boat was that no man should ever walk on anything so unstable. Perun created warriors to stand on firm ground. This shifting, heaving nonsense was for fish, not men.

But then the square sail—striped red and white—caught the mountain wind, and they flew forward. Yaropolk forgot to breathe for the shock of it. Magnus saw his face and laughed. The rest of the crew joined him.

But their laughter died quickly, because the mists were coalescing, not fading away with the passing of the day. Both sides of the lake disappeared, and it seemed that there was nothing but this dark, creeping black-grey emptiness that swallowed them deeper and deeper into the gizzard of a demon.

Yaropolk felt sick to his stomach nearly constantly. Magnus had said that it was Odin who guided his hand against his brother. But what if it was Angra Mainyu? What is that demon was the source of the mountain darkness that had whispered to him seductively at night, only to devour him as soon as he approached?

Everyone else around Yaropolk, their eyes like saucers, gripped their weapons with dew-dripping fingers.

By the time the mists' darkening began to herald the end of the day, something strange happened. Daggers of light passed through the mist, and it parted. It seemed to Yaropolk that the darkness hissed as it faded into nothingness. The grey-black fog rolled away, and the dagger of light turned into a river of golden fire.

The snow on the mountains glowed with a pink light, purple in the shaded regions where no light could pierce through thick woods. For a moment, they were nothing but mountains, and a different kind of song seemed to come from them. Not the ever-present drone of the demonic darkness, but a kind of harmony of many voices, barely audible above the howl of the wind.

They had reached the far end of the lake and were already within the narrows of the river that led into a gorge between foothills. The daggers of light seemed to coalesce around a figure standing on the bank of the river, not a bow's shot away to their right. At first, Yaropolk thought that the sudden coming of the sun was dazzling his vision. But no, there was definitely a man there. He held a cup aloft in his right hand, and something like a loaf of bread in his left.

Magnus, as soon as he saw the old man, started to growl. Yaropolk's skin crawled at the sound.

Then Magnus screamed a series of what must have been curses, judging by the venom with which he literally spat at the old man. The language was unfamiliar to Yaropolk. Probably his native Icelandic.

To Yaropolk's utter surprise, the old hermit laughed and gave right back to Magnus in the same tongue. Magnus's face turned beet-red, and he looked ready to burst. But he couldn't get another word out, whether he wanted to or not. It was a comical scene, but there was something wrong, something twisted in it.

Yaropolk felt giddy and unmoored, and for a moment, a stab of hatred for the old hermit passed through him. But it had no purchase, and after it passed, all Yaropolk saw was a man dressed in some brown sacking, barely holding in place from the ravages of time and weather. He had a shock of white hair and a foaming beard with a dirty yellow-brown streak from chin to tip, as though it had been painted on. His eyes were a dark brown in a face that was even darker brown from constant sun.

When Yaropolk's eyes met the old man's, their light dimmed for a moment. But then he smiled, and Yaropolk felt a sense of welcome and warmth. It was almost like getting drunk for the first time.

Oleg ordered that all the boats stop at the hermit's shore for the night. He lived in a flat area that seemed scooped out of the crags by the river. On three sides, the small field was bordered by sheer cliff faces. The bank of the river formed the fourth wall, at a ford filled with rounded, whitish pebbles. On the far side of the clearing, where the tallest cliff loomed over this strange little haven, a hut stood. It might have been made of nothing but driftwood, held together by old rope. Yaropolk didn't understand how it didn't fall over every time the hermit entered it.

To complete the odd picture, a crazed goat jumped around the field. It had long, twisted horns, and it constantly ranged back and forth, as though it were looking for another goat to head-butt. And since it could find no one, it simply pretended, butting at the empty air.

The hermit had laughed, when asked about it: "Oh, poor tyke, he's a little wrong in the head. We both are. Brothers in silliness."

Yaropolk had encountered medicine men and shamans of various stripes. They always carried with them an aura of importance that he often had to admit was nothing more than self-importance. But this hermit never passed an opportunity to laugh at himself. And it was done not in a way to invite compliments or retorts from his listeners. He simply thought of himself as a rather silly old man living a largely pointless existence in the middle of nowhere.

But he exuded a peace that attracted Yaropolk powerfully, if only because it was a counterweight to the darkness inside him. It suggested that there might be other joys, other elations that Yaropolk had not seriously considered before.

And so when everyone had fallen asleep, Yaropolk visited the old man.

The inside of the hut was as bare as the outside. A pallet in a corner, half covered in goat droppings, a sputtering fire in a dirty pit, and some sort of mat—that was the extent of the decor. A pot of some brown liquid bubbled on the fire.

"Tea," said the hermit. "One vice among many."

"Where do you get tea, old man?" asked Yaropolk, astounded. Tea was a rare luxury in the Khaganate of the Khazars.

"The Lord gives, the Lord takes away," he answered.

"Which lord is this?" asked Yaropolk, his ears perking up. He had known that this would be a useful visit. Perhaps this old man could illumine some of the darkness inside him.

"The only one," answered the hermit.

"Oh," said Yaropolk, and his enthusiasm deflated in an instant. "You're a Christian."

"Don't sound so disappointed," laughed the old man and handed him a clay cup that looked like it hadn't been washed in years. The smell wafting from it was like earth and rosemary mixed together. The taste was sour and bitter at once. An aftertaste of sweetness teased his tongue, then faded.

"That's... that's very good," said Yaropolk.

The hermit chuckled as he picked up his own cup. "So..." he said, breathing in the fresh-steeped tea with the hunger of an addict. "Iskander's gold, is it?"

"Did Oleg tell you?" asked Yaropolk.

The old man shook his head. "Magnus. He's like Charon, you know. Only has one job to do."

"You mean he's taken others before us?"

The old man nodded once. "And none of them have ever come back with any gold. Well, except for Magnus. He makes a pretty penny for himself every time."

Yaropolk was offended. He didn't believe the old man, and now he thought there might be some old grudge between them.

"You Icelandic too, then?" he asked.

"Me? No. Greek."

"Like Iskander!" Yaropolk exclaimed. He felt foolish as a child, immediately.

"In some ways, yes." He smiled in a self-deprecating way that made Yaropolk like him even more.

They chatted like this for a while, mostly about nothing, but throughout, Yaropolk couldn't shake the feeling that the old man was probing, and that Yaropolk's answers were revealing more than he liked.

It was morning before Yaropolk realized how tired he was.

"How quickly the night passed," said Yaropolk, and began to get up.

"Young man," said the hermit, suddenly serious. "You are different from the rest."

"Magnus says that I'm transparent to the gods."

He meant it to sound important. But he felt small, pathetic.

"Oh, that's obvious," said the old man, which deflated Yaropolk even more. "It's not that. It's that the darkness hasn't gotten to your heart yet. I would have thought that murdering your brother would have made you a slave to the darkness. But it hasn't. I find that curious."

Yaropolk froze in place. He had said nothing about his brother to the old man.

"Are you... are you a wizard?" he asked, his hands beginning to shake as they still cupped the tea.

"No," said the old man somberly. "Nothing like that."

But he would not elaborate any more.

The silence between them stretched. Yaropolk didn't move. He was afraid of breaking the silence. It seemed sacred, somehow. But sacred to a different god. Perhaps to that pitiful god of the Christians.

"Yaropolk," said the old man. "What you will see in the coming days will be terrible. It may break you, if you don't die in the fighting. But somehow I think you won't. Something tells me you're meant for something else."

He stirred the fire pit restlessly, then fixed Yaropolk with his eyes, which seemed to glow in the half-light of early morning.

"I won't insult you with counsel. You will follow your own path, as any man must. But a parting wish from a new friend?"

Yaropolk was amazed. Was the old man actually asking *his* permission? He nodded, faintly aware of the sweat sticking to his palms.

"The darkness is powerful. But it is ouroboros. In the end, it eats itself."

Yaropolk attributed his unease during the next day to the tea and lack of sleep. But Magnus' coldness to him suggested something else. Had the old hermit cursed him in some way? Was there some charm or spell woven into him that Magnus could sense?

But the journey soon banished all thought. The wind stopped blowing on the following day, and the rowing began. Those four days of non-stop work that made his memories of scything seem like blessed rest. All around him, Yaropolk sensed the resentment of the men like it was a physical thing that they passed from one to another. Magnus began to sing ballads in his oddly-inflected Russian, telling of legendary Perun stealing thunder from his father to give as a gift to his own worshipers. Then he sang songs with strange melodies, telling of Iskander's many adventures, always ending with his failure. Somehow, he always managed to set up the failure as an opportunity for all brave men to finish the work the great Iskander had started.

Then the river ended. It was time to climb.

The four days of rowing now became a fond memory.

Yaropolk couldn't help it. As he gripped the rocks, half climbing and half scrabbling up the mountain path leading deeper into the mountains, he realized that the old hermit's words had cracked his trust in Magnus. He found himself gaping at the Icelander without noticing that he was doing it. Magnus never caught his eye, but somehow Yaropolk knew he could sense the change. It frightened him. He didn't want Magnus as an enemy. Touched by the gods he might be, but Magnus seemed almost god-like himself at times. No sense testing his anger.

They finally saw their first village. It was like a swallow's nest in the crags—impossible to imagine people actually living in this place. As he saw it, the darkness swelled inside Yaropolk like an overripe fruit. Then he saw the young maids in their red-gold headscarves, with skin the color of milky tea and eyes that sparked between fear and interest.

He knew. This would be the beginning of the true expedition. The first foray into the heart of the mountain's darkness.

It didn't take long. First it was the taunting as the warriors passed the shy girls gathering in the village square. Then the whispers began: *did you see the gold around their necks? Those necklaces look like fortunes to be made.*

"And why not have a bit of fun in the process?" Droned the voice of the darkness inside him.

He didn't even notice when it began, as though all of them went momentarily blank as the madness descended on them.

Yaropolk later remembered it in slow motion, seeing with eyes as though looking downward from a height. It was like his soul had left his body for an hour as he and the others raped and pillaged and murdered every person in the village, then came back down into his chest when he was done.

He found that the killing was easy. He wondered if that had been the purpose of the accidental killing of Gleb. To prepare him for this. For a more profound sacrifice.

The girls' gold, as it turned out, was not insignificant. Most of it was in the form of baubles and necklaces, but a few of the warriors found actual bars of solid gold in some of the houses. The sight of it made Yaropolk's chest warm with expectation.

The next week was a blur in Yaropolk's memories. The raping and killing continued. But the stores of gold didn't materialize, no matter how much they tortured the locals for information. All they seemed to have were the same baubles and trinkets. Yaropolk had begun to doubt they were even true gold. Something about them felt false.

Worse than that was the daily loss of himself. The mountains were draining him of life. The elation of the early days was ragged now, edged with a desperation at the thought that perhaps it was all a lie. Angra Mainyu had gotten his worship, as he had from Iskander's ravages. In Yaropolk's dreams, he now saw himself dying under the same bleak sun that had felled Iskander.

Eventually, Oleg himself tired of the search. Angry at not finding anything, he turned the armies back toward the Silk Road. And then the murdering and pillaging became even worse, because it was no longer for pleasure. It was resentment uncorked.

Magnus, Yaropolk noticed, was largely absent during the pillages. He hardly spoke in those days to anyone. One evening, as they sat huddling in stinking cloaks by a dying fire, he finally broke his silence.

"You Rus," he said with disgust in his voice. "I thought we were of the same tribe. Thor's children. But you are of Loki."

Yaropolk found himself too exhausted to be angry at that. "Be honest, Magnus. Did the others you brought here end any better than we?"

Magnus didn't answer. He avoided Yaropolk's gaze.

"The old hermit called you Charon, you know," said Yaropolk. "I think he was right. You lead people to death."

Magnus got up and walked away.

—◖✳◗—

Finally, they left the mountains behind, riding through a stretch of the Silk Road that was bordered by tall grasses. It was a quiet evening, the kind when the sky dominates the view so much that Yaropolk felt it would be the easiest thing to *fall* into it, that remaining anchored on earth was the thing that required effort and work. They had seen no merchant caravans for hours, which was strange. It should have been a clear warning to Yaropolk, but he was lost in thought.

As the sun set, the ragged clouds were livid red and purple. Yaropolk remembered when such sights had left him breathless with quiet pleasure. Now, he had nothing but a dull throbbing in his chest.

Then, the world exploded. It was like every single blade of the tall grasses suddenly transformed into a turbaned warrior wielding a crooked scimitar. Moslem raiders, he realized.

*But why are they attacking us?*

With a sinking feeling, Yaropolk's muddled thoughts came into horrifying focus. He should have noticed it before. The villages in the mountains. Most of them had had small minarets. It had struck him as strange at the time. He had assumed the villagers of the Persian mountains to be worshipers of Ahura Mazda.

But no. They had all been Moslems. All the women they had raped. All the old men they had skewered. They were all Moslems.

This was revenge.

The scything began in earnest. This time, the Rus were the wheat.

In a brief respite between quick and mad bouts of swordplay that left two raiders dead at his feet, Yaropolk looked around for Magnus. He was nowhere to be seen.

*He has abandoned you.*

The thought wasn't his own. And it sneered at the edges, just like his father used to.

Something about that thought lit a new fire inside him. He would not die. Not like this. Not hacked down like a dog. And he turned on his attackers.

He knew how to scythe. And so he did.

Yaropolk would have liked to pretend that his prowess with the blade saved him. But it was the quick, almost supernatural, fall of night. Yaropolk found himself in the company of about twenty other Rus, all of whom were wounded badly. Yaropolk himself couldn't step on his left foot without it sending screaming stabs of pain all the way to his hip.

But they were alive. Somehow, they were alive.

They wandered aimlessly through the grasses all that horrible night. Around them, the din of battle and the groaning of wounded men rose and faded like audible mirages. But through it all, the drone of the darkness was like a hand pressing down on them, making Yaropolk's already exhausted limbs leaden with pain.

But through that drone, like a tinkling of bells in an impossible distance, Yaropolk heard the same choir-like music that he had sensed, just beyond hearing, in the hermit's cover.

Whether he chose to or not, his feet kept inclining toward that direction, until he fell from exhaustion and the darkness took him.

He awoke to the pungent scent of tea.

"You're awake," said the hermit. It sounded like a command, not an observation. And Yaropolk felt stronger than he had in days.

He sat up to find himself inside the hermit's house. The door was hanging ajar, and there was no one else in the clearing.

"How did I get here?" asked Yaropolk, his mind still cloudy, though becoming clearer with every whiff of the tea's aroma.

"Rest now," said the hermit.

Yaropolk remained in the care of the hermit for several days. His wounds knit together more quickly than he thought possible. He felt stronger than he had in years.

But in his heart, there was nothing but blackness. He saw in vivid color the faces of every person he butchered. He ached to feel... something... even guilt would have been preferable to the cold nothing inside him.

The hermit hardly said anything, but Yaropolk caught his lingering glance on him more than once. Searching, quizzical, unreadable—the expression Yaropolk wonder that this entire strange interlude of healing might be part of an elaborate ruse or dream. As though he would wake up any moment in Hel, surrounded by the victims of his own carnage.

And in the quiet evenings of tea and silence, Yaropolk's heart woke up. First, an ache, then jabbing pain, then his chest burned with the guilt of memory. But as he embraced that shame, he felt the darkness sloughing off like snakeskin. The darkness had no place near the hermit, as before, and instead of the dark, warm elation the mountains used to give him, he saw in perfect clarity all that he had done.

The pain didn't end, didn't fade. It was like fire that he was sure was consuming him slowly from within. Soon he would be no more than a smoking ember. He remembered Iskander dying under a bleak sun. Now he knew why Iskander had died.

"Yaropolk," said the hermit one morning. "I need you to go hunting for me. Down the river, back to the lake, you'll find a dinghy with a bow and arrow in it. A rabbit or two should do it."

Yaropolk relished the chance to get out of the clearing and move around for a change. But there was no dinghy, no bow, no arrow, nothing. After searching for several hours, he decided to go back and ask for better directions.

As he walked along the banks of the river, he heard the unmistakable twang of a bowstring. That was strange. But what followed chilled his blood. It was laughter. He knew that laughter. It was the laughter of men on the warpath.

He ran, heedless of the noise he made. As he turned the bend of the river and the hermit's clearing came into view, he froze in place. The hermit had been hanged on a stake, and several rag-tag warriors were using him for target practice. One of them towered over the rest.

Yaropolk screamed when he realized who it was.

"Magnus!"

Magnus turned to greet him. His face was as calm as it ever was, even with a bloody dagger in his right hand. Yaropolk kept his distance, his body shuddering. All this was far beyond his ability to comprehend. And of course he had left his sword back at the hut!

"Well met, Yaropolk," said Magnus, and he smiled. To Yaropolk's shock, it was a serene, content smile. The smile of one who has done a great deed for others. "I am glad you are here. Through you, Odin gave a good omen at the beginning of our venture. But you Rus failed him. So it fell to me to offer proper sacrifice. Now the order is restored."

"He brought me back from the brink, you idiot!" wheezed Yaropolk. "I would have died if not for his care."

"You don't believe that, do you?" Magnus scoffed. "These Christians are cannibals. Blood-drinkers. It wouldn't surprise me if he was preparing you for one of his blood rituals."

Yaropolk had believed such things about the Christians all his life. It was common knowledge among the Khazars. Now it seemed the most foolish idea in the world.

"You are a monster, Magnus. The old man was right. When the gods are done with you, there will be nothing left."

Magnus sneered at him, then turned to the rest of his band, whom Yaropolk now recognized as his fellow-survivors of the Moslem raid.

"Come!" called Magnus. "Let us leave the weak to their fate."

As Magnus passed by Yaropolk, he looked at him with genuine pity. "I thought you were one of the sons of thunder. But you are weak, like the rest of them."

Yaropolk's blood boiled. He wanted to claw out Magnus's eyes. But the hermit groaned, and all other thoughts fled. He ran to the old man. His former friends and fellow warriors laughed at him. But Yaropolk wept.

The hermit had been nailed to the post by his hands. Yaropolk looked around for something to pry the nails off, but he could find nothing. He tried his sword, but it only cut the old man's hands, and the hermit groaned the louder.

Finally, he begged him to stop.

"Why?" sobbed Yaropolk. "You didn't deserve any of it."

"Oh, I did," said the hermit. "Why do you think I've been living here all these years? For comfort?"

He laughed, but it came out as cackling and turned into a moan.

"I will avenge you," said Yaropolk.

"You will do no such thing," said the hermit, and his voice commanded. "You have given me a great gift, Yaropolk. To die for another. It is the greatest gift."

"What? What are you talking about?"

The hermit's head drooped. It seemed a monumental effort to keep it up.

"Magnus came here to kill you," said the hermit. "You were the sacrifice he wanted to make to Odin. I convinced him that I would do much better."

Yaropolk crumpled on his knees before the crucified hermit.

"How can I ever repay you?" he said, almost whispering.

The old man smiled. "Remember me in your prayers."

Then it hit Yaropolk. "But what is your name, old man?"

His head drooping, the old man whispered, "My name is Alexander."

# — WAVE RUNNERS —
## Kaitlin Felix

*Gyda the Grim*          *Ragnar Goldmane*

S alt crust stung Gyda's eyes. Beneath her feet, the oak hull of *Sea-Wolf* rocked. Gentle waves slapped against the sides and shreds of leftover stormcloud obscured the brightening horizon. Leaning against the sheer strake, she rubbed a calloused hand down her face. She had not slept.

Behind her, a crew of five women dozed in between benches and sea-chests. Gyda chose her crew carefully. Each of Rán's Daughters, as she called them, brought strength to the ship. Over the trading seasons, they had more than proved their worth.

Astrid was the youngest, at twenty summers. Gyda found her wandering the streets of Dyflin. Next was the Irish Liadan, broad of shoulder and red of face. She spoke little, using her hands to communicate most often. Guðrun and Rúna came together and were as closely-bound as a married couple. They had run from their fathers and a life of wool-spinning and sail-stitching. Finally, there was Eir. She joined *Sea-Wolf* the previous summer when her husband died in a raid. With her skill in sailing and leadership, Eir ran *Sea-Wolf* almost as well as Gyda.

Gyda loved each of them in her way, but love made women soft, and softness did not ensure survival, especially on the sea-roads.

Turning from the cold water, Gyda stepped off the platform and weaved through the sleeping bodies. In the hold, a finger's-length of seawater sloshed against the wooden crates and bundles of fur. Rope lashings creaked with crusted brine. Jarl Olavi's cargo appeared intact.

It should have been an easy night, letting the wind push the knarr east and then south, towards al-Andalus and the Emirate of Córdoba. Yet they had scarcely left the Dyflin port when a howling storm rolled over to tear at the sail and whip salt in their faces. That fickle bitch of a goddess Rán had done her utmost to drag the ship down and steal the cargo along with their lives. But Gyda would rather eat the sparks from Thor's own anvil before allowing the sea to steal anything else from her.

She returned to the prow, resting a hand against the long neck of the mounted beast above her. Great Fenrir, wolf of Ragnarök, faced the coming dawn with teeth bared in a fearsome snarl. Gyda swelled with pride. *Sea-Wolf* was a magnificent ship, and it was *hers*. However long it took to deliver this cargo, she would fight every storm, every sea monster, every water-logged god to do it.

Soft whispers and stirrings behind made her turn. "Good morning, Daughters," she crowed. "Time to carve a scar into this whale-road! Move yourselves, get those *brynja*'s scoured!"

The Daughters jumped at her orders, stowing their sleeping furs and grabbing bags of sand from the hold. Six mail-shirts clinked as the bags were thrown back and forth to scrub away new spots of rust.

The sun rose swift and strong, but no wind arrived with it to blow them south. In ever-growing irritation, Gyda barked her orders. Eir relayed them much more cheerfully, and the women went to it.

"Freya's tits, Gyda, do you have to be so grumpy?" Eir chided her on the platform. She shook her *brynja* free of sand and pulled it over her head. "We're barely awake. Not even Jarl Olavi would—"

"Olavi demanded this cargo be delivered within the week," Gyda snapped. She pulled on her *brynja* to tighten the fit. "They had better row like their arses are tarred to that bench or by noon they will be!"

Eir rolled her eyes but lifted her oar and sat alongside Astrid. Rúna, their navigator, took her place by the rudder. The anchor was drawn up. Gyda gave the signal. The oars dipped and *Sea-Wolf* sliced through the water like a serpent through grass.

The morning burned clear and fresh as it always does in early Autumn. The momentum of rowing whipped their hair and dried their salt-crusted clothes. By noon each of them blushed with a sun-glow.

Gyda smiled into the wind. Perhaps they would reach the coast of al-Andalus in a couple of days. She would be back in the Jarl's hall in a few more, cargo-hold full of silks and silver dirhams for her trouble. Visions of how she would spend those coins danced in her mind.

"Rest," she called from the platform. The women groaned, leaning on knees and against each other. Salted meat and hard bread were passed around, all washed down with Eir's stash of good mead. Njörd sent a strong breeze soon after, and the sail was let out to catch it. Once again, *Sea-Wolf* skimmed along the water, faster than the shining fish alongside the hull.

Weeks ago, a secret trade agreement had been struck with the Emissary from Córdoba, a man name Ishraq. Jarl Olavi chose Gyda and her Daughters to deliver the first goods to al-Andalus to seal the agreement.

Gyda could hardly believe her good fortune. Two years of supplying Dyflin with trade had brought her little renown or silver. She wanted more. She wanted a reputation that put respect in men's mouths. With this deal, Olavi would feed her ambition as much as he fed her coffers.

This was a test, though, and Gyda knew it. When news of the deal came out, it would cause no end of jealousy. The other tradesmen under Olavi would protest. Olavi's own son Helgi would be the loudest of them. How Gyda handled her rivals would be the true measure of her competence. If she did well, the Jarl might trust her with even greater tasks.

Custom and tradition dictated diplomatic business fell to men. Even to men who fancied themselves sailors but couldn't steer a fishing boat out of a harbor. Gyda's own husband had been such a man.

Bitterness choked her. That man had put aside all ambition upon their arrival in Dyflin a few years ago. He took to a pathetic life of fishing and selling his catch for a trifle. Middle-aged and childless, Gyda was known in the muddy alleyways as the *Fiskvif* — Fishwife. Less than a half-year later her husband drowned in the river, leaving Gyda alone.

"Never trust a man's ambition," she whispered to the wind.

Something thumped against the hull.

Gyda leaned over the starboard strake, expecting a whale or a shark. Another thump came, louder this time, followed by a low groan.

"Someone is in the hold," exclaimed Eir.

Behind a mountain of canvas-wrapped furs, walrus ivory, and crates of honey, a lump of linen squirmed. Dark blond hair popped out from one end, and the lump cursed.

"Weapons!" Gyda called.

The women pulled out hand axes and long knives. Gyda had a whaling spear, but it was lashed to the mast, too far to reach. She approached, drawing the seax at her waist.

"Whoever you are, you're about to get a blade in your gut-rope," she said. "Stand slowly or shit steel."

The blond lump rose, bracing an arm against a crate.

"Ragnar," the figure said with a stately rasp. "Brings you greetings from Jarl Olavi, may the gods grant him favor." With a sudden lurch, he shoved Eir out of the way and puked loudly over the side.

When he was finished, the stranger turned and collapsed on a bench. Eir glared hard at him, mouth set in a tight line as she rubbed her sore elbow.

"Who are you?" Gyda demanded. She could see nothing of the man's skin that wasn't covered in bruises. His clothes were torn and smeared with blood.

He closed his eyes and turned his head to spit onto the deck. "Torn open again," he muttered, probing the inside of his mouth with his tongue. "Damn."

Gyda walked closer, fist tightening on her seax. "Answer me."

He waved a hand. "I told you my name," he said irritably. "Ragnar. Favored oath-man to Jarl Olavi Sharp-Spear and son of Grettir. I mean you no harm."

"You mean *me* no harm?" She laughed. "You're hardly fit to stand."

Ragnar put his hands over his face. "Can you not do that please? I could do with some water, if you'd be so kind."

When no one moved, he peered through his fingers. "I would drink the sea-water, but you know, not the wisest choice."

Gyda stepped forward and put the edge of her blade to his throat. "You'll get nothing until we get answers," she said. "*That* would be a wise choice. Are you an outlaw? An oath-breaker?"

"You won't get an answer from me until I rid my mouth of the taste of blood and puke," he snapped.

Gyda tilted her head and smiled. "I see. Give him a drink, Daughters."

Several pairs of hands grabbed him. Ragnar yelped as they tipped him over the strake. He dangled, fingers trailing in the water.

"Apologies for my rudeness," he said blandly.

"I will ask once more," Gyda said. "And if we don't like your answer, I think Rán would appreciate a sacrifice and stop sending storms to sink us." The women voiced their agreement.

"I told you already," Ragnar said, voice croaking. "Surely you've seen me in Olavi's hall. I'm rather popular."

Eir touched Gyda's arm, whispering something. She waved her away. "What are you doing here, Ragnar?"

"Haul me up first."

A few of the women loosened their grip, dunking his forearms.

"Alright! I'll tell you. Don't drop me."

Gyda rested on the strake. "Go on. Spin us a tale."

"Lady," Eir pressed. "I know him."

"His face is familiar," Gyda whispered back. "But I still want to know why he's skulking around my ship like a rat."

Ragnar eye-balled the waves. "I am on a special diplomatic assignment."

"What assignment?"

"...It is of a delicate nature."

Gyda nodded, hooming in her throat. "Drop him."

"Please!" Ragnar kicked his legs against the women's grip, trying to hook over the sheer strake. "You like gold, eh? I have gold. A marvellous treasure. Let me back in and I'll show you."

At that, Gyda paused to consider. With a roll of her eyes, she said, "Haul him up."

Ragnar thumped onto the deck, soaked and stinking of fear-sweat. Liadan shoved a waterskin and a length of linen at him. He drank deeply, using the last of the water to swish his mouth out and spit over the side.

"Gods, I hate the sea," he said.

Positioning a sea-chest in front of him, Gyda sat and leaned forward on splayed knees. "If you're comfortable, *Lord*," she said. "We're all keen to hear this tale."

Ragnar pulled the cloth around his shoulders and shivered. "You really would have given me to Rán, wouldn't you?"

"I still might."

He nodded, his face green. "As I said, I have a delicate diplomatic charge. I took passage on your ship, as your destination and mine are the same."

"Really. And this did not warrant even the courtesy of a message?"

"It's a rather new development."

Gyda looked over her shoulder. "Does this sound like truth, Daughters?"

Several of the women shook their heads or scowled fiercely. Eir looked away, brow furrowing.

Gyda turned back and appraised the man. "Here I have a stowaway rat, covered in filth and blood. I'm still waiting for the explanation of this *delicate* matter."

He blanched under her glare. "I was robbed on the way here," he muttered. "The *bak-rauf* took my arm-rings, my sword, and my purse. I could not buy passage, so I hid on-board the night before you sailed, thinking that I would explain once you got underway. Only, there was the storm, and I slept through the morning." He shrugged.

"What sort of warrior loses their weapon?"

"One in a great hurry."

Gyda blew through her nose. His tale held truth, but his expression held something else. Something he could or would not share. The weave of this was yet to be untangled.

"You told me you had gold," she said, changing tack.

Ragnar's jaw clenched. He rose, and the pitch and roll of the ship made him stumble. The women broke apart to avoid being trampled.

Bending behind a stack of crates, He pulled out a small bundle wrapped in thick wool. As he unraveled it, a brief grimace crossed his face. Gyda took note of it before it smoothed away.

He cleared his throat. "I am also called Ragnar Goldmane."

Stepping out of the hold and back onto the deck, he raised the object high to catch the red rays of the sinking sun.

Every eye went to it like a bee to a flower, including Gyda's.

"That's a torq fit for the ancient kings," breathed Astrid.

"That isn't a torq," Guðrun replied, equally thunder-struck. "That's a Roman treasure, surely."

Ragnar lowered the gilded collar and fastened it around his neck, where it gleamed against his upper chest.

Like the mane of a lion, Gyda thought. She remembered the tales told around the hearth fire. Ishraq often shared elaborate stories of beasts from other parts of the world. His cousin Yusuf, a tall man who wore brightly dyed silks that made Gyda horribly envious, would add to these stories, embellishing them for the children who would shriek with terror and delight.

"That is a prize beyond worth," Gyda said, nodding at the large ornament. "I see why you are so named."

"It was a gift," Ragnar said, touching the hammered gold lightly. "From one I dearly loved. A treasure that means more than my arm-rings or my sword."

Gyda stood. "A gift, you say. And you would part with it? Just for passage on an old knarr crewed by forgotten women?"

Ragnar scowled. "I've heard of you, Gyda *Fiskvif*. Gyda the Grim, you are called in the streets of Dyflin. Leader of Rán's Daughters, the swiftest and most reliable cargo-runners. Also the most silver-struck."

Gyda hid her satisfaction. He had risen to her goading. Now to push a little more.

"What would you part with, then? Not this trinket, and certainly not the truth."

Ragnar's tongue scraped over his split lip. "I will not part with this treasure," he said slowly. "But I can give you something nearly as good from al-Andalus. Slaves, or perhaps even a treasure like mine."

"I doubt that."

He shifted, turning to face the horizon. "I know you sail to make the first delivery of the trade deal struck with the Emir of Córdoba. I am here to ensure the deal holds."

Blood rushed to Gyda's head. "That agreement is secret! How do you know of this?"

"I know because I am — *was* — the Emissary's bodyguard."

"Was?"

"Ishraq is dead," Ragnar said flatly. "Murdered. Your agreement with Abd al-Rahman is void."

Curses and gasps flew around the ship. With a cry, Gyda lunged at Ragnar with her seax at his throat. He stumbled, half-falling against the mast-step.

"You lie," she hissed. Her heart pounded. "That agreement was near impossible to forge. It took months of messages, a fortune in silver and goods. And more months of searching for an emissary willing to travel to Dyflin. Without Ishraq, there *is* no trade agreement."

Ragnar stared, his expression lifeless.

"The trip is a waste," Gyda whispered, the realization like a hammer strike.

Abd al-Rahman III was a powerful man, with immense wealth and influence. The news might have already reached his shores, carried by another ship leaving Dyflin before her. What would the Emir do when he learned of this offense? Would he burn *Sea-Wolf* when they reached port? Sell the Daughters as thralls? Kill them?

Gyda looked around her, into the faces of her women. Then she looked at him, at his torn and bloody clothing. At his bruises. At the fortune hanging around his neck. "*You* killed him," she said. "You stole this collar and now you're running away."

Something dark passed over Ragnar's face.

"Watch yourself, Gyda," he said. He stood, pressing back against the mast. Blond hair fell into his face. "Ishraq was killed two days ago." His voice thickened. "But not by me. It's true, I failed in my duty. I go to al-Andalus to salvage my honor and remake the agreement with the Emir."

"Your story *reeks* of falsehood." She pressed the seax closer and a red line appeared on his skin. "You're an oath-breaker. I should cut your throat and feed your corpse to the sharks. Or bring your head back to the Jarl. How would he reward me?" She grinned, all teeth. "With silks, or silver? Or maybe this trinket you wear so proudly."

He glared at her, eyes like flint. Before he could speak, Rúna called out from the tiller.

"Sail!" She leaned over the side and pointed north-west. Every eye turned to see a ship behind them, obscured by the red smear of the setting sun.

"Not Franks," Eir said. "We only just passed the coast of Cornwallum."

Ragnar had gone very still under Gyda's blade.

"Who are they, oath-breaker?" she hissed.

The muscles in his jaw bulged. "It's Helgi," he muttered. "He must be coming for me."

She frowned. "Helgi? No, he's in Jórvík with King Ragnall."

"Ragnall is dead, not a month past. Helgi returned soon after. Look closer at that sail."

Gyda pulled away and squinted. The ship was closing in fast. Across the billowing canvas, an image of two spears crossed over the head of a serpent caught the light.

"That is Helgi's device," she said. "The one he uses when he raids."

The Daughters tensed, fingers touching amulets or weapons. Ragnar saw his opportunity and heaved. Gyda stumbled, nearly losing her grip on the seax.

"Helgi is the oath-breaker," he cried, ripping the whaling spear from the mast and brandishing it. "I will not be given over to a straw-death at the hands of that coward."

The women drew their weapons, but Gyda stayed them with a hand. "Threaten my Daughters and I will rip your gut-rope through your throat and make you choke on it. That will be a straw-death worthy of a liar."

"I am no liar!" Sweat trickled down his face. "Just listen to me. I haven't told you everything. He is a *niðing* and a coward. He will kill all of us."

She paused. Helgi regulated the trade in Jórvík. With a reputation for bloodthirstiness and greed, his heavy taxing made it impossible for his merchants to make a profit. They never bought much from Gyda when she came to port, and so she disliked the man intensely.

Looking up at the sail above, Gyda reviewed her options. The sea-breeze filled the canvas. That sail had helped *Sea-Wolf* outrun other vessels more than once. Enemies and thieves were plentiful on the whale-road. Gyda kept her women well-armed. But in a sea-battle, when warriors made the shield-wall in the bellies of their dragonships and blood ran along the hulls like rivers, Ran's Daughters were too few to fight.

"What will we do, Gyda," asked Eir.

The Daughters watched her with fear on all their faces. Gyda cursed.

"Reef the sail, drop anchor, and bind him," she ordered.

The spear clattered to the deck and Ragnar held his hands out. "You're making a mistake. Please just let me explain."

"I heard enough," Gyda sneered. "Do it."

Ragnar's face crumpled as Astrid, sneaking up from behind, struck him over the head with a shieldboss taken from a crate. He fell unconscious to the deck.

"I don't like this," Eir said, staring at his prone form. "What if he speaks the truth?"

"We will know soon enough," Gyda said, turning back to Helgi's ship. "Pull out the good mead. We're hosting a Jarl's son."

Helgi slammed a fist against the snake-head prow of his ship, growling and spitting curses that curled Gyda's toes in her boots. She leaned against the strake, a cup of mead clenched in one hand.

To her right stood the Emissary's cousin Yusuf. Tall and dark-skinned, he wore his silks and finery with confidence. A sword hung at his hip, the sheath inlaid with ivory and gold. Gyda eyed him warily, but he had yet to speak, contenting himself to watch.

"Give the whoreson over, woman," Helgi growled. "You are sworn to Olavi, and I am his son."

"I am sworn to no man," she answered. "I serve because Olavi pays me. And because he protects me. Why should I listen to you?" She shrugged and drank.

Helgi was an ugly man, with a lean and callous face. His hair was unkempt, and his beard showed remnants of some recent feast. On his arm were three ill-fitting twists of polished silver, ornaments obviously not made for him. He also put off an aroma like the middens of Jórvík itself. He went on blustering, and she went on ignoring it.

The two ships were tethered together to keep from drifting with the current. Rán's Daughters sat on benches among Helgi's crew. Guðrun and Rúna huddled together, ignoring leering stares and comments from the men. Rúna held Guðrun's hand and traced her fingers over the skin. She whispered something, and Guðrun smiled. Liadan sat next to them, watching everyone with narrowed eyes and clenched fists. Astrid snarled at any who tried speaking with her.

Eir, however, had volunteered to stay with Ragnar on *Sea-Wolf*. There had been a set to her face, a stiffness in her shoulders. '*Hide him, Gyda. At least until we know what Helgi wants,*' she had said.

Gyda agreed with her. Better to wait and see what profit could be made.

Helgi talked until the moon rose. Gyda said little, happy to drink and swat his words away like midges on a fen. It wasn't until his boasts turned to threats that she listened.

"My crew is larger than yours," he said pompously. "Better armed. I should just take Ragnar and shove a sword in your belly. Then I'll torch *Sea-Wolf*. Or maybe I'll sell it and fill my coffers with the profit."

She considered his shit-eating grin. "If you did that, you'll have to explain to your father why his best chance for trade with the Emir in al-Andalus ended up drowned in Rán's hall."

Helgi's smile dropped and he flushed. "He chose *you*?"

She took a drink. "You might be his son, goat-turd," she said coolly. "But *I* am the one Olavi leans on to reach his ambitions. You're just the silver-grubbing merchant from Jórvík with no influence of your own."

Helgi spluttered. "I have influence!"

She gave him a placating smile. "I have no doubt."

The sly smirk returned to his face. "What about a trade? This posturing gets us nowhere. A trade could be a tidy way to earn back what you've lost to my merchants over the years."

Now there was a compelling idea. An icy wind whipped the reefed canvas, making Gyda shiver. They would need to untether the ships soon. She opened her mouth, but paused as her gaze fell on a glint of moonlight reflecting from Helgi's twisted silver.

*What about the Emissary?* she thought. That was the hair in the soup of all this. Ragnar knew something. He was Gyda's one bargaining chip, and she wasn't about to give him up.

"Tell me, Helgi," she said, hitching a hip against the strake. "Why do you want this rat so badly that you sailed this far to catch him? Why not try to outrun the news and get the agreement sealed yourself?"

Helgi choked and his face twisted. "I told my father the same. He was a fool to give it to you, *Fiskvif.*"

Yusuf made a noise in his throat.

She turned to him. "You haven't said a word in all this, Lord. The Emissary was your cousin."

Yusuf nodded, dark eyes glassy. "Ishraq was like my brother. His murder must not go unanswered. Your Jarl sent me to ensure Ragnar's capture."

"What proof is there of murder?"

Yusuf blinked. "Ragnar was found with the body. He was covered in blood."

"That is hardly proof."

"I am the one who found them," Helgi growled. "I gave Ragnar a good beating, but he got the better of me and ran like a hare from a hound."

Yusuf nodded. "We learned he hid on your ship only after you departed."

"Did he tell you he stole a fortune in gold?" Helgi added, a gleam in his eye. "I'd wager he kept *that* to himself. A thief as well as a murderer. But I'll get it back, by Thor."

Gyda's pulse jumped. Here was the missing thread, or the beginning of one.

"Ah, so this is about treasure!" She shook her head. "I should have known, Helgi. Do you even care about the trade deal? I bet Ragnar doesn't matter so long as you get your grubby hands on a bit of shine."

Yusuf turned an intent gaze on her, but before he could speak, Helgi stepped close to point a finger in her face.

"Give him up, or I will make certain you remember your place. You'll get nothing but scraps from my father's table. Then we'll see who gets grubby."

Gyda put a light touch to her seax on her waist. "Are you threatening me? That would be unwise."

Helgi scoffed.

"Tell me, is the collar safe?" Yusuf said, leaning forward. "Does Ragnar still have it?"

She nodded, and he sagged with relief.

"I was not informed of its theft." He cast a dark look at Helgi. "The collar is an heirloom, given to our family by the Emir's grandfather, Abdullah ibn Muhammad. It is precious."

"Ragnar told me it was a gift," Gyda said, tilting her head. "From someone he dearly loved. This tale twists like a snake. Nothing fits."

"A gift? Ishraq wouldn't have…" Yusuf cut himself off, brows rising. Then he flushed deeply. "Ah," he said softly. "I see."

Like a hammer strike, Gyda knew what Ragnar had tried to tell her.

She shifted to Helgi. Her mouth was dry as bone. "I think I'll keep this trinket. My payment for handing over your man."

Helgi shoved Yusuf aside to grab her. "You'll get nothing, woman!"

Her seax screeched from its sheath and he lurched back at the sight of steel.

Behind her, the Daughters also drew their weapons.

"Treachery!" cried Helgi.

"It's over, snake," Gyda declared. "Those are Ragnar's arm-rings you wear, and that is his sword on your hip. I wager that you killed Ishraq and framed him."

Yusuf drew his own sword, a cry of rage in his throat.

"Stop!" came a voice. Eir stepped onto the ship with Ragnar following behind her, his face like stone. He still wore the collar, and it reflected the light of the torches.

"Eir? What is this?" Gyda demanded.

"Lady," Eir answered, dipping her head. She carried an axe in one hand. "I told you I know this man. He has told me his tale and I know he speaks true." Her face was washed of color and tight with grief.

"Tell me," Gyda said, softening.

"My husband knew him," she began. "He and Bjarni swore their oaths to Olavi together ten years ago. They were shield brothers. They fought together, feasted at the same table. When Bjarni died, it was Ragnar who retrieved his axe from the battlefield and returned it to me." She held the weapon up. "Ragnar is an honorable man." She handed the axe to Ragnar. He took it, bowing.

"I accuse you, Helgi Olavisson, of murder," Ragnar said, voice heavy with anger.

Helgi scoffed. "This is ridiculous. I should cut out your tongue."

"You will let him speak," Yusuf commanded.

Ragnar nodded his thanks, then continued. "You murdered the Emissary and sought to pass blame. Ishraq told me you approached him with a bribe to turn the agreement to your own benefit. What son would steal from his own father?" He spat on the deck, then looked Helgi up and down, stopping at his hip and the blade hanging from it. "You also stole my arm-rings and my sword, you dung-rat. In the sight of the gods, I challenge you to *holmgang*."

Helgi's face split in a feral smile. "Make the square," he said.

—◄ ✳ ►—

As the moon reached its zenith, the platform was cleared and spears laid down. Gyda watched Ragnar circle Helgi like a wolf. All he had to do was shove Helgi over the boundary, and the fight would be forfeit.

She stood just off the platform. Her Daughters stood among the crewmen. Yusuf also watched nearby, mouth and brow drawn into a scowl.

Helgi wore a helmet and a shield, both decorated with twining serpents. He gripped Ragnar's stolen blade in a white-knuckled fist. Blood already dripped from a blow to his nose.

Ragnar bore no armor except for a shield. He also bled from fresh wounds.

"Kill him, Ragnar," a Daughter yelled.

"Come on, Helgi," cheered the men. Tension roiled across the ship like a wave.

With a cry, Ragnar rushed at Helgi, slamming against him with the shield boss. "You killed Ishraq," he growled, shoving hard. "And blamed me for it. You named me oath-breaker. Murderer. I name you *niðing*! Gutless and without honor."

Helgi snarled and pushed back, angling to get the sword under the rim. Spittle flew from his mouth.

Ragnar broke off, turning quickly to strike with his axe. It clanged off the boss, and he raised his own shield to block the returning strike. "Helgi killed Ishraq in his bed," he yelled, just as the sword took a chunk off the edge of his shield. "As he slept. Only a *niðing* kills a sleeping man!"

Helgi raged. They traded vicious blows, each of them a match for the other. The iron stink of blood and sweat filled the air.

Gyda's pulse raced as she watched. Ragnar was growing tired, slowing with each heavy strike.

"Finish him, Ragnar," she cried. "Kill the pig-shit!"

Helgi roared as Ragnar's axe caught and sheared a large chunk from his shield, leaving it in splinters. Stumbling, he cursed and threw the shield away. He held up a hand to signal for a breather.

Ragnar dropped his shield also but kept his axe ready. "Ishraq refused Helgi's bribes and threats. Yusuf, you heard them arguing late into the night, in the hall. Ishraq feared for his life."

"I heard it, Ragnar," Yusuf said. "But you were still found with his blood soaking your tunic. And you wear my family's gold around your neck."

Ragnar whirled to face him, face red and sweat-streaked. "I *loved* Ishraq! He was everything to me." His hand, caked with dirt and blood, strayed to the gold collar. "He gave this to me as he died in my arms. I must return it to the Emir, to prove Olavi's good faith."

Gyda's eyes went past Ragnar, to a gleam of silver just behind him. "Watch yourself!"

"Die, you son of a whore!" Helgi spat. "When your corpse is cold, I will take that collar and melt it into a buckle for my new sword belt."

Helgi struck Ragnar in the side with a knife. With a hoarse cry, Ragnar stumbled and slammed to the deck. Blood stained the planking. Helgi was on him instantly, flipping him over to press the knife against his throat.

"Worthless dog!" Gyda threw herself forward. She hauled Helgi off and threw him across the deck.

Yusuf joined Gyda and drew his blade. It gleamed with reflected torch fire.

"There can be no denial now, Helgi," Yusuf said. "The Great Emir, may the stars shine on him, will hear of this treachery."

"To me!" he cried to his crew. "Fight them!"

They did nothing, refusing to answer the call of a cowardly leader. Gyda grinned.

Helgi's face changed to a rictus of fear. He backed away, feet hitting Eir's fallen axe. He snatched it, holding it and the bloodied knife out before him.

"Traitorous bitch," he bellowed at Gyda. "I'll burn *Sea-Wolf* and steal your cargo. I'll take it and make the delivery myself. The trade is mine! The *glory* is mine!"

Ragnar limped forward to stand on Gyda's other side. He held a hand against his wound, which oozed slowly through his fingers.

"Did you think I had no friends among the other oath-men, Helgi?" he wheezed. "They know I travel to al-Andalus. I will pay Ishraq's blood-price and throw myself on the mercy of the Emir. My friends will tell your father of it. And of how you seek to supplant him. Jórvík will outlaw you. There will be nothing left for you but dishonor and the fame of a coward."

Helgi launched himself at Ragnar, a scream in his mouth and the axe held high overhead for a killing blow.

Gyda lunged, stepping in front of Ragnar as she buried her seax in the man's guts.

The axe fell with a thump to the deck, and for a moment, Helgi stood still as stone, pressing his hands against the pulsing blood. He gaped, taking a step forward, then another. He fell, striking the strake. Then, he toppled over without a word or even a splash to mark his passing.

Ragnar, Gyda, and Yusuf rushed to the side and looked into the black depths, but he was gone.

"Rán received her sacrifice after all," Gyda said.

"He was a coward to the last," Ragnar said. He tilted his head with a grimace. "And a thief! The bastard still had my arm-rings and purse."

"You have your sword," Yusuf told him, putting a hand on his shoulder. "And now your honor as well."

"I would trade it all for Ishraq," was all Ragnar answered.

—❖—

Gyda stood at the prow of *Sea-Wolf*, watching the sun rise. Behind her, Rán's Daughters drank and laughed among the benches. Eir sang with her clear, high voice. Gyda smiled. It was good to have joy return to the ship.

Helgi's serpent vessel sailed ahead of them, an intimidating escort with Yusuf in command.

Ragnar came to stand beside her. "Thank you, Gyda." He bowed, wincing as his bandaged wound pulled. "You saved my life. And in doing so you saved my honor." The gold collar flashed in the sunlight as he moved.

"I saved this trade deal," she grunted. "See to it that it holds."

He nodded. "I don't know what fate al-Andalus holds for me. Or if the Emir will be merciful. But at least I can pay the debt and give Ishraq's family some peace. That is enough to hope for."

"You should know I would have taken that ornament from your neck if I'd had the pleasure of lopping off your head," she said.

Ragnar laughed. "You would have, wouldn't you? I'm happy you didn't get that opportunity."

They fell silent for a moment.

"Where will you go," Ragnar asked eventually. "Olavi won't have you now you've killed his son."

She drew a heavy breath. "Iceland, probably. I hear there's plenty of land, and settlers. Merchants I can sell to."

He cocked his head, a strange expression passing over his face. "Will you do me a favor?"

"What?"

"Return to al-Andalus in a twelve-month," he said. "If I am alive, I will pay you an obscene amount of silver to take me with you."

She scowled. "To Iceland? What about your oath to Olavi?"

Ragnar looked down at his hands. "Olavi released me. I was going to tell Ishraq the news. Ask him to go with me to Iceland. But then I...it was too late."

She regarded him a moment, then nodded. "If we both live in a twelve-month, I will take you with me."

He sagged in relief. "Grim you might be, and silver-struck, but you are fair, Gyda *Fiskvif.*"

"I will bring you to Iceland...but not for less than your own weight in silver."

His mouth dropped open, and she grinned.

A warm breeze pushed them on, and overhead, white clouds drifted across the dawn sky, promising a day of fine sailing.

# — EXILES —
## Shanon Sinn

*Geir the Young*

My parents met on a raid. My grandfather had just enough warriors to work the oars of our longship, so he was happy when three exiles at the trading post asked to join their crew. They were my mother Thora, and her younger brothers—my uncles—Ismar and Hakon.

Legend has it, my mother chopped the hand off of a petty lord in Norway trying to bed her. My uncles eventually fled the country with her, but not before fighting had cost them two older brothers, their parents, and several nephews and nieces—likely sold into slavery. It was a blood feud unlike any other, uncontainable even by King Finehair. Scores of people were killed on both sides. Rarely in pitched battle. No one would commit to that.

My grandfather's raid was a means for my mother and uncles to raise funds before returning to Norway. Instead, it ended with her carrying my older sister Aesa. A couple of years later, my sister Seala was born. My parents finally had a son—me, Geir—fifteen years ago.

My uncles Ismar and Hakon also started families. The influx of new members into our clan prevented our line from becoming inbred and dying out. My aunts—my father's sisters—had married common enough men, but he was the male heir of our village and had been forced to remain alone. The other chieftains would not allow my father to marry one of their daughters. They loathed us that much.

It was hypocrisy, as the other chiefs had been exiles as well. Fleeing the wrath of King Harald Finehair when he became high chief of Norway and began settling old scores. But our family had come to Iceland later and we were fewer in number. Worst of all, we had settled the land in Sea Dragon's Fjord, a village site no one had considered at all before we did.

Our farmland is sparse and close to shore, hidden in the shadows of the mountains of barefaced cliff rock and windswept vegetation. The fields quickly give way to stands of birch trees rooted in groves around large boulders and boggy pockets of marshy water. Near where the waterfall emerges, from the cracks in the cliff, are the ruins of long dead Celtic priests. Their graves beneath mounds beside a crumbling rock and earthen wall. Apple trees—of all things—are rooted there. For that we are grateful.

We do not harvest the apples without giving thanks and an offering. They say my grandfather's younger brother once did. He was attacked by a wraith with a grinning skull for a face and a long flowing black robe. Others—mostly children—have seen the ghost since. So we give offerings to appease the spirits that reside near the cliff and around the grove before we take anything. The birch trees are given similar respect. We import our lumber and only use the wood around our village sparingly. In contrast, our neighbours have cut clear all of their trees. We will never do the same.

I have not seen the skull-faced ghost myself, but I have been asked at the trading post about the black spirits at the priest house and the dragon that lives in our fjord who sometimes rises and spews out hellish fire.

Truthfully, no one has seen the dragon since before our arrival, but we know it still resides in the fjord, as steam sometimes rises and breaks the surface of the water; seen more often in winter. My mother believes it's a female dragon, but she says it is only her intuition that tells her so, and its faint voice she sometimes hears.

My grandfather used the stories of our cursed land as an advantage, choosing the serpent's image for our shield and sail. Our colors became the yellow of the sea dragon's eyes and black in honor of the ghosts who reside amongst us.

We appease the sea serpent with gifts and song. In exchange, it has never attacked us. Our walrus and whale hunts go unhindered and our enemies leave us alone. Its presence is enough to keep most of them away.

My grandfather was killed during the voyage my parents met on. Our family was nothing more than a mercenary ship from Iceland supporting the Dane's attack on Chartres, unlucky enough to have been caught in a vicious trap and pulled away from the main fleet. The other ships raced by, on their way to attack, as our crew beached the burning vessel and leapt ashore to fight.

He stood surrounded by Franks, killing half a dozen of them before the arrows and dogs took him down. My mother and Uncle Hakon carved viciously into the surviving defenders. She took an arrow in her left leg during the worst of it. My uncle lost the use of his right eye. All while our longship burned hatefully, only a few feet from shore.

My father went berserk that day. Wielding a large battle-axe, he led a counterattack into the right flank of the ambushing Franks.

Their line crumbled and finally fell. My father's axe now hangs behind his chair in our earthen-walled longhouse, notches carved all along its shaft. We will speak to it sometimes.

The remaining warriors of my grandfather's longship moved overland and joined the Dane survivors being mustered by Rollo, who was the leader of the attack. There was a fierce fight, strategy involving sheep corpses to unnerve the Frank's cavalry, and then a sudden end to the killing. Rollo made peace with the Franks that day. Some say he even changed sides.

Only seven survivors returned to our village, including my father, mother, and two uncles. The expedition had been a cataclysmic failure. There was almost no plunder other than what was stripped from the dead. Worst of all, we had lost our only longship. They had been lucky to make their way back home at all. Our dead, including my grandfather and his younger brother, were burned in mass-bodied pyres with all of the other casualties, interned with just enough ceremony to prevent further bloodshed.

When my mother tells me these stories, eyes sharp and deadly as an eagle's, I sometimes sense that these battles—both those of the raid and all of the fights they had been in in Norway—were not as glorious as she tries to make them sound. There is loss in her voice. A tiredness that suggests regret. I wonder how my grandfather especially—our chieftain—had found himself alone that day and surrounded by enemies. Perhaps, he had wanted entrance into Valhalla. Or maybe, he could not live with the shame of losing our only war boat. Who am I, though, to question the stories of our elders? I was only there in spirit. And for that, I can sometimes see the details so vividly I recognize my grandfather's silhouette lying amongst the dead.

Our survivors had been granted some of the Frankish weapons and armor they had stripped off of their enemies. This turned out to be a good thing, as our neighbors failed to understand how such fine arms had been acquired. Their eyes gleamed with envy and confusion, even as they noted the absence of our ship. Our number of capable fighters had lessened, of course, but our reputation amongst the other villages of being dangerous had only intensified. No one had ever seen my mother or uncles before they returned either, and spies would have noticed the marriage celebration that followed soon after. All of this begged to question whether or not a powerful new alliance had been formed with a foreign village.

During the marriage ceremonies conducted by my grandmother, a large wooden pole was erected near our shore. The upper part had been carved into a roaring Sea Dragon, which faced out to sea. The lower portion of the pole was a wood-hewn stack of bare-smiling skulls, piled one on top of the other.

For the following two decades, along with carefully managed assets and meager crop yields, our village's source of sustenance shifted from plunder to ivory. This granted us everything we needed. But things started to change.

The walrus was already becoming harder to find when my father and his hunting group failed to return one day. My uncles Ismar and Hakon had been hunting in another boat to the South of the village before they too were pursued, all the way back to Sea Dragon's Fjord by two unmarked vessels. No colors had been visible. For such daring, one could only assume other war veterans were in those boats and that they were armed to the teeth. Of course, all three vessels were too small and slow to engage in a proper naval battle.

In the council that immediately followed the two neighboring chieftains' visit, my mother said she believed a longship destroyed my father's smaller vessel. If this is true, he did not die in battle.

The chieftains Hlod the Blind and Odd the Elder came late the following day wrapped in rare furs and finely embroidered cloaks.

As the two most powerful chieftains in the area, choosing to stand side by side could only mean a deal for ownership of our village had already been made between them.

My mother sat coolly in my father's chair wearing the armor she had acquired at Chartres. Her bare Frankish sword leaned against her hand rest. Her hair was pinned up wildly in many directions and there was dark makeup surrounding her eyes. Her aging beauty was marred only by the scars across her face.

My sisters Aesa and Seala stood to each side of her as spear-leaning sentinels, shields up, helmets down, suggesting they were personal guards and not who they really were. The rest of us stood around the room, eyes filled with murder. Our blades were sheathed, but our shields were hidden along the walls behind us.

The visiting chieftains were not offered the courtesy of a feast or drink. A dozen armored men stood behind them grasping the handles of their weapons. They had come ashore in two fishing boats. A longship and two more fishing vessels hovered nearby offshore. We could see the shadows of many people and the occasional glimmer of steel in the fading light. With enemies inside our hall and more along our shore it was clear an ultimatum was about to be given.

"There is to be a great meeting of the chieftains," Hlod the Blind said, his milky eyes scanning the general direction of my mother, "and you are to swear fealty to one of us so we can speak on behalf of our whole region."

My mother waited a long moment before she replied. "I find it strange Hlod," his name sounded almost like a curse, "that you are not asking to address my husband."

"Of course, Thora," Odd the Elder said, "can you please summon Chief Gali, so that we may address him?"

"He is out hunting at the moment," my Mother answered, stone faced.

"Which is why we are speaking with you," Odd replied. "There is no time to waste." His eyes were flat and emotionless, as if he did not care my mother knew they had murdered my father.

"We will not be swearing fealty to you this night," my mother answered, "for it is not my decision alone to make."

This was not the Thora I had heard stories of. I would have thought blood would have been spilled by now. She had decided, it appeared, that we could not afford to lose more of our people. Perhaps, she second-guessed the consequences of her hotheaded-ness in Norway all of those years before. Judging by the exchange of words taking place, I could only assume the chieftains were hesitant to sacrifice their warriors, as well. Even in defeat, we would kill many.

It was Hlod who replied. "The rules for the gathering are simple; at least for the first year. Women are not allowed to speak or cast votes. You should know, that I, for one, find this regulation quite preposterous."

If he were not blind, he would have taken a step back from my mother's answering glare.

"We will escort your boat loaded with the summer's trading goods to port for no fee," Odd said, "being that we are aligned in purpose now. Hlod and I will speak on behalf of all of our villages. The others have already agreed. And, to celebrate this final new alliance, your daughters will be found husbands from amongst the free men." His eyes glanced towards my sisters, clearly recognizing who they really were.

Seala does not beat me in training as often as Aesa does, but she is the most fiery of the two. More as my mother once was, I imagine. My parents had often spoken about what they should do with my aging unwed sisters as almost all our village was—once again—too closely related for marriage. But anything less than a chieftain's son was a brutal insult. History, it seemed, was doomed to repeat itself. Seala tipped her helmet up and spit at Odd's feet.

She slowly pulled her helmet back down. A heavy silence hung in the room.

"When is this gathering set to take place?" my mother asked, a bit too casually.

"It begins in two weeks time—Midsummer—but it is expected to last for just as long," Hlod the Blind said. "It will be boring, to be sure. You will be spared old men talking and going on and on about the merits of unification and the new rules proposed for all."

"I would very much like to be spared old men going on and on," my mother said, pausing only long enough for the two chieftains to believe she had answered in their favor. "But alas, we must consult our elders before making such a decision. I do not think it is a secret, that we are pious in our obligations to the gods and to their emissaries who protect us."

The two older men had been stunned into silence. Looking at the faces of our enemies, every last one of them a man, I could see fear in their eyes.

"We will give you our answer in one week's time," my mother added.

Hlod the Blind's mouth opened in disbelief. Odd just scowled.

"As promised," Odd said, "we will escort your goods to the trading post. Our boats will be waiting for your answer at the mouth of the fjord."

"So be it," my mother said.

"So be it," the two chieftains replied, almost in unison.

Our council was swift and our preparations were swifter. It was almost as if my mother had come up with the plan before the chieftains had even returned to their boats. Their five craft cut through the water beneath the pale orange glow of the crescent moon. They did not stop to give offerings to the serpent or make music for her.

In their unification against us, our enemies had finally become that bold.

We had to assume there were eyes watching us. Everything needed to look normal. We could not attack our enemies directly, especially with only one remaining boat. We could not abandon the village to raid theirs either—even if overland travel could be achieved in less than a day—knowing the second chieftain could simply take our land by force with none of our warriors left to protect it.

Every one of us needed to prepare for a fight to the death. That meant the women who had trained their whole lives like my sisters Aesa and Seala. It most certainly meant my uncles, and my father's sisters' husbands, and my cousins, and the tenant farmers. It meant the slaves needed to be ready to fight and die, as well. It was why we had trained harder than any of our neighbors. We would always be outcasts to them, the people who would need to be dealt with sooner or later, once and for all.

It was inconceivable to the other chieftains we would not bring our goods by boat to trade. Perhaps, they knew this was the year we hoped to acquire a new longship for raiding.

Our neighbors would likely know that the cliff face up to the plateau behind our village was treacherous. Overland travel was preposterous, really, as we didn't even have horses. If we did, they would have needed to be stabled so far away from us as to make feeding them near impossible.

My mother's plan was simple, though. Before daybreak, three of us would scale the cliff and travel overland towards the gathering site in order to represent our village. She guessed the meeting was taking place somewhere near the trading post, if the chieftains offering to escort our cargo was any indication.

It was imperative, my mother said—and my uncles agreed—that we be seen and heard at the gathering or our legitimacy would forever be in question. We would each bring a tusk for trade, food for the journey, my father's cloak cleanly wrapped, some bone-carved jewelry, and weapons to kill any sentries who might be blocking our way. We would not be wearing armor.

My mother, one-time queen of ambush warfare, veteran of Chartres and two smaller raids as a mercenary since, would lead the way. Her and I would carry the Frankish swords and shields bearing our sea dragon crest. Draugsi, whose name means "Little Ghost," would accompany us with his bow and those two murderous blades of his. We would travel overland as far away from the most likely anticipated path as possible, in an attempt to make it to the gathering before it began. And when it was time for our village to speak, it would be me, during my fifteenth summer, who would speak on behalf of my people.

I had climbed the cliff often enough as a child, but never with such weight upon my back. We chose the cliff point we called The Ladder near the waterfall by the ruins. It was the easiest path, and the rushing water would make hearing us difficult if anyone was waiting above. Draugsi went first, followed by my mother and then me. It was a steep twenty-minute climb to the water pool. After that, there was another hour of scrambling and bent over hiking. The path twisted away from the village, so that there was no view of the fjord unless we were to go out of our way to find one. As dawn started to break, we found a hollow we could sleep in.

As difficult as it would be, we would only travel during the darkness of the short night and while the lengthy shadows of dusk and dawn crept lazily upon the ground. There are said to be nocturnal trolls in the mountains—and worse; but our primary enemy would need a clear view to see us travelling overland. We had no choice but to gamble on a possible encounter with monsters. The open plateau and wide valleys were our primary concern. Without forests, we would be easy to spot at a great distance. And the summer nights were too short for us to travel during absolute darkness alone.

Draugsi scouted the area, returning just as dawn was breaking. He crept low to the ground and slid into the hollow we were hiding in. He claimed to have seen nothing, not even the presence of trolls.

We took turns sleeping throughout the day, barely speaking. When it grew dark, we began to travel across the plateau as close to the far right ridge as possible, led by Draugsi.

My grandfather had purchased Draugsi as a slave when the man was in his early twenties. His brown skin marked him a man of Serkland, a far-off and foreign land where the sun scorched the earth. We later learned he had once been a bandit in a desert kingdom. Being pursued after his companions were killed, he had intended to hide amongst some slaves until the search ended. I heard the older men tease him when they were drinking sometimes. It would have been a perfect plan, they said, if only Draugsi hadn't been loaded onto a ship whose final destination was Iceland.

My grandfather rarely bought slaves. What need did he have for a frail looking shifty-eyed foreigner who didn't understand our tongue? It must have been his intuition, my father once told me. Either that, or my grandfather recognized a fellow exile when he saw one. Almost thirty years later, the former slave was now in his fifties.

Draugsi had always been treated fair enough—for a slave. He learned our language at the same time as he was given more and more privileges. I have been told that there was always a quiet companionship between him and my grandfather, as if they shared an understanding of life that words could not convey. Draugsi fell in with a female slave and finally found a home at Sea Dragon's Fjord that he never would have been allowed before.

No one treated Draugsi as a slave or asked him to perform the duties of one, because he worked tirelessly in the fields without being asked. As an expert archer, he had been left behind during the raid on Chartres as one of the defenders of the village. The task he excelled at most, however, was when he was sent out to spy on a neighbor's village. He knew the lands surrounding our fjord like no one else did.

It was ten days of arduous travel before we saw our first enemy. We could not continue forward without dispatching him. The man—who Draugsi identified as one of Hlod the Blind's men—appeared alone, as unlikely as that was.

The elevated site offered a wide view of the valley—the direction from which we had come. Our fire at night would have been seen from a great distance, even if we hadn't already been spotted during the day. By walking near the elevated ground in the fading light, we had travelled directly towards him without being seen.

The pool beside him was fed by a small waterfall that fell some thirty feet or more from above. Across the small pocket of water, the stream cascaded into another waterfall that fell a great distance below, disappearing into the shadows. The sound of rushing water would conceal any noise we would make.

The man looked drunk. Every so often, he would get up and piss in the pool and laugh so loud we could hear it even over the falling water. It was an affront to the water spirit unlike anything I had ever seen.

"He is mine," my mother said. Her eyes were still surrounded by the dark paint and her face was covered in dirt from travelling, making her even less visible in the darkness. Draugsi nodded. I wanted to kill my first enemy, but even I could see some careful timing and stealth would be involved. My mother seemed intent on feeding the water spirit.

The next time the man stood to piss, she closed the gap in wide bounds, agile without the weight of her pack or shield. She punched a hole through his back with her sword, which erupted out of his chest, cascading blood into the pool of water. She pulled her blade out as the man fell to his knees. Before he could pitch forward, she hacked off his head.

She must have made more noise than we had realized. Draugsi was up and scrambling across the rocks with an arrow notched in his bow as three or more men came around the side of the rock—a place away from our line of sight. I followed quickly with my sword in hand; confident I was about to kill my first man.

Several things happened almost simultaneously. My mother knelt reverently and pushed the body into the water, clearly in ritual—as if the man had been a sacred sacrifice. The three men stopped dead in their tracks with open mouths and widening eyes. Then, the northern lights began to dance across the sky. I do not recall seeing such a thing so close to Midsummer before. My mother held her sword up to the heavens and beamed a smile towards the gods.

I am not sure why Draugsi did not fire his arrow, as we were evenly matched in numbers. He sometimes interprets the gods in his foreign ways and must have had a reason to hesitate.

Up close now, I could see the men were unsure of what to do. They looked thin and their clothes were dirty. The one in the lead held up his hand in a gesture to calm everyone down and tucked his axe into his belt. The two men behind him did the same.

"Who are you?" my mother asked. She was standing once more.

"I am Rig," the man said. "This is Lenni and Horik. The man you pushed over the falls was named Ivar."

"What are you doing here Rig?" my mother asked. Draugsi and I had not yet lowered our weapons.

"We were told to keep watch for travelers from Sea Dragon Fjord. That if we spotted any, we were to inform the camp down below so the men could prepare."

"Are you Hlod's men?" she asked, sensing otherwise.

"No, Lady, we were banished from the trading port. We have no food and there is no game here. We made camp and were trying to decide what to do next."

I did not recognize his accent then, but I would learn later they were Danes who had been abandoned at port after being accused of stealing their ship captain's mead. *It's simply not true*, Rig would swear to us over and over again. The traders had chased the three men away, telling them if they returned they would be executed as thieves. The Danes had wandered for almost a week with no real food before they were recruited by Hlod's men.

"Ivar and the others arrived several days ago," he continued, "and told us if we supported them we would be fed and given a coin or two each. If we refused, they were going to execute us."

My mother looked at the men for a long moment, appraising them with her cold, hard eyes.

"You are Thora!" Horik, the oldest of them said, breaking the silence. "The shield maiden at Chartres!"

"Yes," my mother answered. "And I would like to make you a far better offer than the one you have previously been given."

There would be six of us against more than a dozen. Two of us had shields. One of us had a bow. Most importantly, the three Danes were thought to be allies. We would also have the element of surprise. Truth be told, the fools should have started arming themselves as soon as the lights began to dance across the night sky.

They had come in numbers thinking we would also be a large party of travelers—if we came at all. Ivar had been put on night watch as he was annoying everyone with his drunkenness. The outcasts had been sent with him, so that no one would have to look at their pitiful pleading faces while food was being shared amongst them.

There was a cliff face that hid the camp from anyone coming from our fjord's direction. Several tents had been set up along the wall and a small fire was burning much too brightly. The Danes claimed their leader was a man that the others called the Ox. He was said to be descended from giants.

Hlod's men thought they could stop us by simply being there, showing themselves in the distance. It was doubted we would come at all. There had been betting and wagers made amongst them. They had a few horses. A rider would be dispatched, the Danes said, if anyone was spotted. The group would slowly back away from us until reinforcements arrived—just to be safe. It was inconceivable we could get so close without anyone having noticed, let alone for us to launch an attack.

My father taught me war craft: never underestimate the enemy; always use the element of surprise in some way, no matter how small; train harder than your foes; conquer fear; be more flexible than your best laid plans. There are many more of his sayings, but these were the ones that came to me as we prepared for the assault.

The first warrior I cleaved had not had time to arm himself. The rest mustered far too quickly. We had crept close to the camp an hour before full light but an alert sentry called the alarm.

The man the Danes called the Ox took out my mother near the beginning of the fight. Lenni hacked at him from behind until they both fell down. Horik, a veteran himself, sewed chaos amongst the rising men with his ax while Rig mimicked him nearby. Draugsi fired arrows from the shadows of the cliff.

Two more strides into the camp and a young man's head hovered as his knees dropped below him. A spear thrust across my shield from another warrior. A backhand of the Frankish blade caused a third to lean away from me. My shield smashed into the spearmen and sent him sprawling. Two axe wielding men rushed towards me shouting to Thor. An arrow in the back of one of them. The second's axe numbing my arm through the wood of my shield.

I pulled to the left instinctively, as the warrior I'd missed came in from my right. My sword slid up the length of his spear and cut his fingers. The axe hammered against my shield once more and pushed me to one knee. There was no time to be afraid. Only a moment of butterflies before the chaos of war.

More men poured towards me. A throat coughed blood. The hurt spearman screaming behind me; not yet a conquered threat. Rig drove into them from the left, yelling and causing confusion. I severed the dying man's leg beneath him, as I rose, taking advantage of a second man's half turned position. My blade went into his side deeper than I intended. Grateful it came free at all. Another warrior running away from me—an arrow throwing him back into the fire. And then, silence. Eerie silence. Except for the moaning of the wounded and the sound of my own breath.

"See to your mother!" Horik yelled, as he and Rig began to dispatch the wounded. The sound of steel on steel rang abruptly and fell silent. Someone retreating had run into Draugsi.

At first, I thought she was dead. I ran to her side, still hyper alert from the battle, yet numb from our forced march and not having had time to mourn my father. There would be time enough later to mourn the dead.

The Ox had smashed her with his shield and sent the much smaller woman flying backwards. Her shoulder had been dislocated and she had been knocked senseless. If Lenni had not sacrificed himself, she would have been dead.

She was barely coherent when I set the shoulder back in place. I was trying to make her comfortable when Drausgi arrived. Behind him, I saw Rig and Horik kneeling beside Lenni. Telling his spirit to save a place for them in Valhalla.

I had never seen anyone touch my mother so intimately before that moment, other than my father. Draugsi's hands went up and down her body. I could barely pay attention. But he explained to me he was searching for hidden wounds and broken bones. He was teaching me how to treat the wounded.

"Unless her mind has been broken," he finally said—with his heavy accent. "I believe she will live."

We rested well into the next day. I had never seen my mother look so weak and it terrified me. She and my father had seemed invincible less than a month before. Now, he was dead and it was no longer Thora the shield maiden resting in front of me. Perhaps, she would never be that woman again.

A grey fox with a white face circled the camp without fear. *Looking for meat scraps*, Draugsi said. The rest of us knew, however, the fox was waiting to see if he would carry my mother's ghost to the Valkyries. Slowly, the ravens arrived. They were much more cautious. Waiting patiently on rock ledges. Making no noise at all.

My mother had trouble speaking at first, but when she began to sit up half a day later her words were as clear as ever. As soon as she caught her breath, she told us, we would set off once more. We would honor our promises to the Danes and they would join us. We would come back and retrieve Lenni's temporarily buried body for a proper pyre once all of this was over. We would not strip anything easily identifiable from the dead and we would leave their horses pegged in the grass, hopefully to be discovered before they starved. The story we would tell anyone who asked was that we had arrived by boat, having travelled along the shore at night.

Of course, no one would believe such a story, especially as many saw us approaching the gathering site from the East by foot, not from the direction of the trading post. Other travelers had told us we could journey with them when they discovered we were heading to the same place. Two chieftains we had never met before, with their entourages of warriors and servants and slaves. Though they themselves travelled by horse, they could only move as fast as their slowest party members on foot.

We had washed in the stream beneath the waterfall. There was no sign of Ivar's body. The Danes would carry our two crested shields and spears they had taken from the dead. Even if someone recognized the men as two of the three outcasts sent away from the trading port, their new allegiance to us would be obvious to anyone who saw them. They were soldiers of Sea Dragon Fjord now. Here to protect their young chieftain and the near legendary warrior Thora, who was that chieftain's mother and advisor. Those same strangers could never have guessed that my mother's cloak had recently been stripped from a dead man. Or that our dark skinned servant was much more important than he at first appeared.

Odd and Hlod had beaten us there by boat. Odd's eyes were wide in disbelief, even though they must have suspected something was wrong when their ultimatum was refused at the end of the week, when they would have learned my mother was absent. Odd leaned towards Hlod and whispered. The blind man's eyes struggled to make out the sight passing in front of them. *A small group from Sea Dragon's Fjord,* Odd most likely whispered, *travelling with other chieftains no less.*

I was tempted to give the men a wink but wanted them to think I was of no consequence due to my age, at least at first.

"What is your name?" another chieftain asked me. I was wearing my father's finest cloak—black with accents of yellow. My mother would no longer be the first of us to speak when we were addressed. Even if it turned out a woman having no voice in the Althingi was a lie.

"Geir," I told them. Then for good measure, so they would not know if I should be taken seriously, I added, "Geir the Young."

My father's distant voice had spoken to me across the wind in the faintest of whispers: *War craft and cunning will be needed Son,* he had said, *in the days and weeks to come.*

I knew I stood in the presence of his killers and I swore an oath to the gods that we would destroy them all.

# — A CLASH IN KAUPANG —
## Eric Schumacher

*Hakon the Fat*

**K**aupang, Norway, AD 930

"Kaupang ahead!" shouted Gorm from the foredeck of the *Fara Happ*, a trading vessel whose name meant travel with fortune.

At the steer board, Sten wiped the soggy strands of red hair from his eyes and craned his neck to see past the mast. They had just rounded the headland that guarded the entrance to a small fjord and approached under oar, giving the shore a wide berth to avoid submerged boulders. On the port shore in the distance lay the scattered quays and tents and shacks of the North's largest trading town. It was known as Kaupang, which in the northern tongue meant marketplace. It was not a very original name, but as long as the trading was good, the whores frisky, and the ale strong, Sten cared little what people called it.

His eyes turned briefly to his crew. Fourteen men in all, ranging from an orphan of sixteen winters named Arne to the gray-bearded Gorm, whose skin was as grooved as the bark of an old oak. Most were from his native fylke of Halogaland, a wild and cold land far to the North, though some came from other, gentler climes. Good men all, who shared Sten's love of the sea and the adventures it offered. But tough men, too, for whether trader or raider, one did not survive long on the whale-road without a sharp blade and a willingness to use it.

"Put your backs into it, men!" Sten called over the cry of gulls. "Ale awaits!"

The men cheered and pulled *Fara Happ* through the silty waters until she lay broadside to the town. Numerous smaller skiffs littered the beach, while several large vessels rested against the wooden quays. He did not recognize them and that was good. Different ships from different lands meant different goods to trade, and that profited everyone. They needed profit—it had been a slow summer of trading for Sten and his men.

"This is the last stop before we head home. Let us make it worth our while." Sten pointed to an empty spot and commanded his men to row to it.

"Ho!" called a warrior from the beach as *Fara Happ's* hull bit into the soft dark mud. The afternoon sun glimmered on the man's byrnie and helm as he approached, though it was his rich cloak and sword that caught Sten's attention. Behind the man marched five other spearmen.

"Look at you!" called Sten to the warrior. "You must have slain Fafnir himself to have earned such finery, Bjarni." For over ten summers, Sten had seen the young warrior parading around Kaupang with the port master, Horik, whose job it was to keep a tally of items coming into and flowing out of Kaupang. The king in these parts was called Bjorn the Chapman, or the Trader, and he was ardent about the taxes he collected in his market. Now, it seemed, Bjarni had been promoted to that role, which was a good thing. He was a fair man, unlike Horik, who fleeced merchants at every turn.

Bjarni grinned behind the nose plate of his helmet. "If I had, do you think I would boast about it, seeing how Sigurd already killed the dragon?"

Sten barked a laugh as he walked toward the prow. "A fair point, Bjarni. So what then? Where is the old toad, Horik?"

Bjarni did not smile at Sten"s characterization. "Old Horik has retired."

"Well, well," replied Sten as he leaped from his ship and sunk to his ankles in the wet sand. "Bjarni the Port Master, then. It has a good ring to it." Sten turned to his men. "Gorm. Grab some others and tie her up." He then turned back to Bjarni. "It is well deserved, Bjarni."

"Thank you, my friend. But if you think flattery will exempt you from port fees, think again."

Sten frowned.

A crooked grin angled across Bjarni's broad face. "You know the rules. A silver coin for your ship. A tenth of your profits upon departure."

Sten's frown stretched, pulling his red mustache down with it. "Robbery," he grumbled as he reached into his purse and produced a coin, which he dropped into Bjarni's waiting hand.

Bjarni's eyebrows shot upward. "A dirham. Been on the East Way, I see," Bjarni commented as he inspected the coin. Unlike many of the coins minted in the West that displayed kings and Latin words, the silver dirhams were covered by the foreign language of Islam.

"Nah. Not me. Got it from a Danish trader in Hedeby for some soapstone cooking pots. Seeing more and more of those lately."

Bjarni dropped it into his purse. "Well, the markets are closed now, sadly. They'll open again in the morning. But I hear the ale is good at Gunnar's tent. There's a trader inside in rare spirits, so mayhap there's a free cup in it for you and your crew." He thumbed over his shoulder at a large tent farther down the beach. As if on cue, a distant cheer erupted from the structure.

"Thanks for the tip," Sten said, then turned to Gorm. "Stay here with the port-side crew and help Bjarni take stock of the ship. Make sure he does not overcount." He winked at Bjarni.

Gorm's old face collapsed. On the deck, the fortunate few cheered and teased their mates, then hopped down onto the beach.

"Fear not, Gorm," called Sten to his man. "I will send some ale, food, and women. But—"

Gorm cut off his leader. "Yah, yah. I know. Do not drink overmuch."

Sten smiled. He had trained his men well. "We will not stay overlong."

Sten and his retinue wove their way down the beach. To their right, fifty paces inland, stood a forest of makeshift tents, stalls, workshops, and pens, all divided by the wooden slats that served as Kaupang's streets. A pall of pit smoke cast a cloak of billowing gray upon the place through which Sten could see people going about their afternoon tasks. Sten thanked the gods for that smoke, for it masked the rank stench of fish guts and feces that littered the dark sand across which he and his men now plodded.

"Mind yourselves," Sten ordered as the group reached the tent belonging to Gunnar. In truth, it was not so much a tent as it was a set of poles supporting awnings that stretched like a cloud above the sea of eating boards and benches and humans beneath. On one end was a large cooking pit over which two pigs roasted. On the other end stood open barrels of ale. Over the noise of the crowd fluttered the trill of a poorly played panflute. Sten smiled and headed for the one empty table he could find with his men in tow.

"Gods, I could eat that entire pig," Arne said as he slid onto one of the benches.

"You might have some competition from that fat fellow," remarked his friend, Knud. They were both roughly the same age, though Knud was taller and lighter in complexion than the brown-haired Arne.

Sten's eyes shifted to where Knud pointed with the stubble on his chin. At the center table sat an immense man both in height and girth, tearing pieces of pork from a thick bone with his teeth that he would then chase with gulps from a pitcher. He did not bother with his cup. As he smacked the pitcher back onto the table, he let out a mighty belch, then patted his huge gut contentedly. The men and women gathered around him roared with delight.

A serving girl appeared at Sten's side. "Tell me," asked Sten after he and his men had placed their orders. "Who is that man over there? The large one," he added conspiratorially.

The serving girl looked at Sten as if he were addle-brained. "Do you not know Hakon the Fat?"

Sten shook his head at her. "No, but I have heard of him."

Sten's eyes traveled back to the hulking man. You could not trade in the North without hearing of the Icelander, Hakon the Fat. As large as two men but as strong as ten, some said. As cunning as a fox and as vicious as a cornered bear, others said. And as wealthy as a king. He had made his coin on walrus, hunting the massive beasts in early summer, then bringing his ivory and walrus hides to marketplaces across the known world. His thick mustache and rolls of fat, and his ivory bracelets and flipper-sized hands, put Sten in mind of the very mammals he hunted.

"So that is Hakon," remarked Rollo as the girl departed. He was the second oldest man in Sten's employ. Like Gorm, Rollo had the skin of someone who had spent a life at sea, though unlike the older man, he had lost the hair on his head and possessed only a raspy mess of gray that clung stubbornly to his jawline and chin.

The serving girl returned with two pitchers and a tray of wooden cups. As she placed them on the eating board, Sten grabbed her arm gently. "Bring us four more pitchers. One for Hakon, and three for us."

She was about to reply when Sten pulled his purse from his belt and placed it on the table. "Do not worry. I am good for it."

With a curt nod, she vanished.

"What are you doing?" Rollo asked.

"Making friends," replied Sten.

"I do not think men like Hakon make friends," grumbled Rollo.

"We shall see," said Sten.

The serving girl appeared at Hakon's side and placed a pitcher before him.

"I did not order another, girl!" he bellowed, though his size prevented him from turning fully to see her. "Do not think to over-charge me." He smashed the eating board with his hand, rattling the trenchers and cups upon it.

"He ordered it for you," the girl explained quickly, pointing at Sten, who lifted his cup in a silent toast to the ivory trader.

Hakon's thick brows bent over his eyes as he stared at Sten. Then, slowly, he lifted his pitcher and returned the toast. Both men drank. "Come!" Hakon called to Sten with a wave of his hand. "I would know who has purchased ale for me and why."

Sten walked to Hakon's table and climbed onto the bench where men had cleared a space for him. He did not consider himself a small man—indeed, in Halogaland, he was known as Sten the Stout on account of his size and strength—but seated before the giant that was Hakon, he felt absurdly small.

Hakon lifted his pitcher and filled Sten's cup, then he fixed his eyes on his new guest. "Who are you?" asked Hakon after releasing another belch that reeked of stale food and drink.

"My name is Sten Thorbrandson from Halogaland. I am a trader. Like you."

"And what do you trade, Thorbrandson?"

Sten shrugged his wide shoulders. "Pelts and antlers. Sealskin. Polar bear fur. Soapstone pots. Some whale oil." As he spoke, his eyes shifted to a long, jagged scar on Hakon's forearm.

Hakon saw the look and pulled up his sleeve to reveal the entire scar, a jagged purple thing that stretched like an overfed earthworm from his elbow to his wrist. "A bull walrus gave me this. Their tusks can be as sharp as a blade if they hit you right. Nearly killed me, it did." He rolled his sleeve down and once again took up his interrogation. "Why do you buy me ale with your hard-earned coin, Thorbrandson?"

Sten took a guzzle of ale. "Your name is well known. I would know a man of your stature."

Hakon's laugh shook the rolls of his body. "You flatter me." And just as quickly, the laughter stopped. "Is that because you wish to trade with me?"

The question took Sten by surprise. "For now, no. I wish only to trade names. Though let me think on it and come back to you. I am certain we can think of something to barter."

Hakon grabbed the new pitcher and poured himself some ale. "A pity," he said as he poured. "We leave at sunrise to attend King Bjorn in Tonsberg, if the weather permits of course. I have recently come from the East Way and paid a hefty sum in ivory for the silks and wine and spices the king is so fond of. It has been a long journey and a costly one. The rivers of the east took two of my ships and some of my men. The Rus taxes and Arab traders cost me even more. But fortune seems to be smiling on us now. Besides Bjorn, we have news that King Erik, Bjorn's half-brother, is also in Tonsberg, so mayhap our dealings there will make up for my losses."

"I wish you much fortune in your dealings, Master Hakon."

Hakon guzzled the remainder of his ale, belched again, and sleeved the foam from his lips. "And you in yours, Thorbrandson."

Sten stood and, with a final nod at the Icelander, departed.

"Well?" asked Rollo when Sten sat.

"It seems there are two kings currently in Tonsberg. Hakon goes to meet with them after sunrise. I do not think it will benefit us at all, but it is good to know. More importantly, I have now met Hakon, which could be of use to us."

Rollo grunted and turned his attention back to his food.

Later that night, Sten lay on his bed of furs in the aft deck of *Fara Happ*, his stomach content, and his head swimming in the glow of ale and ideas. The infamous trader Hakon was traveling to the king's hall in Tonsberg to trade, and Sten could not stop thinking about it. He wanted to trade with a king. To step into the king's hall and offer him something of such value, the king could not help but lavish him with praise and silver. All it took was silk and wine and spices. Wine he could get. But silk and spices would require a longer, more treacherous journey and more men. Or, a partner like Hakon...

And with that thought in his head, he decided to pay Hakon a visit in the morning.

The cry of gulls circling over Kaupang's waterway woke Sten from his slumber. Grey light was just beginning to brighten the world, though the sun had yet to show itself. Sten tossed his furs from his shoulders and sat up, rubbing the sleep from his face with his calloused hands. Across the deck, his men stirred as the morning came alive.

"Up, men!" called Sten as he rose to his feet. "We have work to do." He tossed Arne a small sack of hack silver. "Go find us a cart for our goods. Take Knud. Rollo—find us a chicken that we can sacrifice for luck. The rest of you, pull our goods from the holds." Sten glanced over at Hakon's fleet of ships, where men were beginning to stir. "Move now. I would like to be set up and selling when the market opens."

"Aye, Sten," Arne called as he and Knud disappeared over the ship's prow.

Slowly the sun peeked above the eastern horizon, invisible behind a sheath of grey clouds save for its light. Sten studied the sky, trying to resolve whether the clouds would dissipate or thicken. He felt no moisture in the air, but the gods were fickle. The clucking of a hen captured Sten's attention. He turned to find Rollo walking toward the ship with a protesting bird cradled in his arms. Behind him, Arne and Knud muscled a large cart over the sand.

"Little lass seems to know what's coming," Rollo called.

"If I was cradled in your arms, I would be fighting mad, too," Sten joked.

Rollo frowned and adjusted the hen for a better grip. Just then, the bird managed to shift its weight and break free of Rollo's hands. It flopped onto the sand in a fit of flying feathers and flapping wings and ran helter-skelter for the town. "Hey!" Rollo called and gave chase. He dove for the crazed hen and managed to get a hand on it, though it quickly broke free. Gorm and another crewman, Tove, hopped from the deck and joined the pursuit. Some of the other crews laughed at the scene, but not Sten or his men, for they did not like the ill omen it portended.

So preoccupied were the onlookers that they did not initially hear the warning blast of the sentries' horns. It was only on the second blast that Sten turned his eyes east, across the water to the finger of land that protected Kaupang. On the third blast, others took note. Sten turned his eyes south, to the headland at the mouth of the fjord, where something had drawn his gaze.

Just then, a wooden dragon head appeared, followed quickly by three others.

"Warships!" someone yelled.

Sten's stomach twisted at the sight. Though warships did not necessarily mean strife, these were coming at speed with their prow beasts on, which meant that they were coming for trouble.

The others knew it, too. Sten's crew had stopped in their tracks, their heads swiveling from the ships to Sten and back again, their hands on their blades already. On the shore, Bjarni's own war horn blasted. Townspeople scrambled from their dwellings with their children and possessions in tow. Traders stood tall in their stalls, not sure whether to run or guard their goods. Bjarni and his men began forming a small shield wall up the slope from the beach, hastily lining themselves to face the unknown threat. Behind Sten, Hakon was frantically calling for his men to ready the ships to sail.

"Get aboard! Everyone," Sten called to his paralyzed crewmen. "Arne! Knud! Untie us."

But the warships came faster than Sten and Hakon could get clear of the docks. In unison, they turned their dragon-headed prows to port and came to a slow halt a spear-throw from the shore. In their foredecks stood armored men, their helmets and spearpoints glistening in the dim light. Sten waited on his ship, which now floated close to Hakon's just beyond the docks. For a long moment, the world came to a standstill. Men waited at their oars. Ships' helmsmen, like Sten, held their steer boards and their breaths. Only the gulls seemed mindless of the danger as they floated and cried overhead.

Then, suddenly, a man climbed onto the gunwale in the prow of the largest ship. His cloak and mail and sword marked him as a lord. Like Sten, he had a shock of red hair that hung to his shoulders. "My name is Erik, son of Harald Fairhair," he called to the shield wall on the beach, "and I am now your king."

"Where is King Bjorn?" called Bjarni from the beach.

"Bjorn is dead." The red-haired man hoisted something he had been carrying at his side. A man's head.

The silence stretched as men came to terms with this sudden change. Sten glanced at Hakon, who sat on a mighty chair on the aft deck of his ship, frowning as he tapped the handle of his battle hammer. He then turned his gaze to the beach, where Bjarni and his men shifted restlessly.

"Your lord is dead, and with it, your oath to him," called Erik. "Lay down your weapons and you will be spared. Fight, and you will die."

Sten gripped the steer board tighter. Anyone could see it was folly to fight. Bjarni's troops might have been able to resist one ship's crew, but not four. "Lay your weapons down," Sten urged Bjarni under his breath.

"I give you my word," added Erik.

Slowly, reluctantly, Bjarni and his men sheathed their swords and dropped their spears. Sten exhaled and Erik motioned his ships forward. All save one, which blockaded Sten's exit to the sea.

That ship's helmsman came to the gunwale of his ship. "Back to the docks!" he called as he motioned for Sten and Hakon and the rest of the vessels to return to their moorings.

Sten gazed again at Hakon, who had not moved. Instead, he seemed to be judging something, for his giant head shifted from the beach, where Erik and his warriors were now disembarking, to the docks, to this warship blocking him. Sten thought he knew what was on the man's mind. He had five vessels. Six with Sten's. In total manpower, his force surpassed that of the ship before him. Yet, like Bjarni, he probably realized that engaging one ship meant engaging them all, and he did not have the strength for that. So in the end, he gave the signal to return to the shore. Sten followed reluctantly, his stomach knotting at the uncertainty of what awaited.

It revealed itself soon enough. No sooner had Arne finished tying *Fara Happ* to one of the posts along the shore then a troop of

Erik's men appeared at the docks. "You men," the group's leader called to Sten's crew. "Disembark."

The crew looked at Sten, who nodded. "Do as he commands."

The men rose from their oars in a chorus of curses and grumbles and leaped off the vessel into the shallow water.

"Search the vessel," commanded Erik's man.

As Sten and his men looked on, the warriors climbed aboard *Fara Happ* and began rummaging through the items on her deck and in her hold. They stacked the shields and loose weapons in a pile. As a trading vessel, it was not particularly well-armed. Most of the men carried a blade on their belt, but Sten also kept several additional spears and bows. The crew also possessed helmets and armor they had acquired in trades, and these, too, Erik's men tossed on the pile.

"What are you doing?" Sten asked incredulously. "Those are our possessions!"

"Keep your lips tight, trader. Erik will decide what is yours and what is not. He has taken Kaupang by right, and everything in it is now his to control."

"But we do not belong to Kaupang," Sten growled. "We are traders."

The leader was standing a step away from Sten. Quick as a lightning strike, he spun and drove his shield boss into Sten's face, and that was the last thing Sten remembered seeing.

Sten woke with a start, then wished he hadn't. His head and nose throbbed, the more so because of the light flooding into his eyes. He shut them quickly and took stock of his body. He rested on the ground. That was clear. As was the fact that he could move his fingers and toes. Nothing else on him hurt, which, he supposed, was a good thing.

Carefully, he opened his eyes again. Only this time, he turned his head to shield his eyes from the direct light. To his right, he saw Rollo sitting against a wattle fence. Beside him sat Gorm. "Where are we?" he croaked.

The men jerked at Sten's voice, then came to his side. "You are awake," said Gorm, not attempting to mask his amazement.

"What happened?"

"That bastard knocked you senseless is what happened," explained Gorm. "Broke your nose, too."

Sten's thoughts locked on Gorm's words. "Where are we?"

"In a bloody pen," he said, his voice rising with his anger. "They caged us like animals while they steal from us."

Sten closed his eyes. "Help me sit," he said as he reached out his arms. As his crewmen pulled him to a sitting position, a wave of nausea washed over him, and for a moment, he thought he might puke. Something oozed over his upper lip.

Rollo placed some cloth in his right hand. "Wipe the blood from your nose. I straightened it while you were unconscious, but the bleeding hasn't completely stopped yet."

Sten dabbed at the blood and opened his eyes again. Around him sat the crews of Kaupang's trading vessels, including Hakon the Fat, who perched on the one stone in the pen. Hakon still carried his hammer, and each man, his blade. That, at least, was something.

Outside the pen strode several warriors who appeared to be Bjarni's men. Sten asked Gorm about them.

"Erik gave them a choice. Bend their knee to him or be penned with us. They chose to bend a knee."

Sten grunted at the news. "What is their plan for us?"

Rollo chimed in at this question. "Erik has graciously decided to only take half of our trade goods for his father, Fairhair." He spat in the dirt beside him. "The rest, he left on our ships."

Sten clenched his fists at the thought of losing so much wealth. "Where have they taken it?" he asked through gritted teeth.

"The storehouses down near the shore. They will hold us here tonight, or so they say, then let us leave on the morrow.""

Sten forced himself to think of other things. "How is the crew?"

Gorm shrugged. "Bitter, but hale."

Sten nodded and climbed slowly to his feet. "I must speak with Hakon."

Sten waited until his nausea passed, then wove his way through the crowded pen to the giant trader. Hakon regarded Sten coldly. Gone was the gregarious man with the grand plans and the pitcher of ale in his hand.

"What do you want?" he asked.

"What do you intend to do?" Sten responded. He spoke in a hushed voice to avoid being overheard by the wandering guards.

"I intend to get my goods and my ships and sail from this cursed place," Hakon growled.

"When?"

"Tonight. Erik has gone inland to the royal hall," Hakon continued. "He will feast to his victory, no doubt, which leaves Kaupang mostly free, save for Bjarni and his men, and a few of Erik's warriors." Hakon spat at the mention of the men. "They moved our goods to the storehouses for safekeeping. We'll wait, and then we'll strike." He tapped the handle of his hammer with his thick hand.

Sten nodded. Simple enough, he thought, so long as Erik and his other warriors stayed away. If they returned that night, it would not go well for them.

Hakon cast his eyes beyond the pen to watch for nearby guards and said no more. Sten moved away without another word. When he reached his crew, he whispered the plan to Gorm, asking him to pass it on carefully to the others. And then he settled down to wait.

Night came again, and with it, apprehension. Sten lay on the ground, his racing heart now replacing the throbbing in his head. His fingers toyed with the seax handle on his belt. It was a long stabbing blade given to him by his father. He had not had to use it often, nor did he relish the idea of using it against Bjarni and his men. Still, Erik had robbed him, and so he must fight. If for honor and nothing more, he must fight. Around him, he could hear men breathing, feigning sleep. He hoped it would be enough to fool the guards.

Hours past. The moon shifted. Sten dozed.

When it happened, there was no warning. Just a crash of wood that ripped Sten from his slumber. He jumped to his feet and paused to gather his crew.

"*Fara Happ* crew. To me!" he hissed.

They gathered about him, then moved forward with the rest of the shadows, heading for the break in the fence through which men now poured.

Even before he got to the break, men began to shout ahead of him. Someone screamed. Metal flashed in the moonlight. Sten yanked his seax from its sheath and pressed on, staying close to the man in front of him. Arne lumbered to his right. He knew not where the others were, though he suspected they were close.

Then he was through the break and running for the storehouses near the beach. Some paces before him plodded the giant form of Hakon. An armored man stepped into his path and jabbed with his sword. Hakon batted the sword away with his hammer, then slammed his left fist into the man's face. The man dropped.

As Sten passed Hakon, a glint of metal flashed to his right. He dropped to a knee and stabbed at the form. His blade met resistance, then sunk into something softer. Flesh, perhaps. The form crumpled to the dirt and Sten ran on.

Near the storehouses, he spotted Rollo and called his name. The gray-beard spun. "Get to the ship! Grab anyone you can find."

"What about you?" Rollo called in return.

"I will help here."

Rollo did not hesitate. He turned and disappeared into the swelling crowd of shadows.

Sten moved to the press of men standing at the doorway of one of the storehouses. Near the door lay several armored men and the bodies of two traders. More men were inside, passing goods out the doorway to the crowd. Sten elbowed his way in, then grabbed a bundle of goods. As he turned, he spotted Gorm and four others from his crew. "Grab a handful and get it to the ship!" Sten called to his men.

"You heard the man!" Gorm called and moved into the press of bodies.

Sten jogged with the burden, surrounded by others like him. He carried a jar and what felt like pelts. Shouts and curses rose behind him and he quickened his pace. Someone off to his right cried out in pain. Sten dodged left, down an alley, then right again toward the beach. He could smell the water now. Ten more paces and he was out in the open and on the sand. Before him were the dark outline of ships and toiling men. He paused long enough to locate *Fara Happ* in the darkness, then sprinted toward it.

"Rollo!" he shouted as he came closer.

The man's head appeared upon the gunwale.

"Take these!" he cried, hoisting his armful up to the awaiting hands of his crewman.

Rollo grabbed the goods and pulled them aboard.

"Who's here?" Sten asked.

"Most of the lads," he said.

"I am going back for Gorm. Make sure we can leave as soon as we get back."

"Aye," Rollo shouted as Sten turned away and raced for the town.

Men rushed toward him in the darkness. He ducked behind a stall until they had passed, then he moved on. Here and there, he caught glimpses of metal in the moonlight. Shouts and screams filled the air off to his left. Sten zigzagged right, through the scattered stalls and houses, his eyes moving from man to man in the hopes of finding Gorm and his other crewmen. And then, suddenly, they were there, running toward him with arms full. Even in the darkness, he knew Gorm's gait.

"This way," he called and ran back the way he had come. He angled left, trying to put some distance between himself and those fighting off to his right. In his hand, he gripped his seax, his eyes darting left and right, expecting trouble.

And then they were through and on the beach.

"There!" Sten shouted. "Head for the ship!"

They hustled past him, running awkwardly on the sand with their burdens.

Sten was about to follow when someone shouted his name. He turned to see Bjarni sprinting for him, sword in hand. Behind him were two others.

Sten cursed and ran. Ahead of him, his men had just reached his ship and were hastily passing their goods up to the crew. Behind him, the footfalls of Bjarni and his men were drawing nearer.

"Halt!" Bjarni yelled.

But Sten did not halt. He ran on, willing his feet to push him faster. Gaining his ship, he scampered aboard awkwardly. On the deck, Tove and Knud poled *Fara Happ* into the water. The rest of the crew had weapons drawn, ready to protect their leader.

"Take us with you!" called Bjarni from the shore.

Sten spun and saw Bjarni and his men wading into the water, reaching for his ship. "Hold!" Sten called to Tove and Knud.

"We are doomed if we stay," Bjarni pleaded his case. "Please."

Sten studied Bjarni's young face, knowing that as soon as Erik appeared, the port master faced an impossible situation. It did not excuse him, though, from his wrongdoings. "You stole from us," Sten growled.

"No. Erik stole from you. We are Bjorn's men."

"You bent your knee to Erik, then did his bidding."

"Please," Bjarni implored and glanced back down the beach where more armored men had suddenly appeared.

"Sten, we need to go!" Gorm growled.

"I have silver," Bjarni suddenly blurted. He then jingled a fist-sized sack on his belt.

Sten smiled. "We split it evenly among the crew."

"Sten," Gorm's voice was urgent now. The armored men were coming closer.

Bjarni glanced back at the warriors, then at Sten. "Done!"

"Toss your weapons up to us," he called. "Hurry!"

Bjarni and his men complied. Gorm and Rollo grabbed them and hurried them to the aft deck.

"Come aboard!"

Bjarni and his men scurried over the gunwale as Sten made his way to the steer board. "To oars!" he yelled as he worked his way aft. Tove and Knud poled them free of the shore as the crew slipped their oars into the oar holes and readied themselves to row.

"Sit there and keep quiet," Gorm snarled as he pointed Bjarni and his men to a spot in front of the mast.

Nearby, Hakon was on his ship, roaring commands from his giant seat. His ships were loaded and just pulling clear of the docks.

"Pull, you bastards!" Sten called as he glanced back at the trading vessels and the chaos of the beach. He then turned his gaze on Bjarni and his two men and wondered just how much silver they had upon them. It was not a large bag but it had been enough to sway Sten's opinion of him. Sten turned his eye to the goods they had wrested from the storehouse. Several stacks of pelts and four jars. It was not a lot, but at least he had something.

Sten called out to the former port master when the ships had cleared the headland. "Bjarni, open those jars, eh? Tell me what is inside."

Bjarni did as Sten asked. "It looks to be spices."

Sten looked at Hakon's ships and smiled. They were larger than his and pulling farther away with every stroke of their oars. Around him, the crew laughed loudly, drawing the puzzled look of his newcomers.

"What is so funny?" asked Bjarni.

"The gods have smiled on us, Bjarni," Sten declared. "Men—we are headed back to Hedeby."

# — SIF THE FAIR —
## Jordan Stratford

*Sif the Fair*

*I counsel thee, Stray-Singer, accept my counsels,*
*they will be thy boon if thou obey'st them,*
*they will work thy weal if thou win'st them:*
*wouldst thou win joy of a gentle maiden,*
*and lure to whispering of love,*
*thou shalt make fair promise, and let it be fast,*
*none will scorn their weal who can win it.*
— Havamal 129

The threshold of months from Thorri to Goa.

The river is clear, but ice still snags on the shoreline like a child clinging to a mother's apron. Snow in the mountains, too, though not as low down than in previous years. He can imagine the torrent of water, spring melt in a mad rush to roar through the forest and fill the river, his river, and break up the remaining ice.

Sore after three days rowing upriver. What aches to burning, in order; the palms of his hands, the back of his neck where it becomes shoulder, and the bottom of his ass where flesh meets board. But it's not enough to distract him. Not from rowing—he is already distracted from the endless endless endless drumbeat of it, but from *her*. Or how he imagines her to be, when he gets there. She's fixed in his head like a star.

They know, too. The crew. Ale-talk around fires, every hand here knows which heart belongs where, after nights when there's nothing else to talk about, and all the silver at market spent in their heads before it touches a purse. But yes, they all know about the woman. They don't tease overmuch, both because she is their shared destination, and it's his boat—they'd like to sail with him again, if they can.

The Byrding ship, lighter and more nimble than a heavy knarr, perfect for the tight, shallow waterways, and light enough to beach each night. With a crew of five—though more is better, and the two passengers they take upriver do not shirk from rowing—she can handle the most spirited of whitewater, and when the gods are gentle, open ocean for sprints. He admires the color of the boat, the same color as the mead they'd brought south to other markets, places he still can't pronounce, places of pointing and hand waving and haggling in the common tongue of silver. This for that. Furs and spun wool and honey downriver, silver and whatever months-long caravan's goods he might bargain for. A loop of color—amber and grey southward, but northward always a riot of rich reds, orange, cobalt blues, beads in purples in hues for which he has no words. Aromatic hardwoods, fragrant spices. A world away from the cedar and birch and salmon, of wet sheep and hewn wood.

It had been a good circuit. The crew was quick to take to the temperament of the boat, the river kind to them, and no wind to speak of. With no marked destination, only the need for alertness after some three nights for signs of riverside, makeshift markets. To see what had been dragged north from the wider world. All he had was this byrding, a bag of silver, a hold of trade goods, and the air in his lungs. And of course the trust of his companions—leaner winters could mean he was merely a slit throat in his sleep from having all of this, the duly-won holdings of another trader.

But no time for dark thoughts, as the Fates had been kind, or at least their gaze was upon some other rower those nights. Either way, he was grateful. He thinks about the music, new songs to him from strange instruments in impenetrable tongues. The campfire flirtations of women, scolded and laughing in turn, tattoos down their jawlines. Frankish wine, even, though he had no taste for it. The nights had been warm before the row homeward, upriver, and into the rain. Over now.

He inhales the smell of the boat itself, and there too is the scent of the crew and their sweat, the rain-soaked wool and dried fish. Wax and tallow warming in the early morning, the smoke from the tripod brazier, just arms-length too distant to offer any warmth. He contents himself with the sun. His shoulders hurt. His ass hurts. The salt in his eyebrows sting when he sweats.

Finally they approach the lake and the going is much easier. No current to fight against. They can already see their destination, a slowly emerging forest of masts. Banners. Tents on the shoreline. The hammering of staves into rocky beaches for makeshift pens. There will be goats and cattle to trade, soon enough.

Jomsborg. Or at least its outskirts.

The lone dock is full, they'll need to beach farther back. He likes that, though. Let the barkers have the dock. This shipment, he's confident, has gravity. He takes his exile as an honor bestowed—setting apart from the fair should, he hopes, set them apart from the fair.

He's the first in the water, its cold a shock. The stout line cutting into his shoulders as his feet find the sliding stones of the lake's bottom. The crew laughs at his first gasps, and he meets this with a whoop of his own. An appreciative thunder on the gunwales for putting his heart into this task. It is a good day.

He dares to scan the crowd for a face, sees a shimmer of braid—but it's not her. Back to work. The rumble of lakeshore stones against the hull is as warming as the crackle of hearth. The crew wastes no time in establishing a relay to get every cask and basket and chest ashore, the passengers still earning their keep even though it is, at this moment, concluded business. There's goodwill in the gesture, but also the sense of excitement. The fair, the market: look what we brave companions have brought from southern lands.

Someone sets a fire, and the crew builds the pile of stores around that. He hauls the bundle of tenting a few strides away, and begins to unfold it. Steam rises from the canvas in the sun. Somewhere, music has begun already. A stray cat wanders through, sniffs in appraisal.

He self-consciously reaches for his purse—the silver is there, the fee, to trade here. For her. A price to be paid, well worth it for three days of rowing and all the money he had in the world, save this. Three days of hard navigation, though no open sea, mercifully.

He thinks back on the men who sold him this shipment, how they'd turned, their garb strange, flashes of silver and gold, and an iridescence like salmon skin in the sun. And more of the sun about them, too. Kohl-eyed, they had refused mead, but were decent company regardless. They had turned south for another run, and presumably another. But this, for him, this was the first harvest of his efforts that year, and it all came down to a woman. He knew she'd be fair.

Because she *was* the fair.

When he'd first heard her name, he thought it meant *fagr*, beautiful, or golden. Golden-haired. And while blonde, hers was more of an ash. Her beauty was apparent, but one forged in challenge and early wisdom, not some bestowal of natural attractiveness. He could see it, but suspected others could not. Of course, he admitted to himself he may be muddied in the matter, fancying himself as understanding a woman he'd scarcely met. Sif the Fair.

She was the fair because she was the market, and the arbiter. She was the fair because this was her land, and no trade took place without her approval, no dispute parted unsettled. If you wanted to trade, you traded here, by her rules, and her say, and no transgressors would be allowed to return.

There were other fairs, other markets, certainly. Even just an hour up the lakeshore was Jomsburg itself. A few more days and this shipment would fetch more in Birka, Uppsala. But for short hauls, sheltered rowing, and the guarantee of no betrayals, hers was the most welcome of moots.

Because *she* was the fair.

It was not just goods. She oversaw the trade of silver to gold, when necessary. And of gossip. News. Matchmaking, too, when it came to it, though she herself took no husband. The irony of her name, Sif, meaning bride, was not lost on him. He tries not to let himself dwell on this last point, and consistently fails.

It takes an hour or so to unload the ship—everything comes off, to suggest bounty. Barrel and crate and jar, some still sealed for only the most certain of sales. The more aromatic goods encased beneath layers of flax and beeswax. He thinks of his beard, and in a flash of vanity, wonders if he has time to comb and oil it.

The first of the customers arrive, inquire, exchange news, leave. No trades until she had taken her silver and approved each vendor, but still, there are discreet little forays for intelligence gathering. Let the word spread.

An easy winter meant more variety at market, and hands without the burden of grief or the distraction of hunger. Already, they say, the fair is more elaborate, more eye-catching, than in previous years. But this talk of mild winters brings its own shadow of darker years to come. A grim price to be paid later for a full belly now, always.

A visitor. Not a visitor, a challenge

My spot, he asserts. He's broad, iron-eyed, quick tempered by his gait alone. He wants the tent, the goods, the boat gone.

This is met by calming words, quotes of wisdom, appeals to fellowship. All rebuffed.

My spot, is the only claim made. Move, the only request, with increasing menace.

Further inducements to calm are met with a shove, but no blows can be traded here, so none are returned. He steps back, palms raised, so the madding onlookers can see he bears no malice, prompts no quarrel. In whatever accounting is to follow, he must be known to be the defender in this matter.

The challenger's hand moves to hilt, laterally drawing the first thumb-width of the flat seax slung under his belly.

Eyes alone halt this: any naked blade would have them both banished from the fair, and none looking forward to the open straits to Trelleborg. Even the challenger, head aflame, can see this.

One of the passengers, only halfway into his first ale, and seemingly attached to the tent, rises. A stout enough man, some grey in his beard, though a hand shorter than the challenger. His movements are steady. Confident. He interposes himself.

A game of *fang* is proposed, there on the beach, to settle the matter. This is met with great approval from the crowd, though the challenger sees the certainty of his claim become riskier at their reception. What was a point of business and threat has become a point of honor.

The two are ushered away, already purses are out, odds taken, backs patted, as the combatants unburden themselves of cloak, belt, shirt. They circle and appraise one another.

A lunge from the challenger, deftly avoided by the passenger's sidestep, but he is unprepared for a pressed attack, and finds himself engirdled by the challenger's arms.

The passenger makes a hop of sorts, giving all his weight to the challenger, who topples forward as the passenger rolls from his grasp. The stones are hard on backs already sore from rowing and the shifting of cargo.

Angered, the challenger scrambles to grasp the other man's ankle, which is expertly danced away. The crowd laughs, the passenger winks, and throws himself on the beached challenger to much applause.

Unfortunately he underestimates the challenger's superior strength, and once again finds himself locked around the waist, and wriggling like a rabbit under a hawk.

The trapped man's feet finally find purchase on the stones, and enough leverage to raise his body and twist, breaking the hold and rising. It is not enough to continuously escape in this game, though. He allows the challenger to rise, catch his breath, reset. There's a thunder in the passenger's chest which hasn't made its home there in some years.

This time the challenger waits for a move. The passenger begins with a classic opening, raising the hands to his opponent's shoulders, making an opening too generous to resist. The challenger again lurches to embrace the passenger, whose arms have anticipated this counterattack, and in one move pin an arm, drop, grab a knee, and then lift and throw. It is inelegantly done, but a move that shows the skill of his youth is not completely spent. Keeping the challenger's arm imprisoned, the passenger turns as he walks almost atop the downed man, before lowering himself with an audible groan and locking his opponent's torso to the ground.

After a few seconds of struggle, it is apparent the match is over, and there are dramatic *ohs!* from those with losing bets. Children run to the wrestlers with horns of water, as though receiving thanks could bestow some of the exhibited strength. The matter settled, the men rise to cheers, their clothes restored. The passenger does not return to the tent—he has offers of ale in other parts of the fair, and copious attention.

Finally, Sif deigns to visit them. There, in the market tent on the river's edge, some half hour after the wrestling's excitement has faded like the peal of a bell. She wears a simple brown apron dress, pinned with two woven-copper brooches over a shift of yellow flax. Spattered by spring mud, she's the fairest woman he's ever seen.

She keeps no record except what her head recalls. He grins at the sight of her—is that a smile returned? This interrupted by a giant of a fellow who picks her up in a little-sister fashion, roars with delight at reunion. She tolerates it. He withdraws.

Some of the crew settle to playing dice with arriving friends as rumors of their haul spread throughout the market. There's livestock bleating in the background, a boy chases a stray goose. Finally she approaches him. Only him.

He asks how she is doing, she laughs at the three proposals of marriage today; one offered the bride price of a door hinge.

A hinge?

It was a very nice hinge, she replies.

He says he has goods from the center of the world, hand over hand. Woods from Africa, copper bars from Cypress, spices from Arabia. Scrolls of learning in *arabisku tungumal*, if she has anyone to read them. Shimmering silks.

These last he removes from their waterproof chests, scraping the wax away with a small knife. At once the light catches the fabric, glinting now-emerald-now-purple in the morning light, shifting hues like the scales of a fish. Her hand reaches out and touches the sleekness of it.

She nods, and he misses its meaning at first. He freezes, but there is no further prompt from her. Finally, foolishly, he understands and reaches for his purse, his last remaining silver. She takes it without counting, and another, affirming nod.

For that moment he is trusted and respected by her. It warms him in a way he hadn't expected. It shakes loose words that come out in a tumble.

He explains what he knows of the world, which he admits isn't much. He has never seen a monkey but tries to describe one: A baby, covered in hair, with a tail. And clever. She laughs, says he's making it up, but he can't be sure he isn't.

I have a gift for you, he says.

I'm done with marriage proposals for the day, she answers.

It's not like that, he says. But even if it were, if you've heard three today then hearing a fourth would only be fair.

It would, she agrees.

He slips the silver ring off his little finger. It's tight, so he licks his knuckle like a dog and she's on the brink of laughter, but his efforts are successful. The silver ring glints in the light.

A stone, or glass bead in the center, in amethyst.

She accepts it with a small bow of the chin. Examines it.

Something is written here, she says of the stone. She cannot make it out.

It is a name, he says. The name of their god, the Arabic god.

Just one, she teases.

But he is serious. Explains how in *arabisku* all gods are one god, and our gods are either names for their one god, or are *draugr*, which they call *djinn*.

Our gods are *draugr*? How can all gods be one? How can Freya be Tyr? It makes no sense to me, she says.

He relays, poorly, what has been explained to him: that all gods have magic, and as far as he understands it, then the Arabic god *is* magic—*seidr* or *galdr*—itself.

Even the *draugr* have magic, she says.

He tries again.

They put all of the world into a single word, into one word. All sorrow, all triumph. All justice, all mercy, in one solitary word, and it's inscribed on this ring he has given her.

So you're giving me the whole world, she says.

And that gladly, he admits.

For what price, do you give the entire world?

Only that you accept it from me, it's all I ask, he says.

Well, she says, I was going to give you a kiss, but as you settled early, we have our bargain struck.

That's fair, he admits sheepishly.

For that kiss though, you'll have to come back the next fair, and make me an offer.

I'd like that, he says.

She gives him a smile that lingers, and turns to the next stall for business.

Have a good market day, she says over her shoulder. You'll do well.

She heads off to the next tent, to make her rulings, eject any deal-breakers, collect her due.

She is, after all, the fair.

# — SKY OF BRONZE —
## R.F. Dunham

*Zoskales the Zealot*                    *Vlad the Cursed*

**T**he knife of rejection cuts deepest when the one who wields it stands within your heart. A proverb Zoskales had thought himself familiar with.

Yet the blade of experience was far keener than the cudgel of cold knowledge. A bitter truth that colored his entire existence.

Zoskales allowed the thoughts to churn in his mind while holding them at distance from his heart. He stood on a small rise, south of Baghdad, the city he had called home for the better part of three decades. He drew the hood of his cloak higher, shielding his eyes from the glare of the rising sun on his right. His grip tightened around his staff and he turned from the vista.

Baghdad might be home, but he would not be at home until this journey was brought to a satisfactory ending.

"Ready to go?" a voice asked in heavily accented Arabic.

Cringing at the botched pronunciation, Zoskales nodded in answer and set off down the road.

"You know, you don't talk much for a teacher," Vlad said in his rumbling voice.

Zoskales lifted his shoulders in the suggestion of a shrug.

They walked in silence, Zoskales with head pointed straight ahead, stride just fast enough to be hurried. Vlad kept pace easily with his long legs, arms swinging at his sides as he took in the landscape around them.

Though there was not much to see for one such as Zoskales, Vlad's eyes seemed perpetually wide with wonder. The endless flat plains, punctuated only by sparse, scruffy vegetation were a sharp contrast from the lush hills to which he was accustomed.

Before long, his efforts to restrain his curiosity faltered and a profuse stream of inquiries began to flow. Zoskales answered not a single one but this did little to stem the flood. Vlad's questions ranged from who lived in such a place, to what they ate, to how they lived, to the nature of wildlife, to patterns of weather.

"Why are you even here?" The first words Zoskales had spoken since leaving the city came out as a rasp—harsh, accusatory, and thoroughly disconnected from anything Vlad had said.

The big Northman fell silent, his mouth still in the process of forming his latest question about the herd of goats he had seen perhaps a thousand paces back.

"This journey is not for you," Zoskales said. "You are not Muslim."

Vlad focused his attention on Zoskales. "And you are?"

Zoskales sputtered and stopped walking, turning to face his companion directly.

The two of them standing in the middle of the nearly deserted road could not have made for a stranger pair. Zoskales clutching his staff, slight of frame, dark skin and light beard shaded by the hood of a coarse traveling cloak. Vlad staring down past a scar that intersected his right eye and was crossed by a twin wound on the same cheek, his pale skin already growing red from exposure to the unrelenting sun.

Zoskales finally managed to shape his expostulations into words. "Of course, I am! What kind of a question is that?"

Vlad shrugged. Then began walking again.

Zoskales scrambled after him. "I have been practicing the *shath*[7] for over thirty years and you question my faith?"

"Do you not question your faith?"

A heartbeat passed. "No. I question yours."

Vlad shrugged again. "That is fine. I question it, too. That is why I journey. For answers."

"The *hajj* is an expression of faith, not a quest for it."

Vlad cast a look at Zoskales, but said nothing.

They lapsed back into silence for a time after that. Vlad resumed his perusal of the surrounding land, without accompanying questions. Zoskales resumed his steady stride, but with eyes cast downward and pace somewhat slowed.

The true reason for Zoskales' *hajj*, for taking it now, was buried deeper than he cared to look. He preferred to content himself with the same explanations he offered up to those around him. He was getting on in years and had yet to complete *hajj*. What more reason did a devout Muslim need? The question behind that answer was one no one had asked. Zoskales included.

Yet something in Vlad's eyes, in his probing words, even in his prolonged silences, asked it. The pressure of the unspoken inquiry swelled like a sandstorm on the horizon until Zoskales threw up his hands and turned to his fellow traveler. Something had to be said, if only to cut off the compulsion of the probing silence.

---

[7] In Sufism, the Islamic mystical tradition, a Shath is an ecstatic utterance which may seemingly be outrageous in nature.

"Do you know what it's like to be cast aside?" The question sounded like an accusation.

Vlad met the teacher's eyes, raised an eyebrow. Then nodded slowly as he looked ahead again. "I know something of this. Yes, I know something of this."

Zoskales didn't look at his companion long enough to see the flicker of despondency in his eyes. "Of course you do," he said, with a wave of his hand. "You're an exile, or some such thing. But such a rejection is communal, not personal. The sting is less, is it not?"

Vlad's shoulders lifted then sagged in a ragged sigh. "If you say so."

"I do. It's when the spurning is close that it hurts the most."

Zoskales was no longer looking at Vlad as he spoke. The Northman walked with his eyes straight ahead, gait stiff, fists clenched.

"Betrayal by your own blood. Not just friends. Not a village of primitive savages. Not even clan or kin. But your own flesh and blood. The loss of that, my pale friend. That is what costs you everything."

Vlad said nothing. His jaw was clenched tight under the braids of his dark beard, his shoulders were hunched. His eyes were hard, fixed on some undefined point in the distance.

"Those relationships, those bonds, which are formed not by choice or happenstance but by the hand of fate itself. It is those relationships which no man can bear to see sundered." Zoskales' voice grew in volume as he spoke, rising from an anguished mummer to the resounding timbre of an orator.

"Like that between a father and his daughter." Vlad's words were soft enough to be carried away on the faint breeze yet cut through Zoskales' declamation like the very knife of rejection itself. Both men stopped walking as if at an unseen signal.

The two men—the two fathers—locked gazes.

—⟨ ✳ ⟩—

The silence had become more comfortable by the fourth day. The traveling companions spoke only when necessary. They communicated well enough in the simple matters of food, shelter, and rest, but left the deeper matters to simmer unspoken beneath the surface. The monotony of travel formed a comfortable patina of familiarity between the two men. They spoke and worked together with an ease that suggested an acquaintance of more years than they in truth possessed. Yet to other pilgrims on the road, they presented a most odd pair.

Zoskales was thin and wiry, wrapped in the complex robes of a mystic, with brown skin the shade of strong coffee. Vlad was a contrast in every way. His broad build and considerable height would have been enough to strike a stark counterpoint to the Ethiopian Muslim on their own but the greatest disparity in the appearance lay in the Northman's pale skin.

For all their apparent differences, one who looked longer at the unusual duo might begin to note the similarities beneath the surface. A shared lassitude in their movements. A slight downward cast of their heads. A flicker of suppressed grief in their eyes.

Two opposites who were nonetheless concordant. Like parallel lines, never touching yet moving towards the same destination.

Zoskales cast glances at Vlad over the flickering light of their camp fire. They were two days south of Zubala, perhaps one third of their journey now behind them. The farther they traveled, the more crowded the road became as the flow of pilgrims heading to Mecca became steadily more dense. By unspoken agreement, the two travelers kept their distance from other pilgrims whenever possible and their camp was isolated.

The fire made feeble efforts to push back the irony of the desert night's chill but the men were huddled in their robes with shoulders hunched and tense.

Despite prior resolutions to the contrary, it was Zoskales who broke the silence. "Did your daughter reject you, too? Is that why you're here?"

Vlad raised his head slowly and met Zoskales' eyes. The faint suggestion of a rueful smile crossed his scarred face and he shook his head. "No. Everyone else did. But not Astrid. Never Astrid."

Zoskales scowled. "And you pretended to know what I—"

"No, my Astrid, she died." Vlad was no longer looking at Zoskales.

Zoskales' retort died in the air over the fire.

"Do you think we will meet them soon?" Vlad spoke without inflection.

Zoskales waved a hand, embracing the turn of conversation without acknowledging what had come before. "They will not interfere with the travel of pilgrims."

"We've heard stories—"

"And stories is all they are. The Qarmatians are Muslims. Whatever else they are, they are Muslims. They will not attack pilgrims making the *hajj*."

"Is that what we are?"

Zoskales looked up sharply. "It most certainly is not what you are."

Vlad's mouth turned downward in a grimace. Or perhaps it was a frown. "And you? What are you, Zoskales?"

"I am a Muslim. Journeying to Mecca to complete *hajj*. Yes, I am a pilgrim."

Vlad met his eyes, held them for a long moment. Then shrugged.

"You, on the other hand. Are not a Muslim. And therefore, not a pilgrim."

Another shrug.

"What is that supposed to mean?" Zoskales demanded.

Vlad shrugged again and Zoskales surged to his feet.

"Do you mean to insult Islam? The religion to which I have devoted my life?"

"Religion means little to me." Vlad shrugged.

"So your insult is intended for Allah himself!"

Vlad sighed and shook his head. "No. I have no desire to attract the anger of more gods."

Zoskales had his finger raised, mouth open to continue his diatribe. But he paused, sat again, and said nothing.

The silence stretched between them as the fire burned down and the night's chill pressed in. Zoskales sat uneasily, shifting his weight and looking everywhere except at Vlad.

Vlad stared into the shrinking fire, not moving a muscle.

As the glow of the last embers was fading, Vlad spoke. "Ahmad ibn Fadlan is one of your people, yes?"

Zoskales cocked his head. "Yes. Well, he is Arab. I am Ethiopian, but—"

"You are both Muslims," Vlad clarified. "You follow the ways of Allah."

Zoskales nodded, leaning closer.

"These ways fascinate me," Vlad said softly. "Allah is very different from the gods of my people. He does not strive to maintain his position against other gods. He does not demand sacrifices and rituals of his followers. He offers mercy—"

"There are rituals, expectations that must be met."

Vlad shook his head. "It's not the same. Not the same at all. Ibn Fadlan told me of the ways of Allah and—"

"Wait, how do you know Ibn Fadlan? You told me you only just arrived in Baghdad days before we left on this journey."

"Ibn Fadlan journeyed to my homeland. I was told his journey was well known."

Zoskales nodded. "Ah, yes. I know of his journey. You met him then?"

"Yes. We became good friends and, as I said, he told me of the ways of Allah."

"That is why you have come then? Because you want to learn more of Allah and His ways?"

Vlad took a deep breath. "It is somewhat more...complicated than that." He stared off into the darkness beyond the faint glow of their dying fire until it seemed he would say no more. "Among my people, I am known as Vlad the Cursed. My gods, the gods I have known all my life, cursed me. My family turned from me, all except my Astrid, my youngest. My village cast me out in the belief that doing so would end the years of famine. My name became an oath for children and old men to spit upon and my home was lost to me forever."

Zoskales let the words settle before giving an answer. "So you seek a new god. And hope to find Allah in His holy city."

Vlad shook his head. "I don't seek a new god. Or a new religion. I seek Allah the Merciful. I seek his blessing."

The big Northman ended the conversation by unrolling his sleeping mat and stretching out upon it. Zoskales followed suit a few moments later but neither man would close his eyes and embrace sleep for many hours yet.

Smoke was the first sign they saw of the attack. Thick, black, and angry; reaching far higher than any cook fire.

Vlad and Zoskales increased their pace. The Ethiopian walked with knuckles white on his staff, his legs stiff, eyes darting about in a furtive search for hidden ambush. The Northman's stride was steady and smooth, a grace that belied his bulk suffused his motions. His gaze fixed on the billowing pillar of dark smoke.

They were just north of the crossroads at al-Nuqra. Evidence of the Qarmatian presence had lined the sides of the road for the last two days. Zoskales insisted, in both conversation and a private string of muttered utterances, that someone else was responsible for the violence.

"Muslims would not inflict such horrors on each other," he said. "Not to those on *hajj*."

Vlad never argued. Yet his jaw became tighter with each fire-gutted caravan and looted corpse they passed. By the time the flames themselves were in view, the burly warrior's purpose shone in his gaze with brutal clarity.

When they crested a dune and came within sight of the raiders, Vlad didn't hesitate. Like an arrow loosed from a bow he raced down the southern slope with nothing but his bare hands for weapons. By the time Zoskales realized what Vlad was doing, his cry of surprise and objection was too distant to make a difference.

Left with no other option, Zoskales hiked up his cloak and chased the astonishingly quick Northman into hopeless battle.

The pilgrims were huddled between the raging fire that consumed all the supplies they had brought for their journey and a swirling circle of six mounted men waving broad-bladed swords over their heads. Vlad's only sliver of an advantage came from the utter idiocy of his strategy. Armed, mounted warriors never expected to be assaulted by a single unarmed man on foot.

The Northman reached up and yanked the first raider from his mount, dumping him headfirst to the sand with a loud snap.

The man did not cry out or stir.

The others reacted with battle-honed speed to bring their full attention to bear on the newcomer. Two of them swept down on Vlad with swords raised. Vlad squared himself to the nearest one, and met the charge head on. He dodged the blow with a fluid, lithe motion that sent one attacker barreling past without harm. But he could do nothing about the blade arcing for the back of his neck.

Zoskales' staff of Ethiopian acacia intercepted the strike. The staff was splintered and sent spinning off into the sand but it was enough to turn the blow and keep Vlad's head on his shoulders.

The warriors drew up on their mounts, studying the two unlikely combatants.

"We claim the right of *hajj*," Zoskales said. "For ourselves and these others." He gestured at the pilgrims, still huddled by the flames, too scared—or shocked—to flee.

The identity of the raiders as Qarmatians could no longer be called into question. They bore Sulayman's own standard, one with which Zoskales had grown quite familiar during the attempted siege on Baghdad some years prior.

The warriors gave no reply to Zoskales. At an unseen command, they raised their swords and closed on the two companions. Five swords fell in a flurry of death that could be neither dodged nor parried.

A blinding flash of light and dull *thump* reverberated through the desert. The light lasted only a fraction of a moment and the sound was so deep as to be felt more than heard. When the light faded, the raiders lay on their backs in the sand, their mounts fleeing in five directions. The fire behind the pilgrims was gone, leaving not even a wisp of smoke or a cooling ember behind.

The Qarmatians stood up on shaky legs, exchanged glances with each other, then turned and fled with no regard to the vectors their mounts had taken. Vlad and Zoskales stood alone and unmoving until the pilgrims began to stir. Vlad shook off the stupor first and moved to help the others salvage what was left of their belongings. It took Zoskales a moment longer to join in the effort.

Once the pilgrims were on their way again, the companions stood side by side.

"Thank you," Vlad said.

Zoskales continued to stare after the retreating pilgrims. "For what?"

"You called on the power of Allah to save us, did you not?"

Zoskales snorted. "I did no such thing. Besides, Allah does not intervene in such matters."

Vlad raised an eyebrow at the teacher. "Then why are we standing here talking to each other rather than lying on the sand next to our own heads?"

Zoskales waved a hand. "Such flashes are not unheard of. A mirage, a trick of the desert."

Vlad turned to fully face his companion. "A mirage. That is how you explain what happened?"

Zoskales nodded, still not meeting Vlad's eyes.

"And the sound? How do you explain that? Another mirage? And the fire? That was never there to begin with, was it?"

Zoskales started walking. "Coincidence." He stooped to collect what remained of his staff. After a few moments of inspection, he tossed it aside.

Vlad followed behind, hands raised, footsteps heavy. "Coincidence. An unexplainable convergence of impossible events and you, the teacher of religion and practitioner of mysticism, believes it is all nothing but coincidence."

Zoskales plodded ahead without turning or responding.

"You really have nothing more to say? You, a follower of the ways of Allah, believe your god to be completely removed from actual experience. Doesn't your religion teach—?"

"What my religion teaches is meaningless." Zoskales snapped, whirling back to face Vlad. "Allah does not touch the realm of man."

Vlad stepped back, eyes going wide at the outburst.

"I lead others to experience the very presence of Allah," Zoskales said, voice still ringing with frustration. "A presence I have never touched for myself." His head hung down and his voice became a rasping whisper. "I am a liar, my life's work naught but deception and fraud."

Vlad sighed and stepped closer, laying a hand on the shoulder of the smaller man. "Your lack of experience does not mean there is no reality behind your beliefs."

Zoskales looked up, a flicker of ire dancing in his eyes. "Beliefs," he scoffed. "What do I know of belief? What do you know of it?"

Vlad said nothing. He only turned and began to walk south, toward the crossroads and the flow of travelers branching toward either Mecca or Medina.

Zoskales stared at the Northman's back, breath coming in shallow, ragged heaves. Finally, he shook his head as if clearing it of unpleasant thoughts and followed.

The next five days of travel were fraught with peril. Qarmatian raiders grew both more numerous and more bold the closer they came to Mecca. Though Vlad and Zoskales avoided any further direct confrontations, the signs of Qarmatian attacks were all around and fear was a stench that pervaded every gathering of pilgrims along the road. Remaining aloof from the other travelers was no longer an option. To travel in isolation was to invite the sword of the Qarmatians.

The air along the road was abuzz with rumors and warnings concerning the holy city.

*Sulayman himself was in the city.*
*An attack was imminent.*
*Pilgrims were being turned away at the gates.*
*Mecca already burned.*

Each new tale contradicted half of those that came before it, making the task of sorting truth from lies, separating exaggerations from reality, impossible.

Zoskales and Vlad no longer spoke to one another.

The patterns and routines of their journey made communication unnecessary when it came to setting up and breaking camp, cooking food, and carrying on the mundane tasks of travel.

Speaking was no longer a tool, but a luxury. A luxury in which neither man indulged.

They walked wrapped in the cloak of their thoughts, shrouded in the veil of their emotions. Each looked often at the other. But never at the same time, leaving them both ensnared in the isolation they believed the other intended to impose.

When the walls of Mecca came into view, unmarred by billowing clouds of smoke, Zoskales looked to Vlad with the glimmer of a smile in his eyes.

Vlad was staring straight ahead, so Zoskales glanced away just as the Northman turned his own gaze toward the teacher.

Each strode on in silence, haze of solitude firmly in place.

They entered the city on a swelling tide of pilgrims. It seemed that Sulayman was indeed at the gates, but had been denied entrance. This fact bolstered the confidence of pilgrims who had journeyed far under the looming threat of an incomplete *hajj*. If Sulayman was willingly remaining outside the city, then tensions must have been diffused.

Or so went the excited speculation among pilgrims eager for relief from the dread that had hounded them for weeks.

Vlad and Zoskales took a room in the city and spent one more night in the uncomfortable silence of solitary company.

They awoke to chaos.

Screaming in the streets. Smoke filling the air from unseen fires. The clang of metal on metal. The shouts of men filled with both anger and terror.

Sulayman and his Qarmatians were in Mecca. The streets of the holy city ran red. The final, unthinkable sacrilege had begun.

There were few places within the city walls that had not been cast into havoc and disarray. Those places not under direct attack were thronged with pilgrims scrambling to escape. Yet the flow of desperate, terrified humanity was far from uniform. Some fled one way, some fled another, all running from the sword and towards a gate, but it seemed that no two people moved in the same direction. The result in some streets was a congested snarl of bodies that made little progress moving anywhere at all.

It was in the midst of such a constriction that Zoskales and Vlad found themselves when a horde of Qarmatian blasphemers swept down on them. The bedlam of bodies pressed against each other escalated to absolute pandemonium in the space of a single heartbeat.

Zoskales was being jostled from all sides at once, unable to see where the threat originated or discern which direction they should take to escape.

"Vlad!" He shouted over the chaos. "Can you see them?"

Vlad was an island of rock in the turbulent sea of the thrashing crowd. He grabbed hold of Zoskales, locking them both in place. "There." The Northman pointed to his left.

"Then take us the other way," Zoskales said.

But Vlad began shoving his way closer to the epicenter of the disturbance.

"What are you doing?"

"I have to save them."

"Save who?"

"Someone. Anyone."

Zoskales tugged backwards, but Vlad kept pressing on. "You're not going to be able to save anyone. Not in all this. We have to get out of the city."

"No!" Vlad bellowed. "I will save her this time!"

"Save who?"

Vlad stopped, the crowd continuing to churn around him in growing panic. Without saying anything else, he turned and began forcing a path away from the attackers.

With Vlad clearing a path, they made their way free from the press within a few minutes. They hadn't gone far when the sea of people gave way to streets that were virtually deserted.

"What was that about?" Zoskales demanded, though he didn't slow down.

Vlad said nothing, he just continued to walk alongside Zoskales, staring straight ahead with eyes that seemed to be seeing something other than what was before him.

They walked in a tense silence for a time then found themselves surrounded by another churning crowd without warning. The thunder of hooves was behind them and Vlad threw Zoskales to one side as he dove to the other. A horse charged through the space where they would have been, riding down others who lacked the agility to get out of the way. The crowd bled away as quickly as it had formed, leaving Vlad and Zoskales in an almost empty street again.

Vlad stood staring at a trampled body that lay abandoned in the dust. Zoskales picked himself up and went to stand next to the Northman. He tugged on Vlad's arm, but the big man wouldn't budge.

"Vlad, come on. Vlad. We have to move." Zoskales spoke in a rasping whisper that was incongruous with the distant screams that formed the auditory backdrop of the holy city.

"I failed her." Vlad's voice was hoarse and a broken sob punctuated his sentence.

Zoskales looked more closely at the body, the person, that lay at Vlad's feet. A young woman, likely in her mid-twenties, dark hair splayed about a face that pointed up at the hard sky bronzed by the light of dawn and the blaze of a hundred fires.

"I failed her again," Vlad said in between sobs that shook his shoulders like an earthquake.

"This is not her, Vlad." Zoskales laid a hand on one trembling shoulder. "This is not your Astrid."

Vlad flinched at the sound of his daughter's name but did not pull away from Zoskales.

"This burden is not yours to carry. Do not take it up. These deaths are not on your head."

Vlad's sobs became silent, though they still sent tremors through his body. Slowly, the quavering subsided and he allowed Zoskales to lead him away from the grisly scene.

"These men who slaughter and kill," Vlad said softly, "you say they are not Muslims. They do not follow the ways of Allah."

Zoskales shook his head. "No Muslim would do these things. To desecrate the holy city itself; it is unthinkable."

Vlad plodded on, head nodding in rhythm with his steps. "I can follow no god who kills his own followers. Not another one."

Zoskales looked up at Vlad, eyes narrowing as he found a new understanding of the Northman and his journey.

Vlad met his eyes, tears painting furrows through the dust that caked his face. "The gods, my own gods." His voice broke then, chest heaving with fresh sobs. "They took her from me. As punishment for my affront, retaliation for even thinking to seek the ways of another deity."

Zoskales' mouth opened but no words came to fill it.

To call their escape from Mecca easy would be to devalue the catastrophic loss of life that marred that day. But Vlad and Zoskales made it out of the city without encountering any more Qarmatians. They drew no attention to themselves and managed to get lost in the flood of pilgrims-turned-refugees as it poured through the gates and scattered to the winds. Fractured families filled the road and there were few clusters of travelers that were not weeping as they walked. Mothers huddled close with children, no father in sight. Fathers clutched small babies to their chests, eyes glazed over with pain, grief, and lingering terror. Most heart wrenching of all were the children who wandered alone amidst the press. Few of them cried aloud. They moved with stiff gaits, noiseless tears streaming down their faces, eyes reflecting haunting memories that the young were never meant to bear.

Zoskales and Vlad moved in a daze, just another pair of refugees, albeit a rather distinct pair. The throng of people became thinner at each crossroad and as many succumbed to exhaustion and collapsed into makeshift camps along the road.

By evening, the Ethiopian and the Northman were alone on the road. Neither had spoken a word since leaving Mecca and neither had shown any inclination to stop walking. As they passed clusters of travelers gathered in shanty tents, hollow eyes peered out at them from the gloom, twinkling in the fading light.

The sun sank below the horizon to their left as they trod on. As the light and heat of the day faded, stars popped into existence, starting in the east and spreading across the sky like a blanket of diamonds unfurled in the heavens.

Still they continued.

Long after the only light remaining was the silver gleam of the stars, they walked on. Not a word spoken. Not a glance exchanged.

Without warning, the air around them was filled with a shimmering golden light. It gave off a warmth that dispelled the desert night's chill in an instant without being uncomfortable. The glow seemed to wrap itself around them like a gentle embrace, soothing the rigors of travel and the horrors of the desecration at once.

Vlad stopped first, eyes on the road ahead, and he put a hand to stop Zoskales. The teacher responded to the gesture but his eyes remained downcast.

"Are you seeing this?" Vlad asked.

Zoskales shrugged, seeing nothing but the golden glow cast on the dirt at his feet.

"Are you seeing this?" Vlad said again, voice raising in pitch and intensity.

"A hallucination," Zoskales muttered, still not raising his eyes. "Brought on by exhaustion and…" He trailed off.

Vlad snorted. "It is no wonder you have lived so long without experiencing your god. A vision dances before your eyes and you squeeze them shut to block it out."

Zoskales looked up sharply then, a retort poised on his lips.

A retort that died as he finally saw what Vlad was seeing.

A man stood on the road before them, the source of the baffling radiance. He wore a white robe that reached to his ankles and was threaded with a delicate gold embroidery. His skin shone like burnished bronze and his eyes blazed with a fire that was both terrifying and comforting.

"Zoskales," the glowing man said in a rich voice, resonating with authority and compassion. "You have been known as 'Zealot' for the fervor others see from the outside. But I call you 'Zoskales the Faithful' for the persistence that has defined you from the inside, even when your belief wavered.

"It is this faithfulness that your students and, most importantly, your daughter, have learned from you."

The words struck Zoskales like a physical force and he staggered to his knees, sobs shaking his body like the throes of the seizure. The light that emanated from the robed man seemed to concentrate around Zoskales, swirling around him and enfolding him in ethereal arms.

The man's gaze shifted from Zoskales to Vlad, who stared with eyes wide and lips parted.

The glowing man smiled with fondness and spread his arms. "Vlad."

Without hesitation, Vlad rushed forward. Though he was both taller and broader than the stranger, he seemed to fold into the embrace, enveloped in arms that shouldn't have been large enough to encircle him so completely.

"You have been known as 'Cursed' for the misfortune that has befallen you. But I call you 'Vlad the Dauntless' for the courage that drives you forward through the darkest of nights.

"It is this courage that will rescue countless daughters from the grip of evil."

Vlad sagged in the man's arms, beginning to weep loudly. He would have fallen to the ground if not for the strength in the arms that held him.

The two men stayed like that for longer than either could keep track of. Neither noticed when the light faded and the stranger departed. Dawn was beginning to bronze the eastern horizon when they stood and faced each other. No need for words to pass between them. Each saw the renewal of purpose, of faith, of hope in the other's eyes.

The two fathers locked gazes—and smiled.

# SO DO I WRITE,
# — AND COLOR THE RUNES —
## Bjarne Benjaminsen

*Suleiman Silverbeard*

*I know that I hung on a windy tree*
*nine long nights,*
*wounded with a spear, dedicated to Odin,*
*myself to myself,*
*on that tree of which no man knows from where its roots run.*

*No bread did they give me nor a drink from a horn*
*downwards I peered;*
*I took up the runes,*
*screaming I took them,*
*then I fell back from there.*

(From the Old Norse verse "Hávamál", a part of the *older Edda* poems)

**M**aster, I dare not listen to another word.

The younger man shook his body, as if shuddering with cold — while staring icily at his teacher. Yet the room was damp from the heat of the Persian summer. The sun was high in the sky outside the tower window, mercilessly overflowing the city of Shiraz with rays of heavy gold. Only a very slight wind moved through the chamber, teasing the skin with a cool tingle: The small relief only served to make the undeniable power of the sun even clearer to the mind.

With fingers trembling, the apprentice put down his cup of wine on the oaken table.

— What you are saying, master, stings my heart.

The older man smiled beneath his silvery beard. Bowing his head lightly, he invited his apprentice to keep talking. Clutching his robe, the younger man spoke:

— Master, please tell me, is this some kind of trick upon my devotion? How can this be at all compatible with what you have taught me before? I cannot make sense of your lesson.

— Young Farroukh, my talented boy, said Suleiman the silver-bearded mystic. — Why does it upset you so, for me to challenge you with a tenet?

The learned old man welcomed the breeze on his open face. He gracefully held his cup up against the sun, making it shine with the peering reflection of the power above. The master of the order had dedicated his life to holy veneration, as is described in the hadith[8]: *"To worship God as if you see Him; if you can't see Him, surely He sees you."*

Yet today his tongue had spoken strange and disrespectful words, in wicked disregard of the Quran itself!

— I am confused, master. Are you putting me on? cried Farroukh the apprentice. — I don't know what to make of this!

---

[8] A hadith is a saying of Prophet Muhammad

Yet the revered Sufi master spoke gently, appearing untouched as a drowsy camel. His lips formed crystalline, rational sentences:

— Only through careful consideration of diverse propositions, we may steadily bend our minds towards the truth. This is the principle of all philosophy, the attitude of intellect shared by all the great thinkers of yore. Have I ever taught you otherwise? Why then, should we not strive in the spirit of Aristotle, Plato and blessed Socrates? It is by no means the first time we have discussed hypothetical positions. Tell me then, what makes you so upset as to avoid an open-minded approach to my claim?

Farroukh the Sufi apprentice, with royal blood running through his veins, stood still for a moment. Suddenly he threw his hands up in the air, spun around as if to walk away, before turning back to confront his teacher once again. Wild-eyed and ghoulish he seemed, struggling to keep his composure while pressing an answer out through his clattering teeth.

— But master, surely you must agree: This horrible tenet is something entirely different from any of our earlier studies. It is not an upward glance! We are not moving into the higher realms of the spirit, but downwards.

The apprentice fell to the floor with his hands raised, wailing:

— We are not peering towards that which holds the world together and makes it beautiful. If philosophy is taking us in this ungodly direction, then to what aim are we applying our intellect?

— You find today's lesson to be devilish? Suleiman asked, lifting his one brow. While not smiling still, the old mystic remained calm as the summer breeze.

— I didn't say that! the apprentice replied, backing off a few steps, shifting his gaze towards the ornamented door. — But, he dared continue, — Is it not a horrid thought indeed, to say that God is —

He refrained from finishing his sentence.

Suleiman the Sufi master suddenly hardened his face. With an angry gesture he put down his half-emptied cup of wine on the oaken table next to Farroukh's.

— God is what? Suleiman demanded. — Say the word!

— I won't! Farroukh replied, stepping closer to the door.

Suleiman the Sufi had his hand on the sheath of his scimitar.

— Say it! Say what you think of my tenet!

— No! No, I cannot say it. It is not true, shouted the apprentice.
— God is Great! God is the One, tying the world together, making everything beautiful. God cannot be at loss, wandering the earth, searching for the truth. God is the Truth: He is not Small!

Suleiman drew his sword, throwing rays of gold across the room, roaring with fire!

(Rendered from the diary of Farroukh Farhadan,
10th Century A.D.; 3rd Century A.H.)

*So it is told of Odin, king of the Aesir, that he and his brothers formed the world from the dead body of Ymir, the appalling giant. The giant's blood became the mighty sea, and from his dead limbs the Aesir made all the mountains and landscapes of the Earth. After having made this mess of a world, for all creatures to thrive in, the brothers vaulted the dead giant's skull over their Creation, thereby forming the sky above us. Between the cracks in this monstrous skull, light shone through.*

*— There is a crack in everything, Odin pondered, watching the skies from his sitting place on top of a dark, grim mountain. — That's how the light gets in.*

*The king of gods put his hat on, reached for his staff, and took to wandering off into the steep and rocky hills.*

*— I came, I saw, and I want to know more, he uttered.*

*For although he was the constructor of this strange breathing ground we call our home, he did not fully comprehend what he had done. What kind of a place was this hammered discworld that he had made from blood and* meat? By killing the ancient giant, he and his brothers had given way to new forms of teeming life that rose from the soil. Was it really a good deed they had done? Or was this dirty act of creation merely the beginning of an endless line of suffering, from which there was no way out again?

Really! What was the meaning of it all?

And so Odin wondered. Two ravens followed him through the night, eventually becoming so safe with the bony figure as to settle on the brim of his hat. Croaking.

(From *The Adventures of the Ragged God* by Teddy Partridge, loosely based on the verses of the Old Norse *Edda*)

"The blueman who became known on Iceland as Suleiman Silverbeard, came from the East. Some say he had been a sort of king or a mighty chieftain in his homeland, and that he had resided in a tower of gold. What is certain is that he encountered Tollef, son of Egil, in Miklagard. This was while Tollef and his men were serving in the guard of the great King Leo the Wise at the city stronghold. Suleiman had wandered into the city a few years before Tollef arrived there.

The legend bespeaks how Suleiman Silverbeard saved the king's firstborn son Constantine from a terrible illness, when no other learned man in the city of Miklagard knew how to help. Despite the blueman's unchristian origin, King Leo and his Queen Zoe took him into their hearts then. The royal family made the Easterner a member of their innermost circle, to come and go at the palace as he wished. But among the courtiers it was rumored that Suleiman's medical tricks were not grounded in the blessings of the light, but rather in the dark devilry of Suleiman's mysterious past.

— He is of the devil, they said.

— He respects nothing and no one but his own curiosity, they gossiped.

— His heart knows not how to humble itself before God, they spoke.

There was one courtier in particular, the renowned sword-bearer Proximus, who took a particular disliking to the queen's darling doctor from the East. Proximus plotted how to get rid of Suleiman, since Queen Zoe lent her ear to the blueman before taking advice from the sword-bearer.

One night, Tollef Thundervoice was drunk with Christian wine. High-spirited at the tavern, he got into a quarrel with a fellow guardsman named Skarphedin of Denmark, son of Skjalg the Seafarer. During the ensuing fight Tollef killed Skarphedin and two other Danes.

Later that night, Tollef went to relieve his winey bladder in the street, before falling asleep in a shed nearby. His friends were still at the tavern, when six of Skarphedin's kinfolk came by. They had heard what had happened there, and were eager to use their axes. Five of Tollef's closest friends at the royal guard were killed by the Danes that night.

Leo the Wise was furious to hear of these senseless killings. As his Norsemen could no longer be trusted to work together, he had reason to fear for his own protection. What was more, punishing the troublemakers was not an easy task, since the mischief had been done by his own closest guardsmen.

The great king then called for Suleiman Silverbeard, asking his advice on the matter.

— This is what I think, Suleiman said. — I will invite the Norsemen to discuss the matter, under my roof. What medicine is to the body, an open-ended dialogue is to the soul.

The greatest Roman nodded his head, for he knew the strange powers of his Easterner friend's mind at work."

(From the Saga of Tollef Thundervoice,<br>written down in Iceland 13th century A.D.)

—◖✳◗—

*Odin, king of the Aesir, was hungry for wisdom. He sent his ravens out in the world, and they returned to tell him of all they had seen and heard.*

*— What is there out there today that I do not already know? the top-notch god would ask.*

*— Croak! Croak! the first bird, named Hugin, would answer.*

*— Croaaaak! Croak! the second raven, named Munin, would add.*

*And Odin did a magic gesture with his hand, by this giving the birds the gift of speech - after which the two feathered creatures started making more sense.*

*On this particular night, Hugin and Munin told Odin of Mime the moody giant:*

*— The Well of Wisdom is hidden in Mime's backyard, they croaked.*

*— And the old fellow guards it well! Hugin said.*

*— Anyone who wishes to drink from the Well of Wisdom, must pay Mime a high prize, Munin nodded.*

*Now Odin had a very special eye on the left side of his face. It was such an eye that the owner — Odin himself — could throw it up in the sky, from where it would take a closer look at any particular place Odin wished to examine. Naturally, Odin threw his eye up in the sky and looked down upon the giant Mime, the greedy guardian of the Well of Wisdom.*

*— How come he guards his well so well? Odin asked himself, having already decided to visit Mime and hear his prize.*

*And upon Odin's request, Mime answered later that day:*

*— This eye of yours, that you use to spy on me and all the world: I want it!*

*So the deal was done. Odin gave his spying eye, this tremendous instrument of power, to Mime, in exchange for a sip from the Well of Wisdom. The outside world in exchange for an "inner eye", so to speak.*

*And Odin saw that the deal was a good one.*

(The Adventures of the Ragged God (excerpt)
by Teddy Partridge)

―――( ✳ )―――

"Dear Sully!

Lately I have thought a lot about our nightly conversations, and have reread both Plotinus and Dionysos the Areopagite with your propositions in mind. This thinking has led me to strange places of the soul. Seeing and believing in the One, which I before regarded as the ending point of all rational thought, still does not clear my soul of uncertainty. Rather I have stepped into an abyss of unknowing from which I know not how to climb out of.

As you have suggested, there is indeed something to be said of the world even after the One has revealed itself to the soul. There is indeed a strangeness about it all. I am only getting more and more bewildered as to why the One had to commit oneself into thinking the world into Being in the first place?

Only God can comprehend His own will, and I — mere mortal soul — have no right to question Him. But having reached so close to the One as you and I have, having been united with Him beyond the world, the soul still cannot stop moving. It is as if God himself is on a quest, and we mortals are but instruments to be used for His experiment.

But then, if God is truly on a quest, how can that at all be the case? What is it that God — forgive me for spelling it out — then seems to be lacking? How can God ever be less than perfect, while still holding the answer to our existence?

To be serious in one's search for God, leads — some way or another — to non-clarity of the mind. Yes, my soul is beginning to doubt His very omnipotence.

But how can this be? These thoughts have puzzled me so, I haven't been able to sleep for days. I am torn apart, having lost the One in a cloud of unknowing — yet still my very soul seems to be still moving, searching, approaching its misty goal.

It is as though God was standing right in front of me, but my eyes were so blinded by His appearance that I couldn't face Him — and then, turning away, I realize an even greater message written in my own footsteps.

My sweet friend, am I — by spelling out these sensations — committing a terrible blasphemy?

Please come back to me, so we can once again share the wine of wisdom through the long hours of the night. Proximus is long dead now, and the Emperor Leo is forever thankful for what you have done for us. He bears you no grudge.

Constantine often asks about you. He is doing terrific, already becoming skilled at all kinds of sports — and with quite a talent for philosophy, as well. Surely this is his father's blood running through his veins.

We all miss your reassuring voice among us. Your room at the royal palace is kept ready for your homecoming.

Yours truly,<br>
Zoe Karbonopsina, Queen of the Romans"<br>
(Letter of confidence, originally sealed,<br>
dating to approximately 910 A.D.)

*Odin, king of the Aesir, resided in the great hall of Valhalla. From his mighty throne, the Lidskjalv, he pondered the ways of the world — while his two ravens brought him news of the strange happenings taking place out there. The world was no less mysterious now than it was on the day Odin and his brothers slayed Ymir the mighty giant. With all the knowledge gained through years of investigation, Odin still felt like a child in the world — his one eye gazing wide-open at everything surrounding him, his heart beating with the incomprehensible power that was life itself. It kept moving within him and without him, it seemed.*

*By Odin's feet lay two wolves, and on a little oaken table next to him lay the big head of Mime the wise giant. After the great War of Gods had left the giant decapitated, Odin had saved the head and brought it back to life. Odin often asked Mime's advice; the godhead and the lost head were very close to each other, indeed.*

*Now for all of his kingly affairs and responsibilities, Odin was prone to dismiss the high life of royalty. The highest god would often leave his throne and his fine wine, and take to wandering the Earth in the guise of an old man. He preferred walking in the middle of all Creation, dressed in simple garments, getting his boots dirty, rather than watching it all from a dull distance.*

*He was the kind of dreamer that didn't stop at just words.*

*— The Word is only the beginning, he would tell Mime the table-head.*

*— You know, after the beginning comes the middle of it: A long and winding road, a walk on the wild side, a real life natural mystique blowing through the air, man!*

*— And then where does it end, my friend? asked Mime.*

*Odin fell silent. He knew for certain that his own death would one day come. He didn't like it. But he never tried to rise above it all, never pertained to become something greater than the Way of the World itself. He didn't care to be a conceited godhead — and he certainly didn't wish for such worshippers, either.*

*It is said that Odin and his wife, Frigga, at times would live from tilling the land — like an ordinary peasant couple. Perhaps praying to their own kind?*

*— Indeed, life is as strange as ever, Odin told Frigga one day, as the sun set over fields of carrots and cabbage.*

*Frigga, who is rumored to be the wisest of all beings that ever roamed the Earth, smiled back at him and did a little funny dance on the green.*

*She was very much like a child, Odin thought, lifting his head, spreading his arms like wings, making a pirouette in the air behind her.*

(*The Adventures of the Ragged God* (excerpt)
by Teddy Partridge)

———⟨ ✳ ⟩———

Farroukh knocked on the great brass door.

— Enter, young pupil, said the low, clear voice of master Suleiman from within.

The Sufi apprentice put his shaking hand on the handle, pressed down, and pushed the heavy door open. The old room in which the many conversations with the Sufi master had taken place, lay in darkness — except for a single lit candle on top of the oaken table. Behind it Suleiman was standing with his back to the door. He was writing big, artful letters on a fine piece of cloth — the calligraphy spelling out a quote from the Holy Quran:

*"The servants of the Most Merciful are those who walk upon the Earth in humility,"* the quote began.

— Master, Farroukh said, bowing his head.

Suleiman said nothing. Not knowing what to make of the situation, the younger man stood still, breathing slowly, awaiting his master's next move.

Suleiman kept dipping his pen in ink, laying it on the cloth in grandiose swirls. He took his time, not turning to look at his pupil until the work was done. Then he held the piece up for the younger man to see. The quote now read in full:

*"The servants of the Most Merciful are those who walk upon the Earth in humility, and when the ignorant address them, they say words of peace."*

— What do you think of this quote, my dear Farroukh? the silver-bearded Sufi asked.

— It's a Holy quote, an address from God, Farroukh answered. — I am merely a servant, my thoughts on the matter mean nothing. But I intend to follow up on God's command and humble myself in all matters of life.

Suleiman's eyes seemed oddly humorous, reflecting the candlelight.

— That is a clever answer, pupil Farroukh, the master spoke. — It sounds like the answer of a very humble man, doesn't it?

— Thank you for saying so, master, answered Farroukh; his eyes seemed to awaken and sparkle.

Upon this, Suleiman let go of a small laugh.

— Very well, then, my son, that will be all for now. We both have to ponder today's lesson a bit by ourselves, before we rest for the night.

— We do?

Farroukh's voice sounded shrill, whether with excitement or from bewildered tension. Last night's conversation had started with a point of blasphemy, and ended with Suleiman drawing his sword and whirling about like a madman. Now would today's lesson end on this undecided note? What kind of a religious teacher was this strange old man after all?

Farroukh had come to the tower for a thorough understanding of the holy doctrines of Islam. Yet he couldn't get his head around his master's ways.

— Certainly, the Sufi master replied, and gestured his apprentice to the door.

Farroukh left the room, holding his hand to his heart and bowing his head slightly. Suleiman the tower dweller stretched another piece of cloth up on the wall, dipped his pen in black ink, and wrote in fine swirls:

*"He gives wisdom*
*to whom He wills."*

The Sufi master blew lightly at the candle, and so the room fell dark — only a small, silvery stream of light shone in from the crested moon directly outside the tower window.

> (Rendered from the diary of Farroukh Farhakan,
> 10th Century A.D.; 3rd Century A.H.)

"After Tollef had made his deal of peace with Sigurd the Slayer and the other kinsfolk of Skarphedin, the Icelander honored Suleiman Silverbeard with this verse:

*You took up the words,*
*bound the wolves,*
*we raised our swords screaming.*
*Sigurd and I stood as one,*
*honor restored while no blood fills*
*the empty cup.*

Suleiman's words, as well as the way in which Tollef had saved Sigurd's life from the nightly assassins, ensured the peace among the Norsemen of the Emperor's guard. Tollef and Sigurd would remain friends for years to come.

The silver-bearded courtier then invited Tollef to dine with him in his chamber, overlooking the strait running through the city.

— You are—from what I hear—not a Christian, brother Tollef? Suleiman asked, pouring the wine.

— Since I arrived here in Miklagard, I have been somewhat busy with matters of the shield and sword. I have not given much thought to what goes on inside the churches, Tollef answered.

Suleiman spoke no more of the Christian teachings that night. Instead he queried the Viking about the gods of his homeland. The two men stayed up all night, Tollef recounting all the verses and stories of the Aesir that he could remember.

— These are bold teachings you have presented me with tonight, Suleiman said.

— Verses and songs, that's what we call them, Tollef answered. — I don't know about teachings.

No other people were around, as the two men drank their cups empty.

(From the Saga of Tollef Thundervoice,<br>written down in Iceland 13th century A.D.)

*Odin hung from Yggdrasil, the tree of the world. He was bleeding, he was screaming, the sap of the tree was running through his veins. The roots of the Yggdrasil spread all over the known realms, and Odin took it all in, his blood wild with knowledge, his heart pumping to the beat of the music of all living things. Odin was searching for wisdom, and it was not a joyful ride.*

*— Why on earth are you doing this to yourself, man? asked Ratatosk, a squirrel who lived in the tree, and a lover of gossip.*

*Odin didn't answer. He kept screaming.*

*— What's the point of all your wisdom, if it means all that pain? Why, isn't life about being happy? the squirrel went on.*

*Odin opened up his one eye to stare at the animal. It was as if some of the tormenting sap flung itself at the poor thing from the vessels of the eye. The squirrel in turn fled up the stem to be lost in the leaves above.*

*— Oh my God, said the king of gods.*

*With swollen lips he started singing:*

*- What a feeling!*

*Being's believing*

*I can have it all,*

*now I'm dancing for my life!*

*He was the king of gods, and at the peak of his golden quest — yet very much like any mortal he struggled to hold it all together. He was a wild and crazy heavenly father. But oh! how his heart could dance!*

(*The Adventures of the Ragged God* (excerpt)
by Teddy Partridge)

"Proximus the sword-bearer did not approve of Tollef's friend, Suleiman the blueman. The courtier regarded Queen Zoe's close relation with the Easterner as unbecoming a lady of the throne. He dared not however raise this concern directly with the great king. Instead he let his words of discontent fall whenever he spoke privately with other members of the court:

— This silver-bearded medicine man may seem gentle on the surface, but we do well to remember that he is at heart a Mohammedan heretic, said Proximus. — While seemingly respecting our Holy Faith, he brings poison to the Kingdom with his wicked curiosity.

Tollef never heard these words spoken from Proximus himself, but the ill-spread accusations still reached him as rumors.

— Your friend Suleiman has many enemies here in Miklagard, Voluntaria told him one night in bed. — They say he undermines the Great Kingdom with his curiosity, and spreads poison in the queen's ear.

— Who says this? Tollef wondered.

— This is the opinion of Proximus himself, Voluntaria answered. — A powerful enemy to have in this city, don't you think?

Now Tollef naturally agreed, but he did not yet fear greatly for his friend's life. For the guardsman knew that the priesthood was quite happy with Suleiman. The Patriarch himself enjoyed long conversations with the silver-bearded thinker.

But then one night in her chamber, Voluntaria told him more among the red cushions:

— They say Suleiman has poisoned the queen's mind with beastly thinking, and that the two are now committing adultery in the most ungodly fashion. This less than royal behavior can bring down the Hand of God upon us all! she shivered, pulling her blanket to cover her own naked body.

— Oh be quiet, woman! Tollef thundered. — None of this is true. But even if it were, the gods couldn't care less. What is the queen's nightly affairs to them — when they are living their own wild adventures as we speak?

Suleiman in turn learned of this rumor from his friend Tollef.

— I know the king doesn't believe any of this, the wise man spoke. — I am sure King Leo must have heard these nasty stories a long time ago, yet he has not taken any kind of action against me thus far.

But as the weeks went by, it became ever more evident that Miklagard was becoming a less safe place for Suleiman. Not only did the courtiers avoid him, quite a few of the priests were starting to withdraw from his company.

— They are afraid, lest they shall be numbered among the companions of the Beast, Suleiman said.

Tollef had planned to leave for Iceland that summer. Now he pushed forward the time of departure for the sake of Suleiman the sage. With the blueman's safety in mind, the two friends left Miklagard by late spring. A strong wind blew from the East, leading Tollef Thundervoice and his men homewards.

Tollef quoted:

— *My ship is filled with gold and dried meat,*
*a fine prize for my sword-arm's friendship.*
*Yet the greatest prize of all for men*
*is wisdom aboard the vessel.*

(From the Saga of Tollef Thundervoice,
written down in Iceland 13th century A.D.)

———( ✳ )———

"Your Highness, light of the world, beloved sister, mother and daughter in One, and dearest friend, Zoe Karbonopsina Queen of the Romans,

I was thrilled to read your letter. It reached me through Sigurd the Slayer, one whole year after you sent it, still sealed and enclosed in your miniature box. As your heart must know, I am thinking of you every day, missing your gracious company, warm smile, high intellect, good humor and serene soul. There is nothing that could sound more relishing to me than to return to Miklagard and staying close to your virtuous grace for the rest of my life. I am glad to hear that you now regard the palace safe grounds for me.

However, it is no longer fear for my life that keeps me in this frosty Ultima Thule, far from your kind face and dignified posture. It is, rather, due to the close proximity of this island to the Will of God.

Forgive me if this may sound very strange, or even unheard, to you. As you very well know, I sincerely extol the virtues of your priesthood, your city of Constantinople, and your holy shrine at the Sancta Sophia. After I was driven from my homeland by jealous minds, I found a blissful haven under your generous wings. My spiritual studies were invigorated by our fearless friendship.

I had always taken an interest in the figure of Christ, even during my Shiraz days. The Christian vision of God humbling Himself, becoming flesh and taking on the pain of this world, held a strange—yet confusing—appeal. Through being surrounded by your Christian artifacts and rituals, drinking with you, relating to your experience of the holy, and opening up to the fruitfulness of Paradox, the way of the Christian God became more alive in me. For this I will always be grateful.

In all these years I would still be reluctant in accepting Christianity as the true faith, for I was too well bred in the philosophy of the Undivided One. The mighty appeal of Christianity's claim, that God once lowered himself to the level of man, is hardly compatible with the strict demands of science. God must be One, and he must be omnipotent, or else He is not Great as He must be. This is pure logic.

Yet I once proposed to you a more radical idea of the Humble God than even your Christian doctrines proclaim. This idea is hard to utter in the civilized world of today. My intentions are good, but easily leads to being misunderstood. Still here—among the barbarians—I have come across stories and visions that made my hair rise and my beard tingle with excitement.

I thank you for sharing your thoughts again on this most serious of matters. You are moving towards the light with impressive strength of character. For the paradoxical truth of the human soul is precisely as you say: After having been there—staring at God's eye through our inner lights, so to speak—we return again to the flesh—and then we experience a lowering of the whole principle of existence. It is as if God comes along with us into our unelevated bodies. As if God is in the smallest of things, and the smallest of things is the whole secret? The closer we reach to God's true being and the mystery's end, the more it all reveals itself as nothing but an endless mystery. Being close to Him means not knowing the answer.

For God himself is always moving and searching?

But how can that be?

This enigma exists beyond the boundaries of pure logic, making us all seem like ragged madmen?

There will come a time when I will tell you more of all this and how it connects with the heathen Northerners with whom I live. In the meantime, dear friend, I advise you to ask some of your husband's Norsemen to recite some verses of Odin for you.

I am most happy to hear young Constantine is doing so well in body and soul. He is dear to me as if he was my own son.

Furthermore he is my beloved prince whom I will follow through sweet and bitter times. Please bring him and the wise Emperor my regards. Certainly I am looking forward to the bright future when we will be together again.

Yours humbly, Suleiman"<br>(Sealed letter dating to approximately 911 A.D.)

*Odin, king of gods, frequently left his throne and his palace, to go strolling across the world of men, dressed in cheap and simple clothing. People called him by many names, such as "Old man", "Hey Father", or just plain "Mister". Only a few among them ever got to realize who he truly was, this grey-bearded passerby, a stranger in the night with one eye missing under his uncultivated eyebrow. But anyone who took the old loafer in, let him sit by their fire and eat by their table, was left with a peculiar sensation. Something of the old man would stay behind in their home after he had left them. A wondrous memory would bring uplifting colors to the house. An amazement would fill the air like songs reaching the ears from afar.*

*— Who was this fellow with the big hat? some farmer might be asking his wife at the lunch table.*

*— You're asking me? his wife might answer. — Then I'm asking you, sir. He came in here with you last night. Where'd you find the guy, anyways?*

*— Oh, he was just there, walking by my side, said the farmer. — I mean, I didn't even notice where he came from. It was like he had always been there, you know what I mean? As if he belonged here with us. Yeah. I just brought him home without thinking any more, didn't I?*

*Listening to this, his wife calmed her voice and let her eyes move about the room, as if comparing her own house to something in her own memory.*

*— You know, I know exactly what you mean, she said. — You know, we didn't even ask him where he came from when he was here. How odd, eh?*

*— Yeah, that's how it was. Weird, innit? her husband put in.*

*— You can say that again, said the wife.*

*— Weird, innit? repeated the man.*

*— We didn't even think to ask, said she.*

*— But now we're sitting here wondering, said he.*

*— Like the dumbasses we are, she concluded, raising her cup of milk as if to make a toast.*

*— We know so little in this world … her husband agreed.*

*— Well, you can say that again, she added.*

*And in this manner the conversation would keep going, until the farmer finally put on his hat and coat, called for his sons to join him in the field, and walked out the door to fetch the horse.*

(*The Adventures of the Ragged God* (excerpt)
by Teddy Partridge)

"Suleiman Silverbeard then heard words that Proximus was dead, and that the great King Leo held no grudge.

— The king does not believe any of the evil hearsay that Proximus passed around about you, Sigurd the Slayer told the sage in Tollef's home.

Suleiman thanked the seafaring messenger, and Tollef held a great feast in honor of his former enemy that very night. Three sheep were slaughtered and plenty of ale was hauled into the great hall.

As the feast went on towards the dawn, the tasty ale made Sigurd's tongue more daring. He turned to Suleiman Silverbeard, and queried:

— Being my friend, I am sure you don't mind telling me: What kind of bond is there really between you and the queen of Miklagard? Did you not only save young Constantine's life, but also give her the gift of Julian, the secondborn?

Suleiman naturally did not answer this. But neither did he raise his sword at the guest from Miklagard, as he might have done at another barefaced joker. The silver-bearded blueman simply poured another cup for his good friend's guest.

— Let us toast for the blessed news you have brought me today, he said, staring the Dane in his eyes.

But Tollef had overheard the conversation. The lord of the house drank the toast down, then spoke this verse in a thundering voice:

*The friends of Miklagard poured ale,*
*honoring their king of the East,*
*the one friend wise, the other brave,*
*the lost one a curvy snake, tongue of rot and spoils.*

Upon hearing this, Sigurd the Slayer spit in fury and leapt to the table, shouting:

— My tongue speaks nothing other than what my arm will answer for!

Tollef was faster, and smacked his axe in Sigurd's foot. The guest fell to the floor:

— I seem to have lost my standing, he quoted.

With the next blow of Tollef's axe, Sigurd lost his head for good. Tollef composed another verse, one that he is well remembered by:

— *Once I saved brave Sigurd's head,*
*once I let it go.*
*The cup is full, the head is empty,*
*I simply call it even.*

Sigurd's men were fast to leave their ale-cups behind, returning to their ship in a stupor, falling and cursing through the dark morning.

In this way Tollef fought for Suleiman's honor, although the foreigner had not himself called for such action. And in this way Suleiman Silverbeard—who had once in Miklagard sent assassins for Sigurd as a plot to make him Tollef's friend—still brought the actual death of Sigurd in the end.

Suleiman Silverbeard in time became known as a great negotiator and judge on Iceland."

(From the Saga of Tollef Thundervoice,
written down in Iceland 13th century A.D.)

— God is Great! God is Great! sang the Sufis, swaying their bodies, closing their eyes.

The air was hazy with burnt incense; the ten learned masters were gathered in Hussaini's chambers. The dark-clothed figures were like shadowy columns, come alive by magic. Through the high window the sun threw strange colors upon the floor, making the ten faces flare like flames in a dim mirror.

Yes, God is Great, thought Suleiman, throwing his arms around, singing with a lion's deep voice. But in what way? What does it mean for God, the Supreme One, to be truly Great? How do we measure greatness in that which lies beyond the idea of perfection?

Lately his thoughts had veered off into terrifying, unchartered territories of the soul. The God which he sought, the One beyond anything that could be reasoned, or even understood by reading the final doctrines: How could this perfect God have even bothered creating our world, with all its racked imperfections in it?

Isn't it so? Suleiman thought. If Muhammad—peace be with him—is indeed the last prophet, and the holy Quran embodies the last and final words given to mankind by God the Merciful, then from now on, our quest to reach closer to Him must lead us elsewhere? We must search beyond the written word? For the Word is only the beginning: His words are not simply meant to be swallowed and adhered to. He is not like a dish prepared by men. God is not simply our commander, our lives are not to be the lives of livestock. We must measure His words by our own hearts, grasp them with our own conscience, reflect upon them with our very souls.

We must keep on moving, so as to move constantly closer to Him.

— God is Great! God is Great! sang all the ten men as one. The smoke now filled the room, making the whole scene appear as if inside of a cloud.

We know so little, thought Suleiman. Truly, we know close to nothing. Yet here we are, alive in the world. The One has decided to deliver us this way, and to connect us to him through our confused soul. And while our intellect is limited, His is a perfect one. But then what to make of this doctrine, the perfect intellect? The perfect intellect? Is that actually an intellect at all, seeing as it has nowhere to turn its thoughts to without diminishing its own perfection?

The Sufis all dealt with the great limitations of human existence; they all sought and found God beyond the realm of comprehension. Yet the silver-bearded Sufi master could not come to terms with the theological twist at the heart of it all.

The other day he had tried discussing a radical new notion of a paradoxical God with his young apprentice. The youngster only regarded such arguments as dangerous blasphemies, not to be spoken out loud.

— God is Great! sang Suleiman along with the others. He looked at them through the smoke, letting his glance move from face to face. Their eyes were not opened like his, but all closed: Gazing inward, not to bother with the physical realm for as long as the séance lasted.

This is as far as I can come here in Shiraz, Suleiman thought to himself. He let his arms fall, his body go still. His thoughts kept swirling:

I must venture out into the world. I must search within as I walk without. I must keep on moving, so as to walk with my God beside me. God is not a closed book, as much as He is a wanderer along the shores of day and night.

That very evening, Suleiman Silverbeard left his beloved city of Shiraz, to go on a quest that would take him to faraway places — and bring him much adventure and strange understanding.

(Rendered freely from the diaries of Farroukh Farakhan, 10th Century A.D.; 3rd Century A.H.)

*On one of his wondrous wanderings, Odin, king of gods, came to a river. The river seemed weird, as if floating backwards — and when he bent down to drink, the water wouldn't collect in his hands.*

*— Something in the water here, Odin thought. — Does not compute.*

*— This is the river of time, a voice suddenly spoke.*

*Odin looked up and saw a man across the stream, looking back over at the god.*

*— Who are you? Odin inquired.*

*— I am merely a man, a wanderer of the spirit, answered the other one. — I have come to this place in search of God.*

*— In search of what god, did you say? Odin wondered.*

*— In search of the greatest God of all, said the other one, smearing his beard with his fingers.*

*— Well, then, you are speaking of Odin, the king of gods? the well-disguised Aesir asked.*

*The man on the other side smiled at this suggestion, and Odin began to feel angry at the rudeness.*

*— As a matter of fact, I have heard great things about this Odin, the stranger said. — What do you think? Which side of the stream does Odin belong to? The one which we call the Past, or the one which we name the Future?*

*— I think, Odin suddenly roared. — That Odin belongs where the Hell he wants!*

*The king of gods threw his ragged coat, revealing a kingly armor shining with all the colors of the rainbow. Then he took off his hat, shook his hair loose and lifted his forceful head. His one eye glowed vigorously, and a ray of light beamed across the stream at the other man. It made the man's beard shine like silver.*

*— Now ferry me across, sir! Odin shouted*

*— You are he, the man said. — You are the one I have been searching for: The ragged god. I will ferry you across, and then I will walk by your side.*

*— Ragged? laughed Odin, having forgotten all about his fit of anger right away. — Speak for yourself, man!*

*And so the man ferried the god across the river, and the two strolled on into the ancient landscape of Ultima Thule. Their stride was equal, they walked as companions. Man and god, god as man, friendly and curious about each other's place in the world, neither of them quite certain which of them had been created in the other's image.*

(The Adventures of the Ragged God (excerpt)
by Teddy Partridge)

*Better ask for too little than offer too much,*
*like the gift should be the boon;*
*better not to send than to overspend.*

*........*

*Thus Odin graved ere the world began;*
*then he rose from the deep, and came again.*
(Hávamál)

# — ABOUT THE EDITORS —

**Muhammad Aurangzeb Ahmad** is an Affiliate Assistant Professor at University of Washington and a Research Scientist focusing on AI. He has edited two anthologies focused on Science Fiction with Islamic themes or Muslim cultures: *A Mosque Among the Stars* and *Islamicates*. Muhammad is the founder and editor of the Islam and Sci-Fi project which he has been running since 2005. It is the most comprehensive resource on this subject.

**Joshua Gillingham** is the designer of the card game *Althingi: One Will Rise* and the author of *The Saga of Torin Ten-Trees*, a fantasy adventure trilogy inspired by the Norse Myths and Icelandic Sagas. Along with Ian Stuart Sharpe (*Vikingverse* Books & Comics) and Dr. Arngrímur Vídalín (University of Iceland), he produced a humorous phrase book titled *Old Norse for Modern Times*. Joshua lives on Vancouver Island with his adventurous spouse and their two very unadventurous cats.

# — ABOUT THE AUTHORS —

**Linnea Hartsuyker** can trace her ancestry back to Harald Fairhair, the first king of Norway, and a major character in her critically acclaimed trilogy *The Golden Wolf Saga*, published by HarperCollins. She grew up in the middle of the woods outside Ithaca, New York, and studied Engineering at Cornell University. After a decade of working at internet startups, and writing in her spare time, she attended NYU and received an MFA in Creative Writing. She lives in New Hampshire with her husband.

**Sami Shah** is a multi-talented writer, comedian, performer and broadcaster. His autobiography, *I, Migrant*, was nominated for multiple literary awards in Australia, and received a starred review on Kirkus. He's also published an urban fantasy novel about djinns in Pakistan, *Boy of Fire and Earth*, and contributed multiple stories to anthologies.

**Genevieve Gornichec** is the author of *The Witch's Heart*, a novel reimagining Norse mythology from the perspective of the giantess Angrboda. She earned her degree in history from The Ohio State University, but she got as close to majoring in Vikings as she possibly could, and her study of the Norse myths and Icelandic sagas became her writing inspiration. She lives in Cleveland, Ohio.

**Emily Osborne** has a PhD in Old Norse-Icelandic Literature from the University of Cambridge. Her poetry and Icelandic-to-English verse translations have been published in many North American journals. Her poetry chapbook *Biometrical* was published in 2018 (Anstruther Press) and she currently serves as a poetry editor for *PULP Literature*.

**Alex Kreis** is a researcher and writer. His birth was foretold by a witch but was otherwise uneventful. His short story, *The Calligraphy*, won first prize in the Islamic Science Fiction contest. Alex lives in a hundred-year-old house outside Boston.

**Siobhán Clark** is an author, narrator, and host of *The Myth Legend & Lore Podcast*: A place where we can journey into the past and share tales of mythology, legends and folklore, that have captured our imaginations and fired our curiosity! The year ahead is filled with exciting new projects and collaborations, her second novel, and the continuation of *Víðförul — the Women Pioneers of the Vinland Sagas* which she co-writes and produces with Dr. Jóhanna Katrín Friðriksdóttir.

**Giti Chandra** is currently Research Specialist with the Gender Equality Studies and Training Programme (under the auspices of UNESCO) in Reykjavik, teaches at the University of Iceland, and has been Associate Professor, Dept of English, at Stephen's College, Delhi. She is the author o*f The Book of Guardians Trilogy: The Fang of Summoning* (Hachette: 2010), *The Bones of Stars* (Hachette: 2013), and *The Eye of the Archer* (Hachette: 2020). Her (mostly sci-fi) short stories and (mostly sentimental) poetry have been published in various amazing publications. Sadly, nobody cares about her first non-fiction book, a groundbreaking academic work on violence (Macmillan: 2009), although the *Routledge Handbook of the Politics of the #MeToo Movement*, (Routledge: 2021) has been getting attention. Giti writes poetry in April, paints on Tuesdays, has a PhD from Rutgers, and feels that people would do well to learn that a cello is not an oversized violin. She lives in Reykjavik with a husband, two kids, a dog, and a cat.

**Nicholas Kotar** is a writer of epic fantasy inspired by Russian fairy tales, a freelance translator from Russian to English, the resident conductor of a men's choir at a Russian monastery in the middle of cow country, and a Grammy-nominated vocalist. His only regret in life is that he wasn't born in 19th century St. Petersburg, but he's doing everything he possibly can to remedy that error. If anyone knows where he can find a blue police box that's bigger on the inside, please let him know.

**Kaitlin Felix** is an author of historical fiction and fantasy with a Norse mythological twist. She lives with her small family in Switzerland. On weekends she scales the Alps in search of dragon eggs and hobbit-holes.

**Shanon Sinn** is the author of *The Haunting of Vancouver Island* (a BC and Amazon Bestseller) and has been published in the *Times Colonist*, Nelson's *Canadian Corrections* textbook, *Folklore Thursday*, and elsewhere. He has a degree in creative writing from Vancouver Island University where he was awarded the Barry Broadfoot Journalism Award and the Giselle Merlet Creative Writing Award. He has also studied procedure and protocol of recording Indigenous oral histories at the University of Fairbanks in Alaska and Criminology at Douglas College in New Westminster. Sinn is one quarter Nordic.

**Eric Schumacher** is an American historical novelist who currently resides in Santa Barbara, California, with his wife and two children. At a very early age, Schumacher discovered his love for writing and medieval European history, as well as authors like J.R.R. Tolkien and C.S. Lewis. His first novel, *God's Hammer*, was published in 2005 and tells the tumultuous story of Hakon the Good. He has since written several more historical adventure novels, all set in the Viking Age.

**Jordan Stratford** has been pronounced clinically dead, and was briefly (mistakenly) wanted by INTERPOL for international industrial espionage. He has won numerous sword fights, jaywalked the streets of Paris, San Francisco, and São Paulo, and was once shot by a stray rubber bullet in a London riot. He lives in the crumbling colonial capital of a windswept Pacific island populated predominantly by octogenarians and carnivorous gulls. He's the author of the YA historical *Sword Girl* series from Outland, and the Middle-Grade *Wollstonecraft Detective Agency* series from Knopf / Random Penguin, which was adapted to a video game for iOS, Android, and Nintendo Switch,  as well a television series in development.  He is also a First Responder with Search and Rescue and a board member of Story Studio Canada. He has been featured on *c/net, io9, boing boing, WIRED,* and *Reading Rainbow.*

**R.F. Dunham** is a writer of worlds distant and unknown. Through Fantasy, Sci-Fi, Historical, Alternate History, and beyond, his stories explore the intersection of cultures and peoples. It is his hope that reading his stories will give you a glimpse into the hearts and minds of people who see their worlds differently from you. Dunham lives in the peaceful foothills of Central Virginia with his wife, daughter, dog, cats, and a herd of cows.

**Bjarne Benjaminsen** is a Norwegian writer and journalist. His interest in Norse mythology was awakened during early childhood. In 2015 he released the literary fanzine *Kjærlighetsskjelv (Shivers of Love)*, in part inspired by Sufi poetry. A collection of science fiction short stories, *... som duften av en drøm ... (... as the scent of a dream ...)*, was published in 2020. Benjaminsen holds a master's degree of Philosophy from the University of Oslo. In his youngster days he spent months at a time hitch-hiking across Europe and the USA. He was married in Addis Ababa in 2014, and resides with his wife and two children in the fishing region of Lofoten, Northern Norway.